Paula shuddered as the hot breath tickled her ear. When the lips began to caress the sinewy muscle, her head fell back against Wynne's shoulder. She gasped as long fingers slid underneath her top to stroke her stomach.

Wynne was lost. She knew she had crossed the line, but she found herself unable to stop. Her right hand left the confines of the shirt to cover Paula's breast, which she squeezed softly, but with confidence.

Paula turned, her own hands beginning to caress the warm skin beneath Wynne's silk blouse. Their lips met fiercely, with a near animalistic fervor. Paula leaned back into the counter and pulled Wynne's hips closer, and soon both women were pushing against one another, aching for more contact.

"We shouldn't do this," Wynne murmured, burying her mouth in the soft flesh behind Paula's ear.

"We're both big girls, Wynne. We don't have to stop," Paula whispered boldly.

Visit

Bella Books

at

BellaBooks.com

or call our toll-free number

1-800-729-4992

Just This Once

KG MacGregor

Bella
BOOKS
2006

Bella Books, Inc.
P.O. Box 10543
Tallahassee, FL 32302

Printed in the United States of America on acid-free paper
First Edition

Editor: Cindy Cresap
Cover designer: Stephanie Solomon-Lopez

ISBN 1-59493-087-2

Acknowledgments

This is more of a disclaimer than an acknowledgment. I've never worked in a hotel. I've held plenty of other thankless jobs, but my experience in hotels has been on the receiving end of the hospitality. I'm lucky for that. Hotel workers do a lot for a little, and the only time anyone seems to notice them is when something about the stay isn't perfect. Okay, so maybe it is an acknowledgment after all. Thanks to all of you who make it easier for those of us who have earned our living on the road.

Thanks also to Cindy Cresap for her ideas and guidance. I love it how she always tries to work in a word of praise or encouragement every seventy pages or so. I aim to please.

About the Author

Growing up in the mountains of North Carolina, KG MacGregor dreaded the summer influx of snowbirds escaping the Florida heat. The lines were longer, the traffic snarled, and the prices higher. Now she's older, slightly more patient, and not without means, and divides her time between Miami and Blowing Rock.

A former teacher, KG earned her PhD in mass communication and her writing stripes preparing market research reports for commercial clients in the publishing, television, and travel industries. In 2002, she tried her hand at lesbian fiction and discovered her bliss. When she isn't writing, she is probably on a hiking trail.

Chapter 1

Flick. Flick.
Plop!
"Great. Now I'm going to smell like onions all night," Paula groused as she picked the unwanted condiment from her sandwich and dropped it into the trashcan. "Why did you even bother asking what I wanted if you weren't going to listen?"

"I got distracted," her coworker whined, taking an oversized bite from his roast beef sandwich.

"Yeah, I bet I know by what . . . or rather by whom. What's her name?"

"Juliana." He said the name with a dreamy sigh.

"I bet Juliana smells like onions."

"Careful," the red-haired man cautioned. "That's my future wife you're talking about."

"Right. What's your future wife's last name?"

Rusty Wilburn looked away sheepishly. "I don't know yet," he admitted. "But it doesn't matter, because you can call her Mrs. Wilburn."

Paula McKenzie chuckled at her boss. In the three years they had been paired up on the night shift, they had gotten to know each other pretty well, and she knew Rusty could fall in love at the drop of a hat. Too bad he hadn't fallen for someone who worked at a Thai restaurant. Chicken salad on rye was getting old, especially with onions.

From three-thirty p.m. to midnight, Paula and Rusty were the shift supervisors at the Weller Regent Hotel in Orlando, known by everyone who worked there as the WR. The four-star hotel catered to upscale business travelers who wanted something quieter, something with a more personal touch.

Paula had landed a coveted summer internship at this, Weller's oldest hotel, while earning her hospitality degree nine years ago at the University of Florida. Immediately upon graduating, she had come on board as a night desk clerk, moving through all the departments—catering, business services, meetings, training—to the position she now held: shift manager. Two more rungs remained before she could work in Operations, but it was likely she would have to relocate to move up in the chain. Rusty, the senior shift manager, was next in line to move up in Orlando. That was her career goal, though—daytime management and one day, her own hotel.

"Damn it!" Rusty sat up and reached for his napkin, a futile gesture against the mustard stain on his dark blue shirt.

"You did that on purpose," Paula accused.

"I did not!"

By mutual consent, tonight was Rusty's night to deal with emergencies and customer complaints while Paula did paperwork in the second floor administrative offices. But with his shirt prominently sporting a bright yellow stain, she would have to be the one to venture out if the need arose.

Sunday nights were moderately busy, the weekend convention goers giving way to the road warriors headed for another week of business meetings. The housekeeping staff had turned over virtually every room in the last twelve hours, and Paula had spent the entire afternoon conducting inspections and completing employee evaluations. Thanks to Rusty's prolonged trip to the Brooklyn Deli—during which she had to help out at the front desk—she was way behind with her weekly reports.

Rusty had his own pile of paperwork to resolve. Maintenance logs, inventory sheets, and vendor invoices filled his desk. If they were lucky, the staff on hand would find a way to deal with problems so both of the managers could catch up. If not, they would stay late to finish.

"Hey, look who's back."

Paula glanced at the security monitor positioned between their desks. Every five seconds, the image rotated automatically to a different camera, from the main entrance, to the front desk, to the elevator lobby on the first floor, and to the pool area. Rusty grabbed the remote and froze the angle immediately upon recognizing the woman they had watched twice before as she checked into the WR on Sunday night.

"Too bad you're practically married," Paula chided. "What would Juliana No Last Name think of you ogling someone else?" She set her work aside for the moment to watch the beautiful woman exit the taxi and direct the bellman to her bags. Indeed, Paula too had noticed this guest on her first visit a month ago. A woman as striking as this one was hard to miss.

"I'm looking for someone for you now," he answered.

Paula laughed. "While I happen to applaud your taste, I hereby relieve you of your mission."

"Wonder what her story is," Rusty mused. When they had a rare moment of down time, the two would entertain one another with their made-up background stories of the anonymous guests.

"I don't know. She looks like a typical business traveler."

"No, I mean the limp."

They studied the video as the woman paid the cabbie, gathered her purse and briefcase, and hobbled toward one of the small glass entryways that framed the hotel's massive revolving door. Paula was inwardly pleased to see the bellman respond quickly to hold the door open as she disappeared from the camera's view.

"She doesn't act like it bothers her that much," she observed offhandedly. She wasn't interested in making this woman a subject of their game . . . at least not aloud. But she had wondered silently about this beautiful guest, going so far on her last visit as to pull her reservation record.

Her name was K. Wynne Connelly, and she was from Baltimore. She had the standard corporate rate, billed directly to Eldon-Markoff, a travel and tour company headquartered a block and a half from their hotel.

Rusty advanced the controls to watch the action at the front desk. Jolene Hardy and Matthew Stivich worked efficiently to check in the short line of guests.

"Jolene's done a great job, hasn't she?" Paula asked casually, changing the subject to mask her interest as she searched the video for sight of Ms. Connelly in line.

"Yeah, she caught on quick. You've really brought her along well."

Paula had mentored the new hire since her first day as a college intern. Once Jolene cleared probation next week, she would be given more authority to appease guests. For now, she still needed supervision, requiring a manager's okay to waive a charge or to make special accommodations.

"Looks like she needs a hand with that one," Rusty offered, knowing full well that Paula would have to go downstairs to take care of the obviously irate gentleman at the counter. Without the sound on the video, they relied on facial expressions, and this man looked as though he was about to blow his top.

She groaned. "I guess I should wash my hands first, since your future wife put onions all over my sandwich."

Paula stopped in the ladies room to quickly wash up and check her appearance. Today's suit—taupe linen with a navy silk top—was her favorite combination from among the four WR uniforms. In her closet hung its complement, a navy suit with a cream-colored silk blouse, and several coral tops that could be worn on certain days with either suit. From time to time, the hotel updated its fashions, but conservative attire was the rule. After nine years of being told what to wear to work, she had grown accustomed to it, grateful that the corporate directors at least had a sense of style.

From the ladies' room, she proceeded down the back stairs to emerge behind Jolene at the check-in counter. A quick glance told her Matthew had things under control on his end of the counter, but the man in front of her newest clerk was growing louder by the second.

"How can I help here, Jolene?"

"I'll tell you how you can help," the red-faced man stormed. "You can get me the king-sized bed I specifically reserved!"

Paula looked over the shoulder of her harried clerk. "Mr. Thomason, is it?"

"That's right." He seemed infinitely satisfied to be getting special treatment from someone in charge.

"Our reservationist probably didn't make it clear at the time, but we aren't able to guarantee all room types for guests traveling alone. But let me see what I can do." In fact, it was standard practice for the reservationists to read a disclaimer that was often ignored. But arguing with Mr. Thomason wasn't going to solve the problem, and that would make a poor impression on the people waiting in line. Paula searched a moment before using her code to manually override the system. "I can upgrade you to the concierge floor and waive the extra fee for this stay. That should take care of this problem. But in the future, if you're traveling alone, the only way we'll be able to guarantee a king-sized bed is if you book directly onto the concierge level," she advised with quiet authority.

Paula stepped back and allowed Jolene to complete the transaction. Spotting the familiar face next in line, she shifted immediately to an open terminal. "I can help you here."

The guest she had watched from arrival stepped forward and proffered her credit card. "I'm Wynne Connelly. I have a reservation."

Wynne Connelly was even more stunning up close and in

person. The black and white video didn't do justice to her hair, which was dark brown with strands of red. It was cut all one length to just above her shoulders, and full of what looked like natural wave. But the woman's most captivating feature was her eyes, blue-green, like the color of a tropical sea. "Yes, Ms. Connelly, I have your reservation right here, a single room, non-smoking, three nights."

"That's correct." Smiling slyly, she leaned across the counter and lowered her voice. "So if I act like an ass, can I get upgraded to the concierge floor too?"

Paula chuckled and shook her head without looking up. "I tell you what, Ms. Connelly. What if I just do the upgrade anyway and save us both the bother?"

"Oh, you don't have to do that. I was just being silly. But I appreciate the thought," the woman said sincerely, apparently embarrassed to have evoked such a generous offer. "I promise not to misbehave," she whispered.

Paula looked up to see her mischievous smile. "That's okay. We like a challenge," she said with a smirk. "I'd be happy to do it, though. I see by our records that you're making a habit of staying with us, and we want to reward that."

"In that case, thank you very much. I suppose I shouldn't look a gift horse in the mouth, eh?"

"I wouldn't if I were you," Paula advised, once again invoking her business voice. "It's a very nice deal if you can take advantage of the extras. You'll have two phone lines and a fax machine, and high-speed Internet access. Breakfast is served in the private lounge just across from the elevator from six a.m. until ten. Cocktails and hors d'oeuvres are available after five. And if you want to stop in there before turning in tonight, they'll have coffee and dessert until midnight."

"I'll be sure to check that out." Ms. Connelly scribbled her name on the signature card and initialed the rate and departure date.

"Did you have a nice trip into Orlando this evening?" Paula

asked that question of all her guests at check-in—to be polite, of course, but also to kill time while the computer processed her commands. Tonight, though, she was taking advantage of the chance to make conversation.

"It was delightfully uneventful, like all flights should be," Ms. Connelly replied. "And it was wonderful to arrive someplace where it was warm. It was snowing in Baltimore when I left."

"Then I'm glad you're enjoying our weather, at least for tonight." Paula turned to indicate the placard behind her that displayed weather icons for the next three days. "It's supposed to rain all day tomorrow and the next day."

"That figures. I didn't bring an umbrella."

"I have an extra one in my office. If you like, I'll send it up with a bellman later. You can just leave it at the front desk when you check out."

"Boy, you really are accommodating tonight, aren't you?"

"Just that good old Weller Regent service, second to none." For Wynne Connelly, Paula would have thrown in a backrub.

"I couldn't take your umbrella. You might need it yourself. Besides, my coat has a hood."

"No, I won't need it. I lend it out all the time," Paula insisted. In fact, she had lent it only once, to a pretty flight attendant who chatted with her sweetly at check-in . . . much like Ms. Connelly was doing.

"Well, in that case, I accept."

"So do you travel a lot with your work?"

"A fair bit. Our headquarters is here, and it looks like I'll be coming back and forth a lot for the next few months."

"I'm glad that you've chosen to stay with us. We'll do our best to make you comfortable here at the Weller Regent. If there's anything you need, don't hesitate to call, Ms. Connelly." Though it sounded official and contrived, Paula made it a point to look directly into the woman's eyes to convey the offer as sincere.

"Shall I ask for you when I call?"

"If you like." Paula smiled, slipping a business card from her pocket. Departing from her usual business tone, she continued, "Here's my direct extension. I'll be here tonight and tomorrow night as well."

Ms. Connelly pocketed the card and smiled back at her. "I'm sure everything will be fine."

The computer spit out the key card. There was really no more reason to keep the woman at the desk. Paula pushed the envelope across the counter. "This is your room number." She circled 2308 in red. For security reasons, they never repeated the room number aloud. "You'll need your key in the elevator. Just insert it and wait for the green light before pressing your floor. Would you like some help with your bags?"

"No, I can manage. Thank you for everything." Wynne shouldered her briefcase and flashed a brilliant smile.

"You're very welcome." Paula congratulated herself on her timing, quietly applauding whatever forces had come together to cause Mr. Thomason to behave like a jerk and Wynne Connelly to arrive a moment later. It was nice to have finally gotten the chance to meet this beautiful guest, and a special bonus to have the authority to dole out such a treat.

Paula McKenzie, the nametag had said. *Shift Manager*.

Wynne took one last look behind her at the pretty woman before rounding the corner at the elevator. There was now one more reason to look forward to these trips. She stepped into the elevator and checked her reflection in the brassy mirror, smiling demurely as the door closed.

"Why yes, Ms. McKenzie! You may flirt with me whenever you like."

Moments later, she exited the elevator directly across from the private lounge on the concierge floor. Clusters of love seats and wingback chairs held couples and small groups, all conversing softly in the dim light as they sampled the dessert offerings. It was a pleasant atmosphere and one she would try to take advantage of, provided she didn't get hit on. That was the worst part about traveling alone, and the main reason she usually just ordered room service.

Wynne studied the key for a moment and inserted it into the slot. By all appearances, the room was like those she had stayed in before, except for the fax machine and king-sized bed. A quick check behind the curtains revealed a view of the city, rather than another wing of the hotel.

Nice.

She liked the feel of the Weller Regent. On her first trip to Orlando, she had stayed at the Hyatt, Eldon-Markoff's other recommended hotel. She didn't care for the boisterous atmosphere of the Hyatt's lobby bar and its adjacent towering fountain. The Weller Regent possessed a calmer, more distinguished ambience that was perfect for Wynne when she needed a respite on the road.

The décor was warm and inviting, a blend of cream and taupe, not the usual vibrant colors some hotels used to mask stains on the bedspread and drapes. Everything about the hotel was plush, almost decadent. The feathered pillow-top mattresses were the finest anywhere, and the towels and robes were soft and luxurious.

Methodically, she emptied her suitcase and hung up her three crisp suits, only one of which she had ever worn. As marketing director at Gone Tomorrow Tours, Eldon-Markoff's newest subsidiary in Baltimore, Wynne usually wore skirts and sweaters or sometimes pantsuits to work. But the corporate culture was more formal in Orlando, so she had dipped into her savings to purchase eight new suits to get her through the strategic planning project.

Most likely, she would be keeping this travel schedule through the end of April, which was not a bad time to be leaving Baltimore for sunny Florida. After that, who knows? From the looks of things, she might plan herself right out of a job. But if that happened, she would have nice new clothes to wear to job interviews.

That's what this project was all about, streamlining the marketing and sales initiatives for Eldon-Markoff. That meant crafting a plan to link the company's worldwide travel agencies and its tours. Wynne was asked to work on the plan, along with sales director Doug Messner from the Dallas travel agency office. Cheryl

Williams, Eldon-Markoff's vice-president of sales and marketing, headed up the task force. Cheryl was a dynamo and skilled leader whom Wynne admired for her ability to get things done.

But it was clear after only three planning sessions that sales and marketing would operate more efficiently if it were centralized. Now it was up to the team to draft a plan to make it happen. Probably the best she could hope for was a good severance package.

A sharp knock on the door signaled the arrival of the bellman with the borrowed umbrella.

"Thank you," she said, passing the young man a couple of bills.

"You're welcome, Ms. Connelly. And Ms. McKenzie asked me to remind you about the dessert."

"Please tell her thanks, and that I will go see about dessert right now."

Checking to make certain she had her key, Wynne followed the bellman back to the elevator, at once eyeing the dessert table in the center of the lounge.

"May I bring you something to drink?" a tuxedoed woman asked.

Wynne thought about it and passed, deciding she would just grab one of the sweet offerings and return to her room. So many different treats . . . but she should have only one. She took the lime tart with the strawberry on top. And then reached back for a truffle.

Back in her room, she dropped tiredly into the wingback chair. It was almost ten and she had a full day tomorrow. Her leg throbbed from the demands of her trip. Fishing in her purse, she drew out a bottle of ibuprofen. Since the accident two years ago, she carried it everywhere she went, waiting for the moment her leg would start to ache from deep within. A hot bath would soothe the pain and help her sleep.

Flicking on the light in the marble bathroom, Wynne silently blessed Paula McKenzie for the upgrade. Her tub was equipped with massaging air jets.

10

Chapter 2

Monday was shaping up like just another weeknight at the Weller Regent.

At least once a day, Paula walked the hallways from end to end on all twenty-three floors. Mostly, she checked to ensure that fixtures were in working order, doors were not left ajar, and room service trays were picked up in a timely manner, but she also kept an eye out for anything out of the ordinary. So far, she had logged two burned out lights and one that flickered off and on. On the concierge floor, she discovered a wallet stuffed behind a plant in the elevator lobby, likely hidden by a pickpocket who had pilfered the contents.

"Security, please," she directed softly into the walkie-talkie.

"Security here," a male voice crackled.

"I need a security officer in the elevator lobby of the twenty-third floor, please." Paula was eager to get this cleared up quickly, as the sight of a security guard on the concierge floor might unnerve some of the guests.

"On the way. Roger out."

Three minutes later, the uniformed guard arrived and began to document the evidence in the event criminal charges might be filed. They usually weren't, but management always wanted fingerprints when possible to rule out employees. It was doubtful an employee would have hidden the wallet in plain view of the camera in the ceiling. Too bad for the fool who ignored the warning signs advising that the public areas of the premises were under surveillance.

Together, she and the guard carefully opened the wallet to confirm its contents, or rather, lack of contents. But there was a driver's license, and she immediately called downstairs to get the room number of its owner, William C. Jeffries.

"Do we have tape?" she asked the guard.

"We should. I'll check it when I go back down."

"Call me when you find something."

Moments later, Paula's knock on the guest room door was answered by a middle-aged man, apparently fresh from a shower in his robe and with dripping hair. She explained the purpose of her visit, then listened calmly as Jeffries ranted about the hotel's lack of security, demanding reimbursement and threatening to sue for damages if the thief ran up charges on his credit cards. When she assured him the hotel had videotape that would likely show who had hidden his wallet, the irate man suddenly turned docile.

"You know, I'm probably just making a big deal out of nothing. I can cancel all the cards with just a phone call, and as long as I have my driver's license, the only real thing I lost was some cash. I guess that's the price for being careless with my wallet, huh?"

When she exited the man's room, Paula went immediately to the house phone. Some information was not suited for broadcast on a broader frequency.

"Hello, Tim? I think we've got another hooker working the building. If you find something on the tape, let's get the OPD in and see if we can get an ID."

12

∽ಌ∾

Wynne glanced at the check-in counter on her way to the elevators, hoping to catch sight of a friendly face. It had been a long day—most Mondays were when Sunday was spent traveling—and she was looking forward to kicking back with a book, and to making a meal out of the hors d'oeuvres in the lounge. No such luck on the friendly face front. Paula McKenzie was nowhere to be found.

The happy hour fare in the lounge turned out to be a godsend. Room service was nice, but then her room smelled like dinner all night. Going out to a restaurant was less attractive, especially alone, though she had politely refused several dinner invitations from Doug. Her Dallas counterpart was young and single, and enjoyed the fun he could have on an expense account. For that reason, he had opted to stay at the Hyatt, calling the Weller Regent a little too uptight for his tastes. Coming from a sales background, Doug liked meeting new people and striking up conversations.

She settled into a wingback chair in the corner by the window, her small plate loaded with grilled fish strips with lemon and capers, brie and crackers, and fruit. It was hard to avoid calories on the road, but if she kept up her workout on the stationary bike— which she had to do anyway to keep her right leg limber—she could probably stave off the extra pounds.

"Hi, I'm Bill Jeffries. Do you mind if I join you?" A smartly dressed businessman held a cocktail in one hand and a plate of chicken wings in the other.

"Not at all," Wynne answered graciously, her mind rapidly forming words that might send him on his way. "But I have to warn you. I'm at a very exciting part of my book, so I doubt I'll be very good company."

Dejected, the man turned to look for another seat.

"Mr. Jeffries, may I see you a moment please?" As she entered the lounge, Paula noticed Wynne in the corner and smiled. "Good evening, Ms. Connelly."

"And to you, Ms. McKenzie." Wynne was quite pleased to see the familiar face, even though it was clear Paula was in the lounge in her official capacity. It was probably just wishful thinking that she had been flirting the night before, but it was nice to imagine it just the same. It would be great to have a friend here, especially since it looked like she would be back at least a half dozen times or more.

After a brief conversation in the hallway, both Paula and Bill Jeffries returned to the lounge. To Wynne's delight, Paula was heading her way, and she quickly closed her book.

"What are you reading?"

Wynne held up the front cover. "It's Pamela Crenshaw's latest. I picked it up at the airport yesterday afternoon." Crenshaw had written a series of spy novels featuring a military heroine, Major Dana Grant. Each new release vaulted to the top of the bestseller list, both in hard cover and in paperback.

"Oh, I haven't seen that one. But I've read the others. Crenshaw really tells a great story."

"Yeah, but I have to admit, I think she's sort of gone over the top with the Major. It's kind of hard to believe a person can be perfect at everything."

"I'm not sure what you mean. Aren't all of your friends black belt gourmet cooks who can perform heart surgery in the dark while docking the Queen Mary?"

That sent Wynne into a fit of laughter that brought a smile to Paula's face. "Now that you mention it, a lot of my friends are like that. I'm the underachiever."

"I doubt that," Paula said. "So is everything to your liking? Your room, I mean."

"Yes, it's very nice. And the lounge is very nice. Thank you so much for the upgrade. I think I'll lean on the accountant at Eldon-Markoff to let me book up here on my next trip."

"I'm glad you're comfortable. I suppose it's hard to be away from home and your family so much, so I hope we can make it a little easier."

Wynne couldn't tell if Paula was fishing for personal information or just being nice. "You do make it easier and I appreciate it."

"I suppose I should get back to work. If I don't see you again tonight, have a safe trip home."

"Thank you. Oh, and thanks for the umbrella. I'll be sure to leave it at the desk."

"You're welcome."

Wynne watched her leave, first stopping by the host's desk to say hello to the staff and ask how things were going. She wondered how old Paula was. With her long blond hair and soft features, she looked to be in her late twenties or early thirties. But her poise and air of authority were those of someone older, more experienced in the work world. Wynne admired those same qualities in her boss, Cheryl Williams, a woman in her late forties. She found those traits—and Paula McKenzie—to be very attractive.

Have you tried the plunger, like I showed you?" Wynne raised the antenna on her cell phone to get a clearer signal. "Then you should do that first. If it doesn't work, don't use that toilet anymore, and call a plumber first thing in the morning."

The digital clock read a quarter to midnight.

"Mom, I can't do a thing for you tonight. I'm in Orlando," she explained. "Yes, my cell phone works here, same as always . . . I know you didn't know, but this is my week to travel. I won't get home until Wednesday night."

Wynne threw the covers back and stretched out for the bottle of water on the desk. "No, I have to work on Thursday. I can come by Thursday night, but you should call a plumber tomorrow if the plunger doesn't work." With her foot, she dragged her purse closer and retrieved the bottle of ibuprofen.

"I don't know. Maybe Sophie put something in it," a reference to her two-year-old niece. "Who knows?" Two tablets . . . make it

15

three. "Probably sixty bucks or so, maybe more if they have to stay a while. But what else are you going to do?"

Wynne was exasperated, both from her long day at work and at trying to manage her mother's house from almost a thousand miles away.

"You can't just keep flushing it and hope it doesn't overflow. It'll ruin the floor and the ceiling underneath it. Keep it mopped up and call a plumber first thing, okay?"

Settling back into bed, she cradled the phone underneath her chin. "Mom, I have to get back to sleep. I have another long day tomorrow," she pleaded. "I know this was an emergency. Just do what I said. It will be fine . . . Yes, I love you too. I'll come by Thursday night. Goodnight, Mom."

Wynne sighed deeply as she returned the phone to its cradle for charging. One would think Kitty Connelly was the most helpless person on earth. When Wynne's father died four years ago, her mother had come completely unglued. Within a year, her house was in disrepair, her finances a mess. The woman could barely decide what to wear each day.

Wynne painstakingly balanced her mother's household checkbook, arranged for a housekeeper to come by twice a week, and contracted with a handyman to make the necessary repairs. On top of that, she started calling two or three times during the day, just to keep her mother company and make sure everything was okay.

Growing up, neither Wynne nor her younger sister Janelle had realized the degree to which their mother had shaped her entire existence around their family. When both daughters left home, her devotion to her husband had kept Kitty grounded. Without him, she was aimless.

Wynne had hoped for something of a reprieve when Janelle moved back to Baltimore, unmarried and with a daughter of her own, Sophie. But Janelle had her hands full with nursing school, not to mention the demands of a two-year-old.

There was certainly one thing she didn't mind about the travel to Orlando. It was, for the most part, a respite from the day-to-day worries of managing her mother's life. It wasn't that Wynne didn't want to help her mother through this difficult time, but after three years, Kitty Connelly hadn't made a lot of progress toward living on her own.

And the ninety-year-old Tudor house only made matters worse. Maybe it was time to convince Kitty to sell the old place and move into something new—where someone else besides Wynne could deal with things that went wrong.

Paula pulled the pin on the leg extensor and reset it at thirty-five pounds. It was a pain following the Incredible Hulk around the weight room, but she got a small measure of satisfaction knowing he would follow her on his next circuit and also would have to reset the pins.

"How's work been, Val?" Val Harbison was Paula's best friend, and the manager of Flanagan's, a downtown sports bar. It was easy to commiserate about the lack of a social life, as both women were locked into working evenings and weekends. That ruled out clubs and parties, and left them mostly with meeting people through work. On weekdays, they met to work out in the fitness room at Paula's condominium complex. Usually, they had the place to themselves, but not today.

"We've gotten busier these last few weeks, so I guess that means the season's in full swing."

"Yeah, things have picked up for us too. Have you been out with Robbie?"

"Not since we did The Mouse," Val answered, invoking the locals' nickname for Disney World. "I don't think that's going to work out. We can only see each other in the daytime, and I just don't want to spend all my dates at the attractions, then rushing to get to work on time."

"I know what you mean. Knowing you have to go to work just takes the fun out of whatever you're doing. At least I have Saturdays off." On the weekends, Paula often visited her family in

Cocoa Beach, sometimes staying over until Sunday to go to church with her mom and dad.

"I'd kill for Saturdays off. But the weekends are our busiest days."

"Saturdays aren't that bad at the hotel, at least at night. Most of the convention traffic gets in on Friday. I think that's why Rusty takes off then and gives me Saturdays off. A lot of these convention goers only travel once a year, and they don't have a clue about how to survive away from home."

"What do they do?"

"What don't they do?" Paula groaned. "They complain about the price of everything, and they never miss a chance to tell you how they do things up north. They're like eighteen-year-olds when they first go away to college. They want to stay up all night and party in the halls. They smoke wherever they please. They don't keep up with their belongings. They can't find anything, even with a map." Paula slowly counted her reps.

"That would drive me crazy. At least the folks that come in Flanagan's seem to know the drill. They find a seat in front of the game they want to watch, drink their beer, and tip their waitress. Nothing to it."

Paula recounted the story of the man whose wallet was stolen last night by his hooker, and how he had threatened to sue the hotel until he learned they had her on videotape. When she told him the Orlando Police Department could probably identify the woman, he backed off completely, refusing to press charges, effectively ending the hotel's liability.

"Isn't it funny how self-righteous some people can be?" Val proclaimed. "Imagine what he'd have done if you'd found it after he left and called him at home."

"Yeah, or what if we'd called his office?"

"Really," Val huffed. "So have you had any good looking flight attendants lately?"

"No flight attendants, but there is a gorgeous woman staying there who works at Eldon-Markoff. She came in on Sunday night

18

from Baltimore. She's beautiful," Paula said dreamily, grabbing the pull-down bar for her lat reps. "And she has a limp. I'd love to know that story."

"So does she bat for your team?"

"I doubt it. But she's . . . I don't know, friendlier than most people."

"To everyone or just to you?"

"That I couldn't tell you. But I swear when she checked in the other night, it was almost like she was flirting. I told her to call if she needed anything, and she said, 'Should I ask for you?' Doesn't that strike you as flirty?"

"I guess it depends on how she said it. I hope you told her yes."

"I did. And I gave her my card. And I lent her my umbrella. And I upgraded her to the concierge floor."

"Good lord, woman! I'm surprised she didn't go down on you in the lobby." Val whispered the last part so Hulk wouldn't hear it.

"Oh, don't say things like that. My heart can't take it." Paula laughed. "I talked with her for a few minutes last night in the lounge. She's really nice, and she's going to be coming back and forth for the next few months. Maybe we'll get to know each other."

"Does she have a name?"

"She has a lovely name. It just rolls off your lips. Wynne Connelly."

Chapter 3

Two weeks later, the woman with the lovely name exited the taxi and reveled in the warm humid air, glad again to be rid of the Baltimore ice and snow. It was no mere coincidence that her leg felt better after being in Orlando for a day or two, and she looked forward to that.

This time, Wynne's arrival at the Weller Regent went unnoticed by the shift managers, both of whom were on the sixteenth floor seeing to a guest who had fallen ill after dinner. The hotel's physician on call had come to the room and diagnosed acute food poisoning. Predictably, Paula was concerned about the woman's well-being, while Rusty was rejoicing that she hadn't dined in the hotel.

"May I help you?"

"Yes, I'm Wynne Connelly," she answered, presenting her credit card.

"I have your reservation, Ms. Connelly. You've booked a single non-smoking room on our concierge floor for three nights. Is that right?"

"Yes." Without the charges for high-speed Internet access and two meals a day from room service, the upgrade was a virtual wash. Besides, Wynne didn't have the bar bill of her Dallas counterpart, so she refused to feel guilty about indulging in a little luxury at the company's expense. The whirlpool tub was worth it even if she had to pay the extra chare from her own pocket.

Jolene handed over the room key and walked her through the procedures for reaching the concierge floor. Wynne politely interrupted the explanation with the assurance that she already was familiar with the routine and the use of the key in the elevator.

"Would you like some help with your bags?"

"No, thank you. I can manage." Wynne folded her unneeded overcoat over her arm. Turning toward the elevator, she was surprised to see Paula McKenzie rush past her toward the front door, walkie-talkie in hand.

"It's pulling in right now," she messaged in a commanding tone.

The flashing red lights drew Wynne's attention to the entrance, where an ambulance had come to a stop directly in front of the door. Surprised by the sudden commotion, she watched Paula calmly, but hurriedly, direct the attendants to a waiting elevator. Her take-charge manner was impressive. If Wynne ever had another emergency, she wanted someone like Paula in charge. Of course, she hoped never again to have an emergency like the last one.

At her kitchen table, Paula studied the *Orlando Sentinel*'s weather report: sunny and calm, with temperatures climbing to the low seventies; tonight, clear and cool, with a low of fifty-four—a perfect February day.

It was an important day for central Florida, and for the rest of the country too, for that matter. But it was especially significant for Paula's family and all the families like hers on Florida's Space

21

Coast. Tonight at 9:06, the shuttle Atlantis would lift off. Since the Challenger and Columbia disasters, everyone connected to the space industry held their collective breath each time a shuttle launched or returned to earth.

A big orange cat landed with a thud in the middle of the news-paper.

"Hi, Slayer," Paula cooed to her baby. "What's the matter? Are you feeling neglected?"

As if in answer, the cat began to paw at the corner of the paper with his usual persistence. It was hopeless to try to continue to read, so Paula folded the newspaper and stood up.

"Let's go play," she coaxed.

The gleeful feline followed her to the sliding glass door, rearing to bolt the moment it was opened—not that freedom lay on the other side. The door led to a porch, which Paula had enclosed last year with gray-tinted smoke glass to increase the usable square footage of her two-bedroom second-floor condo. The porch ran the length of her living room and guest bedroom, and a single glass-paned door at the end opened to the master bedroom.

As soon as the door cracked open, Slayer dashed out, crashing at once into the glass against first one lizard, then another.

"My fearless hunter," Paula chuckled. One of the bonuses of converting the screen to glass was the cat could no longer rip into the mesh to capture his startled prey. She had grown decidedly ungrateful for his constant presentation of trophies, especially those he brought to her bed in the night.

"Get your toy," she coaxed.

Not surprisingly, Slayer ignored her. But then, Slayer was a cat. He would get his toy when he was damned good and ready.

The orange cat with the big amber eyes decided two years ago that Paula could keep him and feed him. In return, he would bring her prizes from the wild and allow his nails to be clipped on occa-sion. At the time, she was living in an apartment that didn't allow pets. Good thing, too, because Slayer didn't like pets. So when Paula's grandmother died and left her a small inheritance, she used

22

it for a down payment on this condominium to have a place to call her own. Or Slayer's own, as the case seemed to be.

Paula interrupted the play session to take a call in the kitchen. "Hello . . . Hi, Mom." She had expected this call.

She had grown up an hour away in Cocoa Beach, a small upscale community in the shadow of the launch pads at Cape Canaveral. Her father, Raymond McKenzie, had worked as a NASA public information officer since 1967. Neither she nor her brother Rodney shared their father's aptitude in science and engineering, but they had always been proud of their link to the space program. In her whole life, the most difficult days were those in which the Challenger and Columbia were lost.

"Yes, I'll be watching . . . probably up on the roof. It's a pretty good view that high, because there aren't any lights to worry about . . . I don't know, maybe just by myself, but I promise I'll watch."

As she talked on the phone, she gathered her overcoat and purse and finished her preparations to go to work. Lastly, she fed Slayer, who ignored her again. He would eat when he was damned good and ready.

"I'll call you at T minus ten to see if you've heard anything." Once the countdown was begun, it was always possible—likely, even—the NASA ground crew would build in a few holds for specific purposes, so the launch didn't always go off at exactly the designated moment. "Gotta run. Give Dad a hug for me, okay? . . . Yeah, I'll see you all Saturday."

Wynne opened the cover of the report that detailed the market research on co-branding the travel agency with the tour company. The findings were another nail in the coffin for the old guard at Gone Tomorrow Tours in Baltimore. Low name recognition made it less likely Eldon-Markoff would preserve that brand. Rather, they would incorporate it under their own moniker. At least that's what she would do if the decision were hers.

"How was lunch?" Cheryl Williams dropped her monogrammed leather folder onto the conference table, ready for the afternoon's work. At forty-seven, her collar-length blond hair was flecked with gray, and her small frame caused many to underestimate her toughness.

"It was fine, thank you. I feel a little guilty about enjoying your weather so much after hearing that Baltimore got seven inches of new snow last night." Wynne had bought a sandwich at the deli down the street and sat outside on a bench in Eldon-Markoff's courtyard.

"Don't sweat it. Somebody in Baltimore probably deserved it," the vice president quipped. "I saw you outside. You know, you're welcome to have lunch in the executive dining room on the top floor any time you like."

"Thanks, but I think I'll save that one for a rainy day."

Cheryl checked the door and pulled her chair close to Wynne's. "Listen, I wanted to let you know how much I value your input on this plan. You've obviously worked very hard at Gone Tomorrow, and you have a real nose for this stuff."

Both women looked up as Doug returned from lunch and took his seat on the opposite side of the table. Wynne sensed that Cheryl wanted to say more, but Doug's arrival squelched any further personal talk.

"Shall we resume?"

In the concierge lounge on the twenty-third floor, Wynne relaxed with a news magazine, weary from an afternoon of deflecting Doug's objections to everything that threatened his operation in Dallas. The young man was less concerned with what was good for the overall company—not to mention the stockholders—than he was about preserving his own turf. That made their strategic planning sessions more difficult than they had to be. She didn't know how she was going to deal with one obstacle after another from him for the next ten weeks.

"Hi."

Wynne was startled to see Paula McKenzie standing in front of her, a walkie-talkie in her hand and a coat draped over her arm.

"Hi, Paula . . . I mean Ms. McKenzie," she stammered. "Sorry, didn't mean to be so familiar."

Paula chuckled. "Paula's fine. In fact, I'd prefer it."

"Well, in that case, please call me Wynne."

"I don't think I can do that. It wouldn't sound very professional to the other guests. Besides, all my staff would have coronaries on the spot," she added with a smile.

"I guess they're used to the formality."

"I should hope so. I stopped by to see if anyone in the lounge would be interested in going up to the roof to watch the shuttle launch. It's a great view, and it's going up in about fifteen minutes."

"Are you kidding? I'd love to. I was just reading about the Atlantis in this magazine."

"Great. You should get your coat and meet me right back here so we can go up together. I'm going to see if any of these other folks want to join us."

Secretly, Wynne hoped they would all say no, but it was not to be. When she returned from her room with her coat, five other guests, all businessmen, were waiting to follow Paula up the stairs.

"I should warn you, we aren't insured for anyone falling off the roof. Your heirs won't see a penny if you go too close to the edge."

Wynne chuckled along with the others. As she grasped the rail to pull herself up the stairs, she caught Paula looking back. She hated the usual sympathetic looks she got from strangers when she struggled with her aching leg, but that wasn't at all what Paula's expression conveyed. Her look seemed more like encouragement.

Finally they emerged through the metal door at the top of the stairs.

"Can we sit on these?" One of the businessmen gestured to several three-foot-high block walls that surrounded the massive air conditioner units.

"Sure." Then she smiled and added, "But we aren't responsible for dirty clothes either."

25

Wynne waited as the five other guests broke out into the same two clusters as when they were in the lounge, leaving her standing alone with Paula.

"Why don't we sit over there?" Paula gestured to an empty wall and they both began to walk. "I need to call my mother to see if it's still a go."

Wynne lowered herself gingerly to the wall as Paula stepped away and placed her call. Her leg wouldn't have lasted much longer without a rest.

"Mom said there was a six-minute hold. They're going to launch in twelve minutes."

"Your mother follows the launches too?"

"We all do. My dad works for NASA. He's there tonight at the Cape. I'm sure they're all holding their breath right about now."

"What does he do?"

"He helps put together the press kits and he briefs reporters on the technical aspects of the mission. He's been there through the whole shuttle program."

"It must have been exciting growing up with all that."

"It was. We're all space junkies."

"So you're from Florida? I didn't know anyone was actually from here."

"There aren't many of us, that's for sure. The shuttle's going to launch right over there," she explained, pointing to a spot on the southeast horizon. "I grew up just to the right of that pad, in Cocoa Beach."

"So I bet you've seen a lot of these."

"Eighty-eight, to be exact. I've only missed about twenty-five of the shuttles. But if you add in all the rocket launches, I've seen about two hundred."

"You're kidding."

"No, that's what space junkies do."

"Have you ever gotten really close?"

"Yeah, I've been to the press site a few times, but it's not a bad view from the beach at Cocoa. That's where my friends and I used to go."

"And how many times have you come up here to watch?"

"Believe it or not, about twenty or thirty. But night launches aren't all that common."

"Then I really lucked out, not just because I'm here in Orlando to see it, but I have my very own expert right here with me." She rather liked the idea of Paula being her very own anything.

"I'm no expert, but I like being close to it."

"Did you ever dream of being an astronaut?"

"Not really. But I wanted my older brother to be one so he could go live on Mars."

"I would have sent my little sister with him."

"We could have stood on the beach and waved goodbye to both of them. They probably wouldn't even be there yet."

Wynne laughed. "An opportunity wasted."

"Have you always lived in Baltimore?"

"Always." Wynne surprised even herself at the way she groaned.

"Sounds like there's a story in there somewhere," Paula said.

"No, there's not really a story. I sometimes think I might have missed out on things because I stayed so close to home."

"You mean career-wise?"

"Mostly." Wynne didn't talk much about her personal life with people she barely knew. "Now that Eldon-Markoff's bought up our company, I doubt my role will get any bigger. In fact, if things keep going in the direction they're headed, I could be out of a job before too long."

"What would you do?"

"I'm not sure," Wynne answered honestly. "But maybe that's what it would take to get me to move out of Baltimore. Then I might push myself to do something with my career besides just showing up for work every day."

"Somehow you don't strike me as the kind of person that mails it in."

"I'm not really." From what she knew about Paula, Wynne was pretty sure that was one thing they had in common. "But I'd like to have a job with more responsibility. That probably won't happen if I limit myself to Baltimore."

"I know what you mean. I've passed up a few chances to move up over the years because I didn't want to leave Orlando. But if I'm ever going to break into daytime management, that's what it's going to take."

"You must really like it here."

"Orlando's okay. It's a pretty quick shot over to the beach. I'm close enough that I can see my folks regularly, but far enough way that they don't drop in."

"Believe me, I understand that one. My mother doesn't drop in. But ever since my dad died, she calls me for everything and expects me to be there in ten minutes."

"That must have been hard, losing your dad."

"It was. He was a good man." Wynne couldn't believe how much she was opening up. But what she really wanted was to learn more about Paula. "Do you like working here?"

"I love this hotel. If I had to name my ideal job, it would be running this place."

"Well, from what I can see, I'd say you're already doing that," Wynne offered, "and you're doing it very well."

"Thanks, but I'm only helping to hold down the fort at night. I don't get to make the real decisions that affect how things are done. But that's my goal, and like I said, I'll probably have to relocate if I'm ever going to see it."

"Who knows? Maybe things will work out."

"Maybe . . . but I'm not holding my breath," Paula lamented, checking her watch. "Hey guys, two minutes."

Wynne settled back in anticipation of the spectacular show, her mind still turning over what Paula had said about her career goals. Their jobs were very different, she thought, but their ambitions were similar.

She stole a glance at her companion, glad for this casual time together. Though she admired Paula's professional demeanor, she also appreciated her willingness to relax with some of the guests, if only for a few moments. Wynne hoped they might be able to forge a friendship, even if it fell away once her work in Orlando was done.

"There it is!" Paula shouted, pointing to an orange glow on the dark horizon. A bright yellow burst slowly became a towering stream that arced across the night sky.

"Wow!" That was all Wynne could articulate.

"Yeah, pretty amazing, isn't it?"

"Wow!" she said again. Wynne had never grasped the reality of the space program until just this minute. She had read the news, especially the coverage of the disasters, but seeing that trail of fire gave it a personal meaning she had never felt before.

In less than three minutes, it was gone, the glowing orange vapor trail its only visible remnants.

"That was one of the most magnificent things I've ever seen," Wynne gushed with obvious emotion. "I mean, it was almost surreal thinking about those seven astronauts riding on top of all that fire. I just . . . I don't know, it's like I just kept thinking about the people in it."

"That's the same way I see it, and the way most of the folks at NASA see it." Paula seemed very pleased that Wynne was so moved by the experience.

Wynne laid her hand on the shoulder of her new friend. "I can't thank you enough for bringing me up here tonight. I'm going to remember this for a very long time."

"I'm really glad you were here. Not many people get it like you did, you know, that it's not just a bunch of technology strapped onto a giant Roman candle."

"Surely after the Challenger and Columbia, people can see past all that."

"They do for a while, but then they start to take it all for granted again. Believe me, that never happens at our house."

"I don't think it's ever going to happen again at mine," Wynne said sincerely. "Really, thank you for this."

"You're welcome." Paula tucked her cell phone in her pocket

and grabbed her walkie-talkie. "Well, uh . . . I suppose I should be getting back to work."

"That's too bad. I wish we could just go have a drink." It was a bold statement but Wynne had an inkling Paula would be receptive . . . to the idea of talking more, that is. For all her interest in flirtations, Wynne wasn't looking for more than that.

"I wish I could, but I think my bosses might frown on that," she answered with a grin. "Maybe we can do that sometime, though . . . just not here."

"That would be fun."

The men had started to gravitate toward the top of the stairs, waiting for their escort to unlock the door.

"So why do you keep this door locked?" a man asked, obviously thinking himself clever.

"Aliens," Paula deadpanned. "We've had a real problem with them coming in this way. They sneak into the concierge lounge and load up on the hors d'oeuvres. I've seen them walk out with six plates, one in each hand."

"How was it?" Rusty asked.

"Spectacular."

"The launch?"

Paula gave him a suspicious look. "What else would I be talking about?"

Rusty shrugged, but his sly grin gave away his mischievous intent. "I went up to the concierge lounge and Brenda said you took a bunch of people up on the roof. I just wondered if one of them was Lady Baltimore."

"Her name's Wynne."

"Oh, so you're on a first-name basis now. What comes next?"

"Nothing, bonehead." Though he was technically her boss, they had worked together so closely that Paula thought of him more as a brother. And he was the only one at work besides the director she had told about being a lesbian. "We just talked about work mostly. She's very nice."

"You know I'm cool with whatever, don't you?"

"Yeah, but there's nothing to be cool with." She wasn't about to mention Wynne inviting her for a drink. It was bad enough she was probably reading more into it than Wynne had meant. She didn't need Rusty busting her chops for details.

Wynne stepped out of the bath and wrapped herself in a large fluffy towel. Her leg and hip felt wonderfully relaxed, and if she went right to bed, she probably wouldn't even need to take the usual painkillers.

It would be great to have a tub like this one at home, she thought, but the bathroom in her small two-bedroom townhouse wouldn't accommodate a tub that large. Too bad, though. It was funny she slept better here in a hotel than she did in her own home. Then again, there was nothing funny about that at all, she thought dismally.

Wynne had called home before her bath to check in and to report her excitement about witnessing the launch. Her mother seemed to be managing fine on her own this trip, since Janelle had been able to stop by and look in.

As she readied for bed, her thoughts turned back to her evening on the roof. What on earth had made her blurt out an invitation for a drink? Paula had even accepted . . . sort of . . . but she probably had no idea where Wynne was coming from. Hell, Wynne didn't know where she was coming from either.

What she knew was Paula McKenzie beckoned her attention in a way no one had since her last big crush almost eight years ago. Interestingly, that had been yet another strong, independent woman—Marlene Cox, the owner of Gone Tomorrow Tours. Over time, that crush ran its course and dissipated, thanks in no small sum to the looming reminder of Marlene's husband. There

31

was nothing to be gained from pining for a happily married straight woman.

Wynne had pored over her feelings for Marlene for a year or two, asking herself what had ignited that spark, and how could she find it in someone who was attainable. As a new hire, she had been nurtured by her boss, made to feel like an important cog in the company, and eventually given uncommon autonomy with regard to marketing decisions. She answered this trust with hard work and loyalty.

So why was Paula McKenzie stirring those same feelings Marlene had evoked so many years ago? Most likely it was because she was giving Wynne special attention, which made her feel good because it was coming from someone whose authority she admired. That was the pattern, and Wynne had always found it so difficult to connect with women who didn't have those authoritative traits.

The rational part of her said Paula was just doing her job, making guests feel welcome and at home. As for the upgrade, that was obviously a promotion to encourage guests to spend more—and in Wynne's case, it had worked. Sure, she was invited to the roof tonight to watch the launch, but then so were all of the others in the concierge lounge.

But Wynne thought she had seen something else . . . interest, perhaps. There was no ring on Paula's finger that said she had a husband or fiancé, and she hadn't gravitated to the men on the roof. It seemed to Wynne that Paula genuinely liked her, aside from her professional rapport.

When she finished in the bathroom, she hung the towel on the back of the door and turned out the lights. Foregoing the usual nightshirt, she slipped nude between the cool sheets to continue thinking about Paula McKenzie.

Chapter 4

Paula pulled her dark green Mazda Miata into the double driveway of her parents' home, glad for the shade of her brother's minivan. Most likely, everyone was already in the backyard pool getting an early start on their respective sunburns. Though Paula was blond, she had her father's brown eyes, and they both fared better in the sun than the rest of the family.

"Anybody home?" she yelled from the foyer.

"Paula?" Her father's voice called from the kitchen.

"Dad!" Without delay, she went straight to her father to deliver the hug she had been saving since Monday night when the shuttle launched. "Congratulations."

"Thanks, hon, but save it for when she touches down." Everyone at NASA was watchful of the re-entry, just as they had focused on the launches for years after the Challenger accident.

"Tell you what, I'll give you another one for that. But the launch was a beauty."

"It certainly was." Ray turned to pick up the plate of hamburger patties on the counter. At fifty-nine years old, Ray McKenzie still boasted a full head of wavy graying blond hair and a slender physique, the latter thanks to his daily run along the beaches on the Cape.

"You want any help?

"Nah, go say hi to everyone. I've got the easy job."

"Okay, but let's talk later. I want to hear how the mission's going." Her father had a gift for translating all of the technical mumbo-jumbo into interesting stories and facts. When she was in junior high school, she and her brother Rod had made a game of getting their dad ready for the reporters by firing questions at him during dinner. The tradition carried over to this day.

Paula walked through the open French doors to the large screened-in patio, where, as she had predicted, Rod and his wife Adrienne were in the pool with their five-year-old son Josh and three-year-old daughter Jordan.

"Hey, baby!"

"Mom!" Paula hugged her mother like a long lost relative, though they had seen each other only two weeks ago. The launch of Atlantis had brought welcome stress to all of the McKenzies, and they naturally drew closer to share it.

"I thought you were going to cut your hair." Maxine McKenzie snagged the ponytail that protruded from the back of her daughter's USS Columbia cap.

"I chickened out," Paula admitted. "But I made another appointment for the week after next."

"Pauwa!" A very wet five-year-old wrapped his arms around his aunt's legs to say hello.

"Hi, Josh!" Ignoring the fact that her nephew was dripping, Paula bent down for a big hug. Not to be outdone, her niece soon joined them, dripping as well. "Hi, Jordan!"

"So now that you're already wet, you should come on in," her brother shouted from the pool. Rodney McKenzie was a building inspector for Brevard County, an important job in a coastal community that got its share of hurricanes.

"No, thanks. It's still too cold for me." Today was the first day the McKenzies had used their pool since October. Though temperatures would climb only to the mid-seventies, everyone was antsy to hurry spring along. "You guys doing all right?"

"We're good. Did you see the launch?"

"Of course. I even took some of the guests on the concierge floor to the rooftop to watch it." Paula had no idea why she had just shared that tidbit . . . except that she had been thinking about it for days. "Where'd you guys go?"

"I went to the press site," Rod answered. "Adrienne and the kids went to the causeway."

"You went to the press site?" Paula was jealous. She rarely got to go because of work, but the press site at the Kennedy Space Center where her father worked was the best place to experience the liftoff. Situated next to the giant Vehicle Assembly Building, the press site was eight miles from the launch pad. The flagpole and six-foot high digital clock in the foreground were staples of NASA news coverage.

"The next launch is scheduled for a Saturday," her father chimed in. "Let me know if you can make it and I'll get you a pass."

"Cool!" Paula's first thought was how nice it would be if Wynne could come along. It wouldn't be a problem getting her a press pass, but it would all depend on whether or not she would be coming to town that weekend and if she could come a couple of days early.

Today was a typical Saturday at the McKenzie household. Paula and her brother quizzed their dad through lunch about the mission, then she spent an hour or more on the floor with the kids before they settled down for an afternoon nap. She enjoyed the company of her family, but had no idea she was the source of much concern for her mother.

35

Over the last few years, Maxine McKenzie had worried that her daughter seemed to have no life outside of work and these twice-monthly weekend visits to Cocoa Beach. Paula never talked about anyone special, but Maxine wasn't sure if that was because there was no one, or if Paula just didn't feel comfortable sharing that part of her life.

Paula once told her how difficult it was to date someone steady when you were off only two nights a week. But Maxine suspected it was more than that. It was almost as if Paula had just given up on finding someone to be with. Rather, she seemed satisfied to have her job be the center of her life.

Maxine thought she knew her daughter as well as a mother could, and something was different today—something that hadn't been there only two weeks ago. Paula was relaxed and happy, and her only mention of work was the bit about taking guests up to the roof for the shuttle launch. She seemed clearly excited about one guest in particular, a woman from Baltimore.

Wynne grimaced with pain as she crawled across the floor in her mother's bedroom, following the extension cord to its end behind the television. This was not her favorite way to spend a Saturday afternoon. She would almost rather have stayed in her office to catch up.——

"It's no wonder the fuse blew, Kitty. I'm surprised you haven't burned the house down," she muttered to herself. "Mother!"

Wynne counted seven electrical appliances feeding off two adaptors and the extension cord. Three or four at a time was probably enough to overload the circuit.

"What? Did you find the problem?" Kitty Connelly entered the room to find her older daughter sprawled on the floor, her head behind the TV.

Wynne extracted herself and held up the array of cords and adapters. "This is way too much to be plugged into the same outlet." One by one, she identified the plugs—the TV, the VCR, the cable box, the clock, the lamp, the humidifier, and the small space heater. "You're giving the fuse box more than it can handle."

"But I need all of those things. How can I read the TV listings without the light?" she asked indignantly, adding, "And you don't expect me to sit up here and freeze."

"No, but you're going to have to plug some of this stuff into different outlets." One by one, Wynne rearranged things so the clock radio and humidifier now worked off a plug on the far side of the room, and the space heater and lamp used an extension cord that ran into the hallway.

"But it looks terrible to have that running out there," the elder Connelly whined.

"It's only temporary, until you get an electrician over here to put another outlet in this room off a different fuse."

"That's so unnecessary. I've lived in this room for thirty-seven years, and I never needed another outlet before."

"But you have all this stuff now, Mom." Wynne gestured at the various items about the room. When her father died, her mother gradually used less and less of the large Tudor house, creating her own personal space in her large bedroom. "You don't have a choice about this. You can't leave all those things plugged in there. It's dangerous, and besides, Sophie might come in here sometime and play with all those cords and get shocked." Invoking her niece's name would do the trick.

"I suppose you're right."

"Can you find an electrician in the Yellow Pages and tell him what it is you need?"

"I don't know if I can remember all that."

Wynne always hoped for a different answer, but she never got one. It would be up to her to find someone to come over and take care of this.

"Okay, I'll do it on Monday. But you'll have to show him where things go when he gets here." She walked her mother through the directions until she was satisfied that the woman understood. Together, they returned to the first floor of the old house, where

Wynne collapsed on the couch and tried to massage the soreness from her leg.

"It still hurts you so much, doesn't it, sweetheart?"

Wynne sighed at seeing the tears that sprang to her mother's eyes. She tried to hide the pain that dogged her every day, but sometimes it got the best of her.

"It's not that bad, Mom. It just gets a little sore."

"You're going to have to go ahead with that other surgery or it will never get better."

"I know . . . I just can't do it right now." Wynne knew the surgery to bond her splintered femur just above her knee was the last procedure planned for her recovery, but she just couldn't bear giving in to the doctors again and laying up for another four to six weeks. It was especially true now that she had this added responsibility in Orlando. Besides, she would have lots of time to do it if she got laid off.

"Auntie Wynne!" An excited two-year old barreled across the room to deliver a hug and kiss to her beloved aunt.

"Hey, angel. How's my girl?" Wynne adored her sister's child. "How are you doing, Janelle?"

Wynne's younger sister was hot on the heels of her little girl, who had torn through the house after recognizing her auntie's Volvo in the driveway. Janelle was as much like their mother as Wynne was like their father. Like Kitty, Janelle was average height, with expressive brown eyes and black hair. Her sister had done a six-year stint in the navy and was now finishing up her nursing degree.

"I'm good. We've just been to the park, where somebody went on the slide all by herself," Janelle bragged.

Her eyes wide, Wynne turned to her niece. "All by yourself?"

Sophie nodded proudly.

"What a big girl you're getting to be!"

"Do you have to head back to Orlando tomorrow?" Janelle asked.

"No, this is my week to be at home."

"I bet you've been at your office all day," Janelle said with a huff. She made no secret of her displeasure at the amount of time Wynne spent at work.

Wynne had to work most weekends when she was home to make up for being out of the office so much. Her inbox was always crammed full on Thursday morning when she returned from Orlando, as no one else could deal with marketing issues in her absence. In fact, she planned to work at home tonight and tomorrow afternoon to catch up.

"Will you stay for supper?" Kitty asked, obviously trying to insert a little cheer into their conversation.

"No, I need to get home, but thanks. And I'll call the electrician on Monday, but don't use all that stuff at the same time, okay?"

"Whatever you say. You know I depend on you to help me out with those things."

And with everything else, Wynne thought resignedly as she stood to leave.

Wynne tried to no avail to mask her limp as she walked down the steps from the porch to her car. So much in her life had changed since the accident, but the lingering pain was not the worst of it, she thought. Something else had made her a different person.

After almost three hours online, Wynne disposed of the final message in her mailbox. With the time she had put in last night at home and this afternoon, she was now caught up enough to start the week at Gone Tomorrow Tours with her head above water. It would be another frantic week, trying to get everything done—at work, at home, at her mother's home—before heading out again next Sunday for Orlando.

But no matter how much extra work the Orlando project had created, it was hard not to look forward to going. The bi-monthly trips she had originally dreaded had become both a respite from the responsibility and something of an adventure, thanks in part to her new friend at the hotel. Wynne knew she had no business letting her mind wander to Paula McKenzie, but it wasn't something she could stop . . . or even wanted to stop.

No matter how many times she told herself that Paula was just doing her job, it was hard to overlook the feeling that she was going out of her way to connect. Wynne fished her wallet from her briefcase and located the business card she had been given almost a month ago: *Paula R. McKenzie, Shift Manager*. With an e-mail address, she noted.

Paula finished the last of her report to management on the activities of the week. Since it was Sunday night, Rusty was filling in at the front desk to help handle the rush. With her work done, she knew she should relieve him so he too could wrap up his paperwork, but Paula couldn't resist using this rare time alone to check out the company's job postings. She long ago acknowledged it wasn't likely she would advance here in Orlando. Add to that the fact that her life—not just here at work, but all around—was growing increasingly stagnant. As much as she hated to leave this hotel, it might be time to consider making a change. She logged on to the Weller Regent network, wondering if perhaps there might be something open in the DC area.

But the job postings could wait, she realized, sitting up straight in her chair. She had e-mail from KWConnelly.

Hi Paula,

I just wanted you to know that I've followed the news of the shuttle mission very closely and look forward to seeing its triumphant return on Friday. Thank you ever so much for including me last week in that special viewing on the roof. Honestly, I can't tell you how much that meant, or how many times I've thought of that magnificent sight since then.

I look forward to my trip next Sunday to the Weller Regent, and I hope we'll have another chance to say hello.

Thank you again,

Wynne

Paula forwarded the note to the ISP she used for personal e-mail. If she was going to become friends with this intriguing woman, she wanted to do it out of the prying eyes of their network administrators.

Chapter 5

Paula had hoped to be working the front desk when Wynne made her appearance at the Weller Regent on Sunday night, but it was not to be. Instead, she found herself on the fourteenth floor in the middle of a domestic dispute that was growing nastier by the minute.

"Mrs. Frandle, I need to know if you wish to press charges. If you choose to do that, I'll call the Orlando Police Department, and they can be here in five minutes. If you decide you'd rather not, our security staff will escort your husband from the premises for the night, and hopefully he'll cool off." Paula stood in the bathroom with the door closed watching Karen Frandle shake as she held ice to her bleeding lip. "The decision is entirely up to you."

"I don't know," the crying woman said with a sigh. "What do you think I should do?"

"I'm not qualified to give you advice on this. But I'll do whatever you say." Paula would have his ass thrown in jail.

"I'm scared if you take him away tonight he's going to go nuts on me when he gets back," she whimpered. "What if they just took him out for a while and brought him back?"

"I'm afraid we can't do that, Mrs. Frandle. Based on what we've heard and seen tonight, your husband is behaving violently, and it's our policy to remove people like that from the premises and not allow them back." After nine years, Paula was no longer surprised at the incidence of domestic violence, even among couples who seemed to exude an air of sophistication.

"Then I guess we'll just both leave," the woman finally said with indignation. At once, she exited the bathroom and announced they would depart.

"I'm not paying for this night!" Howard Frandle barked as he began to throw his belongings in a suitcase.

Paula had the authority to waive his room charge, and that was preferable to having him remain on the grounds. "I will see that your account is credited."

"Let's get out of here, Karen," he ordered. "This hotel chain will never get my business again."

Paula hoped he was telling the truth. The Weller Regent didn't need guests like him. She waited as they finished gathering their belongings and then walked with the two security guards to escort them from the building. "Give them a parking pass, and make sure you see them leave the premises," she whispered as the foursome exited the elevator and walked toward the parking garage.

A quick look at her watch told her she had likely missed the arrival of Wynne Connelly, and thanks to having spent the last hour and a half in this domestic dispute, she was going to be chained to her desk for the rest of the night.

The alarm rudely jarred Wynne from a comfortable sleep at six-fifteen. "Time to hit the fitness room," she grumbled to herself, knowing full well the thirty minutes she spent each day on the exercise bike was the only thing that kept her mobile.

43

She had been disappointed last night not to have seen or heard from Paula, especially after they had traded e-mails a couple of times last week. But Wynne had to remind herself that while she was at leisure at the Weller Regent, Paula was not. As shift manager, she probably had important things to do, and it was stupid for Wynne to be placing expectations on her time.

On her way to the bathroom, she spotted an envelope on the floor, pushed under her door sometime after she retired at a quarter to midnight. On hotel stationery, the writer had inscribed her name neatly with a slight backward slant. Someone was left-handed, she realized with a smile. She liked learning things about Paula McKenzie.

Wynne,

Welcome back to Orlando. I'm sorry I didn't get a chance to say hello last evening. We had a few emergencies and I ended up in my office until two a.m. getting my paperwork finished.

If I miss you tonight in the concierge lounge, I'll try to call before it gets too late.

Paula

p.s. That was some landing on Friday, wasn't it?

Wynne smiled and folded the note, very pleased to realize Paula had tried to get in touch. It was becoming clear Paula's job wouldn't leave them much time to connect here at the hotel. Getting to know each other would be difficult, but Wynne still wanted to try.

"Okay, I'm ready." Paula gripped the arms of her chair and squeezed her eyes tightly shut. A few snips later and it was too late to change her mind. "Done?"

"I'm done with that part. You want to see?" Carla held out the long blond ponytail.

"No! Finish it." Paula hadn't worn her hair short since the summer she had left for Europe.

Carla spun her around to face the mirror. "Okay, here's what I want to do . . ."

Out of habit, Wynne looked over at the front desk as she walked through the lobby. She had put in a longer day than usual, starting the morning off at a breakfast meeting with Doug, Cheryl, and Ken Markoff, the CEO at Eldon-Markoff. Cheryl had provided her boss with regular updates on the progress of the planning committee, but until today, he hadn't actually met her crew of two.

Now she was beat, eager to head upstairs, grab a bite to eat, and settle in for an early soak in the jetted tub. Paula didn't work on Tuesdays, so she wouldn't be coming around tonight to the concierge lounge. There was no point in hanging out there. But her vigil had been rewarded last night when Paula stopped by briefly to say hello, and to apologize for not having more time.

Wynne rounded the corner for the elevators, stopping short when the reflection from a broad mirror on the opposite wall caught her eye. Turning to face the beauty salon in the small row of shops, she saw Paula—with short hair—draped in a black plastic cape, her dark eyebrows raised in doubt.

"I think I need a manicure," Wynne said to no one in particular. She had just gotten one on Saturday, but here was finally an opportunity to chat with a very captive audience.

"Good afternoon, is there any chance I could get a manicure?"

"Of course," answered the stylist. "Please have a seat and I'll go get Elena."

As she disappeared into the back, Wynne approached to stand directly behind her new friend, whose brown eyes were wide with astonishment.

"Getting a trim?" Paula's long hair had been beautiful, but this was going to look fabulous.

"Just a small one," Paula almost squeaked.

"I bet it'll look great," she said, trying to give some reassurance. "Have you worn it short before?"

"Not since high school."

"It's going to be gorgeous," Wynne said again, this time in a low timbre. She would have sworn she felt Paula shudder. She took a seat facing the stylist's chair and readied for her manicure.

A talkative Hispanic woman soon joined them and began to make fast work of Wynne's impeccable nails. She and the stylist bantered back and forth, mostly in Spanish, and apparently about Paula's new hairstyle. On occasion, Paula would chuckle, obviously understanding their words, but not participating in the conversation.

"They're talking about my boss, Rusty Wilburn," Paula explained. "He's in love with a girl who works at the Brooklyn Deli down the street."

"I know the Brooklyn Deli. I get lunch there sometimes."

"Rusty walks down there every day on his break to see this girl, but he always stops in here first to get advice from these two ladies on how to act and what to say."

"So are they helping the guy, or are they setting him up to crash and burn?"

"Mostly, they're helping. But he's really bashful, so they get a kick out of telling him to say or do stuff he'd never have the nerve to do."

Carla was almost finished with the masterpiece that was Paula's new coiffure. She continued to jabber in Spanish, and this time, all three women laughed aloud.

"Now, she's giving me advice on my love life," Paula translated.

"This should be interesting."

"In English, Carla. And throw in a little wisdom for our guest here," she said, indicating Wynne at the table. "This is what I have to put up with on a daily basis."

"Okay, I was just saying that a man likes to think he's in charge, so even if he isn't you have to make him feel that way. Don't you think that's true, Miss?"

Wynne laughed in amazement. "I don't have a clue what men like, but if they need all of that, why would anybody want one?"

"My sentiments exactly!" Paula cheered, turning quickly to cast a knowing look. In that instant, they connected.

Thrilled at the revelation of that little piece of data, Wynne smiled back, her look a confirmation of their coded exchange.

Paula took the offered handheld mirror to check out the back of her new style. It was short, just barely touching her collar. Carla had styled it puffy on top, spraying it to stay in place. But Paula fixed that quickly by running a hand through it and shaking it loose.

"You're messing up my hair," Carla whined.

"It's my hair, and you fixed it like a helmet. I like it to look more natural."

"Let's ask our guest." Turning toward Wynne, the stylist posed the question. "Which do you like better, the elegant way I styled her hair, or the mop she chose for herself?"

Wynne's first thought was it was pretty hard to run your hands through all that hairspray. "I think I prefer the more natural look," she answered, casting a brilliant smile to the waiting Paula. "In fact, I think it looks fantastic."

"Thank you very much." Paula turned back toward Carla and smirked, mussing her hair again for good measure.

"You hurt me," Carla pouted.

"I'll tip you and you'll feel better," she answered, digging for her wallet.

Wynne did the same for her manicurist, and the two ladies exited the salon together.

"So you're off today," Wynne observed. That meant they both had free time right now.

"Yeah, Tuesdays and Saturdays," Paula answered. "Do you have to go do some work now . . . or anything?"

"No. Could I talk you into joining me for dinner?" She gestured in the direction of the Weller Regent's four-star restaurant.

"I was about to ask you the same thing. But not here. Are you up for a ride?"

"Absolutely. It would be nice to see something of Orlando besides the office, the hotel, or the airport."

"Then let's do it."

Wynne looked down at Paula's jeans. "I should change. Can you give me a minute?"

"Tell you what. I'll meet you in the parking garage on Level 2. Just go down this hallway and out the door," she said, pointing over her shoulder. "Then up one flight of steps. Look to your left and I'll be waiting."

"Ten minutes."

"Great."

Wynne could feel Paula watching her as she walked toward the elevator.

You shouldn't be doing this, a little voice cautioned.

She pressed the button for the twenty-third floor and settled back against the brass rail as the door closed. That little voice could get lost, for all she cared. It was just dinner, and she was going to do it whether she should or not. There was very little in her life that wasn't an obligation or responsibility. Paula McKenzie was a treat.

This is how it's supposed to feel, she told herself, taking on the objections of her conscience. Through the years, Wynne had met dozens of women at parties, at clubs, and through mutual friends. She had followed up with a handful who seemed like the strong and independent type, going out a few times to see if anything sparked. When it didn't—and it never really had—she cooled things and went back into hibernation again. On rare occasions, there would be a sexual spark, but when she played it out, it was never attached to the kind of woman she wanted in her life.

Things were different with Paula, who was exactly the sort of woman Wynne had always envisioned as a partner. And though they barely knew each other, the spark was already there. How else could Wynne explain why she thought about Paula so much, why her breath caught when she saw e-mail from her, and why she was going out to dinner with her, even though the little voice told her she shouldn't?

Wynne slipped on the tan slacks and red sweater she had worn on the flight down last Sunday, grabbing a blazer just in case it turned cool. Paula had been wearing black jeans and a long-sleeved white V-neck pullover, so she didn't want to be too dressed up.

Right on time, she emerged from the stairwell on the second

floor of the parking garage. An engine roar got her attention as she eyed the roadster—top-down—pulling out of a space to draw to a stop in front of her.

"Was this the runt of the litter?"

"Come on, it's bigger than it looks," Paula answered with a smirk.

Wynne gamely complied, bending low to fold herself into the passenger seat. Little by little, she stretched her legs in front of her, surprised to find plenty of room. Leaning over the console, she peeked underneath the steering wheel. "Do you have to pedal?"

"Yes, it's how I keep in shape," Paula answered back, not missing a beat.

"You never struck me as the sports car type."

"This is probably the only thing about me that's not practical," she explained. "But I just love the way it grips the road."

"That's probably because you're so much closer to it," Wynne said with a laugh. "Will I have to drag my foot when we're ready to stop?"

"Yeah, I'll let you know when," Paula teased right back. "Do you like ribs?"

"Are you kidding? I love ribs."

"Great. I've got the perfect place." Paula whipped out into traffic and made for the expressway. "You warm enough? This car's got a great little heater," she shouted.

"You drive around with the top down and the heater on?" Wynne brushed her hair from her face, but to no avail.

"Sometimes," she answered defensively. Paula glanced over at her struggle with the wind. "Here, have a hat. I won't need it anymore." She grinned and ran her fingers through her short hair.

Wynne noted the USS Columbia insignia, took it thankfully, and tucked her hair underneath the band. Now that it wasn't blowing all over the place, this open-air ride was rather nice. Paula had slipped on a jacket, but Wynne was comparing this to the winter in Baltimore, and it didn't seem cold at all.

Fifteen minutes later, Paula pulled into Buck's, a family style restaurant with a sports bar décor. Wynne twisted her body to climb out. "Wait, I'm having a *déja vu*. It's from when I was born."

"Very funny." Paula chuckled. "So I bet you drive one of those road monsters."

"A Volvo sedan. I'd crush this thing like a bug."

"I'll have you know I'm not easily intimidated," Paula answered, tossing up an eyebrow.

"I think I already figured that out about you."

A few minutes later the women were seated across from one another in a booth, the tall wooden seat backs affording them a measure of privacy in this otherwise bustling venue.

"I recommend the pork ribs," Paula announced, "with the hot sauce if you're man enough."

"Then I'll have the pork ribs, with extra hot sauce."

"Ooooo, tough girl."

"Believe me, I am a tough girl," Wynne answered back, now arching her own brow. "And if you're not easily intimidated, I sure hope we never tangle, Miss McKenzie." Though tangling with Paula might be quite a bit of fun.

"Believe me, with all the stuff I have to go through at work, the last thing I want to do on my free time is tangle." Paula went on to relate her Sunday night experience with the Frandles, and to tell a few stories about breaking up drunken parties, and even a fight or two.

"You know, that's something I noticed about you right off the bat that first night we met, when you handled that man in front of me. You had this air of authority about you. I really admire that in people."

"Well, thank you. I have to be like that. And I bet you're really good at what you do."

"I am good at my job. But I don't think that's going to be enough to save it." Now it was Wynne's turn to talk about work, about how the company she worked for had been acquired by Eldon-Markoff, and how she was helping them centralize the marketing operations in a way that would likely put her out of a job.

"The vice president for sales and marketing is great, though. In fact, she's a lot like you in a way. I mean, both of you sort of . . ."

"Walk softly and carry a big stick."

"Exactly."

Dinner arrived and both women dug in, each daring the other to add Tabasco to the already fiery barbecue sauce. The conversation was easy, Wynne thought, like they were already friends. And it was fun to see Paula's playful side. She talked again about her family, and how proud everyone was of the recent shuttle mission. Wynne told all about her mother's ineptitude around the house.

"So I have to congratulate you on that little response of yours to Carla's philosophy of men," Paula said. "How did you know I'd get it?"

"Well, I wasn't sure you had until you spun around in the chair and flashed me that big smile . . . sort of like the one you're wearing now."

"I had to see the look on your face, just to make sure. I thought we were on the same wavelength, but you never want to assume anything."

"What gave you the idea we were on the same wavelength?"

"Oh, I don't know. That first night we met, I just sort of got the feeling you were checking me out while I was checking you in," Paula quipped.

"You did, did you? That's because you were flirting with me."

"Oh, no! You were the one doing the flirting. 'Shall I ask for you?'"

"Yeah, Miss 'Here's my card with my direct extension. If there's anything you need.'"

Paula raised her hands to her blushing cheeks. "This from a woman who said 'I promise not to misbehave.'"

Wynne pursed her lips indignantly for a moment, finally looking down as she nodded her head in mock shame. "I was flirting," she admitted softly.

"I knew it."

"But so were you."

"So was I," Paula finally confessed, and both women laughed.

As they were talking, the waitress dropped by to discreetly deposit their check.

"Thank you for being my dinner guest," Wynne said as she quickly covered the check with her hand. After a brief argument, Paula acquiesced and thanked her, vowing that she would get the bill next time.

Wynne dropped some bills in the tray, grimacing as she stood.

"Are you okay?"

"Yeah, my leg just gets really stiff when I sit for awhile."

"Is there anything I can do? I mean besides marching you outside and folding you into my tiny car?"

"No, I think that'll finish me off," Wynne said, trying in vain to hide the stiffness in her hip and leg.

"I'm sorry. If I'd known three years ago that we'd actually be going out to dinner, I'd have gotten a larger car." The women exited into the parking lot, Paula offering her arm.

"And if I could go back three years, I would stop at that intersection, even though I had the right of way."

"So it was a car accident?"

"Yeah, some kid stole a truck and was trying to outrun the cops. He hit me broadside."

"That's awful. Was anyone else hurt?"

Wynne nodded, feeling the sadness wash over her as it always did when she spoke of that night. "The kid was killed. He was only fifteen years old. I was alone in the car."

"I'm so sorry to hear that. And that was three years ago?"

"Yeah. I've already had a few surgeries on my leg. I need to have one more, but I just can't bring myself to schedule it."

"Will it fix this pain you have?"

"It should. But I'd be out of work for about a month, and back into physical therapy twice a week. I just don't have the time to do that right now." She looked down at where her hand gripped Paula's arm, squeezing a bit before letting go to climb into the small car.

52

"Well, you definitely win the Tough Girl Award, my friend."

As she had done on the ride over, Wynne put the USS Columbia hat back on, tucking her hair just right so it wouldn't blow. "It's great you have this hat," she said wistfully, remembering the sad day the crew was lost.

"That reminds me, the next launch is scheduled for a Saturday. If it works out that you can come down on Friday, I can get passes to the press site right there at the Cape," Paula offered.

The idea of a weekend trip jolted Wynne back to reality. She couldn't afford for her flirtations to get out of hand. "I'm not sure. If you'll let me know the date, I'll check my calendar."

"Okay, just . . . let me know."

From Paula's uncomfortable reaction, Wynne instantly regretted her formal response. "It would be great if I can work it out."

They rode in silence back to the hotel, where Paula pulled into the circle at the main entrance. She reached over and squeezed Wynne's hand. "Thank you very much for tonight. I had a lot of fun."

"Me too."

Wynne folded back the covers and climbed into bed, still trying to get a grip on what she was feeling.

The soak in the swirling water had eased the throbbing in her leg, but she was far from relaxed. What had started out as an adventurous evening had left her a nervous wreck. She couldn't take her friendship with Paula any further, but that didn't make her want it less. All night, she had been looking across the table, wanting to kiss those lips and pull that body to hers. Only in her fantasies, one of which she was going to enjoy right now.

Chapter 6

"What is this stuff?" Rusty couldn't hide his disgust.

"It's called edamame, and you're not supposed to eat the whole thing. Just put it between your teeth and pull out the soybeans." Paula had insisted on something different tonight, despite Rusty's pleas to return to the deli.

"If I'd wanted beans, I could have gotten a bowl of chili and eaten them with a spoon."

"Rusty, I needed a break. You can go see her tomorrow night, and maybe she'll have had a chance to miss you."

"Did I tell you we went out again last Friday?"

"Only about twelve times, but if it makes you feel better, you can tell me all about it again."

"What if we talk about your lady instead?" He gestured to the monitor, which showed Wynne Connelly climbing again from a cab and collecting her things.

Paula had been watching the clock, expecting Wynne to arrive sometime between nine and nine-thirty.

"She is not my lady." Though after their dinner a couple of weeks ago, she was certain the hotel staff was abuzz about her dropping off a guest at the front door.

"You should go on down to the desk and check her in," Rusty suggested.

"Oh, I don't think so. Every single person on staff knows we went out the last time she was here, and I'd rather not be under their microscope. Besides, Jolene and Matthew have everything under control." The view had changed to the front desk, where Paula could see Wynne standing in line, looking around. They had traded several e-mails over the last couple of weeks, agreeing to a movie and pizza on Tuesday night.

"Nobody's going to think anything about it," he reasoned. "Everybody knows by now that she's a regular, and they'll just think you're friends."

"That's exactly what we are, Rusty. But I'd just prefer that people not read any more into it."

"No one cares if you're gay, Paula. Everybody knows that Matthew is, and they don't give him a hard time. And you know you won't get fired, because the WR has a non-discrimination clause."

"I know all of that on the surface, but you know what? If I come out to these people, the next time I have to reprimand someone, it'll be because I'm a fucking dyke, as if that makes my authority less valid. I'd rather it just be none of their business. Besides, it isn't like I have a personal life to keep private anyway."

The pair watched Jolene complete the check-in process for K. Wynne Connelly, who then turned toward the elevators. Rusty advanced the camera to capture that view, and they stared in silence as she stepped aside for passengers to depart, then disappeared as the door closed.

"At the very least, you should give her a call," he coaxed. Rusty couldn't understand why on earth someone who had so much to offer would keep to herself as Paula did. In the three years they had shared the night shift, he had gotten to know her pretty well. She had mentioned only one casual girlfriend in all that time. Part of the problem, he knew, was their awful work schedule. Lucky for him that Juliana worked the evening hours too, and then, only part time.

"Later, maybe."

Rusty was bright enough to realize Paula wouldn't call when he was there. He would have to think of a reason to make himself scarce in a half-hour or so.

Wynne opened her briefcase and spread her materials out on a corner of the conference table. It was a quarter till nine. Usually, they started promptly at eight-thirty, but there was no sign that anyone else was even here. A feeling of dread swept over her as she considered she might have gotten her weeks mixed up, or they had canceled this week and she somehow missed the message.

"Good morning. Sorry I'm late." Cheryl bounded into the room with her typical exuberance and Wynne breathed a sigh of relief. "Let's move into my office to work today, shall we?" She helped Wynne collect her papers.

"Is Doug already here?"

"No, Ken and I decided it would be best to proceed with just the two of us. That might mean an extra trip for you, but we may be able to move through things a little faster with less discussion."

She meant fewer objections from Doug, Wynne knew.

"I'll be happy to do whatever you need, Cheryl."

"I know that about you, and I really appreciate it." She led them into her corner office, where coffee and breakfast rolls were already set up. "I didn't get a chance to eat this morning, so I hope you don't mind. Help yourself."

"No, thank you. I ate at the hotel."

"How do you like the Weller Regent?"

"It's very comfortable. And it's quiet. I like that."

"So do I. There's a nice one in Washington, but the one in New York is my favorite. They also just opened a new one in Dallas and another in Denver."

56

"I haven't had the chance to try those."

"And speaking of Dallas, I'm sure you're wondering why we decided to take Doug out of the loop with regard to the marketing plan." Cheryl's eyes held a conspiratorial twinkle.

"I could guess, but I'd rather not."

"You're very diplomatic, Wynne. And you'd probably be right. It just seemed like it was getting harder and harder to push ahead with Doug's constant objections to the plan, especially once it became apparent that he was opposed to anything that might weaken his own position."

Wynne nodded in understanding. That was Doug in a nutshell.

"That makes me want to ask why you haven't had the same reaction." The words hung in the air for a moment, but before Wynne could answer, she continued. "It's become obvious to me—almost since the day we started this overhaul—that the streamlined sales and marketing plan is going to take away some positions, and yours is certainly at risk. I know you've seen that, but you don't seem to fight it at all. Why is that? Are you eager to be rid of Eldon-Markoff?"

"No, not at all. It's just that centralization is what's best for the company and the stockholders, and that's who I work for. I can see the handwriting on the wall, but that doesn't change what's a good business decision. I trust that Eldon-Markoff will treat me fairly if my job gets cut."

Despite her hopeful words, her stomach had dropped at the confirmation that her job was definitely on the block.

"You will be, Wynne. If you've worried about that at all, let me put your fears to rest."

"Thank you."

Paula pulled into the circle in front of the Weller Regent, waving politely to the valet crew. There wasn't any point in trying to meet Wynne in the garage and sneak out, since everyone already knew she had gone out to dinner with this hotel guest two weeks ago. Besides, that flight of steps to the employee parking level was an unnecessary hardship for Wynne with her injured leg.

She smiled as she spotted her companion waiting outside, and a uniformed man hurriedly stepped forward to open the passenger door.

"Hello, Miss McKenzie. You ladies have a nice evening."

"Hi, Justin. Thanks." Paula shifted the car into gear and slowly edged out into traffic. Tonight, the top was up, as it had rained earlier in the day. "Hello again, Miss Connelly. Are you enjoying your stay at the Weller Regent?"

"Most certainly, Miss McKenzie. I especially appreciate the way the hotel staff coordinates my entertainment schedule."

Paula grinned at her, almost giddy with excitement. She thought Tuesday night would never get here.

"What movie are we going to see?"

Paula explained their choices and they settled on an action adventure flick that had gotten fair reviews. Once they entered the theater, Paula relaxed, oblivious to her companion's sudden case of nerves.

Wynne had started the evening calm and collected, but when they took their seats, her composure began to erode. As her eyes adjusted to the darkness, she lost all ability to concentrate on the film. All she could think about was how much she wanted to hold Paula's hand. She had told herself ever since her last trip to Orlando the only way she was going to allow herself to socialize with Paula was if they kept things at a friendship level. But here in the dark theater, the need for even just a small bit of physical contact was overwhelming. Unable to resist, she picked up the drink from the cup holder they shared and moved it to her other side, raising the chair arm between them. In a not-so-subtle move, her hand crept over to Paula's. She was rewarded instantly by fingers that wrapped around hers and squeezed. Gradually, the knots in her stomach unwound and she gave in to the comfort of Paula's touch. All she had to do was keep things from going too far. This much she could handle.

When they left the theater two hours later, Wynne clung to Paula's arm, limping slightly at the stiffness from sitting still for so long. They reached the pizza parlor in only a few minutes.

"Which is better for your leg, a table or a booth?"

"A booth," Wynne answered, nodding toward an open one near the door. "I've been meaning to tell you, one of the best things about coming to Orlando is soaking in that Jacuzzi tub at the end of the day."

"Sounds like you need one at home."

Wynne shook her head. "I already looked into it. I don't have enough room. I live in a pretty small townhouse."

"Well, there's always another solution."

"Move?"

"Actually, I was going to suggest that you come down to Orlando and stay with us more often."

"Now there's an idea."

"That would really get the tongues wagging back at the hotel."

The waitress interrupted to get their order. Moments later, she deposited two icy mugs of beer at their table.

"Are you out at work?" Wynne asked, sipping the foam from the rim of her mug.

"Not really. I mean, Rusty knows, but he and our boss are the only ones I've ever said anything to. Of course, the whole staff is probably speculating about you and me by now anyway."

"Then maybe I should rent a car and meet you somewhere next time we go out," Wynne offered.

"I hate to have you do that. I should just get over it."

"No, I understand how it is, really."

"What about you? Are you out?"

"Mmmm, yes and no. I don't care if people know, at least back in Baltimore. I don't want to be worrying about secrets all the time. But Eldon-Markoff is another story."

"Don't they have domestic partner benefits? That should be a clue where they're coming from."

"Yeah, but I think the whole industry does that to be competitive. It only takes one person writing your reference to sink your chances of finding a good job. And since I'm probably not going to end up with the company in the long run, the less they know about my personal life, the better."

"Do you have an arrest record I should be aware of?"

Wynne laughed. "Nothing too serious. My dad caught me smoking pot once. That took about ten years off my life."

"I hear you. I was sneaking around in high school with my girl-friend and my parents called me in for 'the big talk.' " Paula used her fingers to make imaginary quote marks. "They were worried because I was spending so much time with Shauna, and since I'd quit hanging out with all my other friends, they thought we were using drugs. Wish I had a picture of my dad's face when I told him what we were really up to."

"You think he would rather it had been drugs?"

Paula chuckled. "I used to wonder. Thank goodness they came around. I didn't outgrow it like they thought I would, so they had to get used to it."

"And they've been nice to your girlfriends?"

"I've never really brought anyone around to the house, except Susan. She and I saw each other for a few months a couple of years ago, but it wasn't serious."

"How did your parents react to seeing you with someone?" Wynne asked.

"They were nice to her, but kind of stiff. She wouldn't notice that, but I did. The thing is, though, I don't know if they were reacting to Susan or the idea of me with Susan."

"Have you ever talked with them about it?"

"Yeah, I've talked with my mom a little. She says she wants me to be happy. She wishes I could find a person to give my attention to, instead of the Weller Regent."

"Yeah, I guess all parents are like that. They want us to be happy, once they get over deciding what should make us that way."

Paula clinked her beer mug with Wynne's. "I'll drink to that. What was it like with your family?"

Wynne chuckled. "Well, it's funny now, but it sure wasn't at the time."

Their pizza suddenly appeared and both women dug in as though famished.

"Something tells me your coming out story is better than mine."

"Coming out took another twenty years off my life. It was when I was in college at the University of Maryland. I was living at home, but I met this woman who lived near campus, and I started staying nights at her place. Mom used to go on and on about what a nice young woman Judith was." Wynne stopped her story to take a drink.

"But then they started getting suspicious, right?"

Wynne shook her head. "Oh, no. It was much more melodramatic than that. You see, in college, your professors don't happen to care if you go by your middle name. They always call you by your first name, and mine is Katharine, just like my mother's. But Judith didn't know that, and during summer vacation when she was home in Connecticut, she sent me this card with a picture of two naked women, and just as a joke, she addressed it to Katharine W. Connelly. Mom opened it by mistake and nearly had a heart attack, and of course she showed it to my dad. Then at dinner, she tossed it in front of me and Janelle grabbed it and started laughing her ass off. Mom was just glaring at me with her arms folded across her chest, and Dad was like 'pass me the potatoes.'"

"Oh, that's hilarious. Your story definitely wins."

"As I said, it's funnier now than it was then. Mom stayed on my case for the next three years or so. Every woman I mentioned, she would ask if that was my girlfriend. Finally when I told her yes, she dropped it. But I have to give the woman credit—she's come around, just like your folks."

The waitress dropped off the check, and this time Paula insisted it was her turn.

"I should probably get back to the hotel," Wynne said. "It's almost midnight, and I have a breakfast meeting at seven-thirty."

Paula offered her arm as an escort and they walked slowly back to the parking lot. When they reached the car, they stopped, Paula guiding Wynne to sit on the rear fender. "You know, there's one real big drawback to me having to drop you in front of a busy hotel."

Wynne began to tremble with the realization that Paula was about to kiss her.

Indeed, Paula stepped closer and placed a hand lightly on her shoulder. "Is this okay?" she whispered as she slowly lowered her head.

Wynne raised her hand and cradled Paula's cheek, guiding the lips toward hers. For the time being, she had tuned out that voice telling her she couldn't have something as nice as this. Their kiss was coy at first, but soon both women were breathing hard, open-mouthed as their tongues danced with a tentative passion. As her free hand made its way to Paula's hip and beyond, a pair of passing headlights stopped them short.

"That was nice," Paula murmured.

Wynne could only nod. She gazed for a few more moments into Paula's eyes, sensing a deep satisfaction at what they had just shared.

"I guess I should get you home."

"Then I suppose one of us should move."

"Oh, that would be me," Paula answered, stepping back to allow Wynne to stand. She unlocked the passenger door and held it while Wynne slipped in.

If it hadn't been for the manual transmission, Wynne would have taken Paula's hand again. She wanted contact for as long as their night together would last.

"So are you coming back in two weeks?" Paula asked.

"That's still the schedule."

"The next launch is the last weekend in April. If you have a chance to check your calendar, let me know if you think you can be here and I'll get an extra pass to the press site."

"I forgot to look, but I will," Wynne promised. That was almost six weeks away, but she doubted she could pull it off.

Paula whipped the Mazda into the curved driveway. "Have a nice day at work tomorrow and a safe trip home. I had a really good time with you tonight."

The valet opened the passenger door and Wynne climbed out, trying as usual to hide the stiffness in her leg. "I did too. Thank you."

"Two weeks?"

"Two weeks."

Wynne readied for bed, her head swimming with the memory of Paula's mouth on hers. If that kiss was indicative of what else they might offer one another, it wasn't going to be easy to maintain control.

For the first time in her whole life, she had found someone who seemed to have the whole package—intelligence, a sense of humor, independence, ambition . . . not to mention the pretty package itself. Paula was the kind of person she wanted for a partner.

But she couldn't give in to her selfish desires. She had to stop herself before things got out of hand.

Chapter 7

"Wow, where'd you get all this energy?" Val had been watching Paula for the last half hour, roaring through her circuit like a woman possessed. Paula was pushing herself to the limit at each station, and as soon as she finished with one, she rushed on to the next machine without a break.

"I don't know. I just feel invigorated all of a sudden." In truth, Paula was still savoring her night out with Wynne last week, and was full of nervous energy in anticipation of Wynne's return.

"You're in love," Val pronounced.

"I am not. We barely know each other."

"That may be true, but you've been in a great mood since last week, and you've talked about the woman almost nonstop."

"That doesn't mean I'm in love. But I do like her a lot." Paula mounted the ab cruncher and started her pulls. "And I think . . . she likes me . . . too," she puffed.

"Well, what's not to like about you? You remember Robbie, the guy I was dating for a while?"

"Yeah."

"He wanted to fix you up with one of his buddies and I told him I didn't think you'd be interested. He said, 'Aw, that's too bad. She's hot!'"

"Just . . . what I need . . . not."

"So what's going to happen with you two? I mean, the woman lives in Baltimore, right?"

"Yeah . . . but she's still . . . got about . . . four more trips here." It was hard to talk and crunch at the same time, but Paula couldn't be still. And besides, she didn't want to think about what would happen when Wynne's work in Orlando was finished.

"And then what happens?"

"Don't know . . . we'll have to . . . cross that bridge . . . when we come to it."

"Slow down. You're making me sore," Val barked. "Are we going to run?"

"Ready when you are." Paula slid off the cruncher and grabbed her bottle of water.

"The way you are today, you'll probably run off and leave me in the dust."

"Only one way to find out," Paula yelled over her shoulder as she took off out the door in the direction of the jogging trail that ran between the condo property and the neighboring golf course. If they cut out to the sidewalk by the main roadway, they could loop around to the other side of the course, a two-mile circuit which they would run twice.

"By the way, I really like your hair that way," Val huffed as they settled into their pace.

"Thanks." And because all conversations eventually had to come back to the woman from Baltimore, Paula added, "Wynne likes it this way too."

"So you write down all of the outstanding checks here and add them up," Wynne explained. "Then subtract that from what the statement says, along with the service charges, and add any

65

deposits you've made that aren't on here . . . and this number should match the checkbook."

Wynne and her mother compared the two numbers.

"Great, and what do we do if they're different?" Kitty asked.

Wynne sighed in exasperation. "Well, that means that you probably either forgot to write down a check, or that your math is wrong."

Together they pored over the account until the mistake was found, finally bringing the checkbook into balance. Despite her frustration, Wynne was pleased to see her mother working so hard to learn this.

"Mom, you have to do this as soon as the statement comes in. If you don't, you'll lose track of what you spend and before you know it, you'll be overdrawn." She bit back the urge to add "again."

"Okay, I'll do my best."

Wynne knew her mother didn't want to be so dependent. She just didn't know how to do these things because her father had always taken care of them.

"What are we going to do about the car?"

Wynne sighed. Her mother had been reluctant to get rid of the Park Avenue, as it was the last vehicle her husband had purchased. But she had never thought to put oil in it, and it finally threw a rod and bit the dust. She called crying from a payphone, and Wynne picked her up and arranged to have the car towed.

"It's a goner. You're going to need a new car."

"What am I going to do? I don't know the first thing about buying a car."

"I'll go with you on Saturday. We'll find something nice, something Dad would have liked." Wynne threw in that last bit for encouragement.

"Thank you, honey. I honestly don't know how I'd manage without all the things you do."

"You'll get the hang of this, Mom." Though her tone suggested they both knew otherwise.

❧

"Did you see this letter from Starquest?" Rusty tossed the paper onto Paula's desk. "They're thanking us for handling their meeting, and they mention you by name."

Paula chortled. "That's because I happened to be walking down the hallway when their chairman was locked out of his room in his underwear."

"Boxers or briefs?"

"Boxers, and they had Wednesday stamped on the leg. But it was Friday."

"People would never believe the things we see in hotels," Rusty said, shaking his head in amazement. "Remember that other guy who got locked out in his underwear?"

"You mean her underwear," Paula laughed. "Or the woman who—"

The phone on her desk interrupted their reminiscence, its caller ID flashing Front Desk.

"This is Paula . . . yeah . . ." She twirled around in her seat and grabbed the remote for the video camera display. "Okay, I see them . . . We'll be right down." Hanging up the phone, she turned to her boss. "Two busloads just pulled up with that country music band. You want to work the front desk or the bellmen?"

Rusty groaned. "Bellmen." They would be here half the night again finishing up paperwork.

Wynne sat solemnly in the back seat of the cab, accustomed now to the route from the airport and no longer taking in the sights.

She should have just booked at the Hyatt, she told herself. No, the problem wasn't the hotel. The problem wasn't even that Paula McKenzie had kissed her, but that she had kissed back.

For the past two weeks, Wynne had berated herself for letting that happen, knowing her own flirtations had helped to bring it about. She had nothing to offer Paula and it was wrong to lead her on. Even if she could keep her emotional distance—and that was a big "if"—it was wrong to give in to temptation for a kiss, because Paula was worth more than just a sexual fling.

"Oh, great," she muttered, eyeing the buses in the circle. The line at check-in would be an hour long. Wynne paid the cabbie and exited when the valet opened her door.

"Would you like me to take your bag inside?" he asked.

"No, I'll take it myself. Thank you."

As expected, the check-in line held more than thirty waiting guests, all of whom seemed to know each other. Right away, Wynne's eyes went to the familiar face behind the counter and her breath caught with surprise at how nice it was to see her again. Keeping her desires in check was probably going to be harder than she thought.

"Excuse me, Miss Connelly?"

"Yes?" Wynne turned to see a tall, red-haired gentleman, more sharply dressed than most of the other staff, but an employee just the same.

"Could I ask you step to over here, please?" As he reached over and lifted her bag, he unlatched the braided rope that formed the queue. Then he extracted a small folder from inside his jacket. "I'm Rusty Wilburn, the senior shift manager. Miss McKenzie took the liberty of checking you in already on the concierge floor. Here is your room key. If you would kindly stop by in the morning and allow us to swipe your credit card, we can spare you this bedlam tonight."

"You are my hero, Mr. Wilburn," she gushed, recognizing the name as the boss Paula often talked about. "Thank you very much."

"No, I'm just the delivery boy. Paula says welcome."

Wynne turned again to glimpse Paula behind the busy counter. "Please tell her how much I appreciate this."

"You know, we've made pretty good work of this, Wynne." Cheryl sat on the floor of her office, surrounded by index cards that mapped the process of their proposed marketing plan. "I'd like to have this drawn up in a slide presentation. Are you any good at that? I never had the patience to learn that program."

"I can do that. Shall I set up my laptop and start laying it out?"

"Sure, why not? We're going to have to put this in front of Ken and Wendell, and it would be easier for both of them if we could explain it all in a slide show."

Ken Markoff, Wendell Martin, and Cheryl Williams were the top three officers in the company, definitely people Wynne wanted to impress. They would present the new marketing plan to analysts in New York at the end of April, hoping the cost-trimming and forward thinking would boost their stock value.

"Oh, and then next time you come down, I want to play with a few scenarios. Would that be hard to do? You know, different slides for each possible outcome?"

"It shouldn't be a problem, but it will take me a couple of hours," Wynne said.

"A couple of hours? You've got to be kidding. It would take Denise a couple of days," Cheryl exclaimed, the latter a reference to her administrative assistant. At once, her hand flew to her mouth as she remembered how close Denise's desk was to her office door.

Wynne sniggered at Cheryl's gaffe, and at the sight of the impeccably dressed executive sitting cross-legged on the floor, her tailored skirt hiked up well above her knees. Their rapport had gotten a shot in the arm when Doug was dropped from the team. They chatted more while they worked, and even had lunch together a couple of times.

"Have you seen much of Orlando since you started coming down?"

"Not a lot. I did get out to dinner at a great barbecue place called Buck's, and last week I saw a movie downtown."

"That's hardly what I call getting out. Tell you what," she said, pushing her nimble body off the floor and padding in her stocking feet to her desk drawer. "I have a gift certificate for Jack Elam's. Do you know that place?"

Wynne shook her head.

"It's the best seafood restaurant in Orlando. I won this in a raffle at the Chamber of Commerce, but my husband's allergic to seafood. Why don't you take it and ask someone to go with you?"

Wynne immediately thought of Paula. Though Paula had sped her through check-in last night, they hadn't yet had a chance to connect. "Thank you, Cheryl."

"Do you know someone to invite? You want me to see if I can find someone to keep you company?"

"No, that's all right. I have a friend here in town I can ask. But thank you. This is very generous."

"It's no big deal. Like I said, Jim won't eat there and I hate to see it go to waste." Cheryl checked her watch and slipped her shoes back on. "I have a meeting with Ken in about five minutes. Why don't I let you start working on those slides? Come on over to my desk and make yourself comfortable."

Wynne settled in as Cheryl left, easily feeling at home in the corner office. It was hard not to daydream just a little about having a job like Cheryl's someday.

Paula was irked at the report left by the two previous shifts on the behavior of their country western guests since check-in. Apparently, many had stayed awake until the wee hours of the morning, prompting several complaints about shouting in the hall-ways and loud music. And today, the first shift housekeepers were unable to rouse them to clean their rooms, leaving three times the usual workload for the skeleton staff on Paula's shift.

It was almost ten o'clock when she got her first chance to visit the concierge lounge, but as she feared, Wynne was long gone. Paula had hoped they would have a chance to get together again tomorrow on her day off, but as they hadn't yet set anything up, she was afraid she had lost the opportunity. The last thing she wanted was for Wynne to think she had simply blown her off.

Checking to see that a light was on in room 2314, Paula con-templated her options. She could knock on the door, but Wynne might not welcome an invasion of her privacy at this hour. And it

70

wasn't a good idea for her staff to see her knocking on the room of a guest, especially if it got her invited inside. The better option was to call.

She considered using the house phone, but decided to return to her office for more privacy. She was thrilled to find that Wynne had already left a message on her direct line.

"Hi, Paula. This is Wynne. It's about nine-fifteen, and I was calling to see if you might be free for dinner tomorrow night. My boss gave me a gift certificate for a place called Jack Elam's, and I hope you can be my guest . . . my driving guest, that is. Anyway, please give me a call in 2314. I'll probably be up another couple of hours. Oh, and sorry about the short notice, but I just got this today. Talk to you soon, I hope. Goodbye."

Quickly, Paula dialed the number, hoping to finish her call before Rusty returned to their office.

"Wynne? It's Paula . . . I was just coming back to my office to call you . . . I'd love to go. Why don't I pick you up at seven out front?" She paged through the organizer on her desk for the number of the restaurant. "If you want, I'll call and get us a reservation . . . It's kind of dressy, but not formal. A skirt or a nice pantsuit will do just fine . . . Can't wait. See you tomorrow at seven."

Paula smiled and sighed as she plopped into her chair. She had another date with Wynne Connelly.

At seven sharp, Paula drove into the circle, her breath hitching as she eyed Wynne in her black business suit, the skirt well above the knee, but professional-looking nonetheless. She was one beautiful woman.

Paula had chosen an olive green silk pantsuit for herself, with a pale yellow top. Most of her dresses, which she purchased for weddings or parties, were too dressy for a simple date, especially since she figured that Wynne had packed nothing of the sort. This pantsuit was one of her favorites, and a welcome departure from the skirt and blazer she wore five days a week.

The two women made casual conversation during the short

71

drive to the restaurant, Paula running down her list of problems with the country western group, Wynne recounting how she had impressed her boss with the first draft of their slide presentation.

Paula noticed Wynne kept her hands folded in her lap, as if maintaining her distance. It was probably nothing. They just needed a few moments together to re-establish the familiarity they had enjoyed two weeks ago, when their flirtations and admissions had eventually led to that kiss.

When they reached the restaurant, Paula turned the car over to a valet and hooked her arm casually through Wynne's as they walked inside. "This is a great restaurant. I came here once with Stephanie."

"Who's Stephanie?"

"She's our hotel director, the Big Cheese. I couldn't ask for a better person to work for. She's probably had more influence on me than she realizes."

"I think good bosses are rare. Otherwise, people wouldn't complain so much about theirs. I like mine a lot too."

"You mean in Baltimore?"

"Both places, actually. The woman I'm working with here is very sharp. It's too bad I won't get to work with her very long."

The hostess seated them at a small table for two that bordered the main passageway to the front door.

"Have you ever noticed that two women in a restaurant tend to get the worst tables?" Paula asked. "Look around. There are tables with two men, and with men and women, and they're all in the center of the room. But all three of the tables by the wall have two women."

"I'm not surprised. I've noticed that when the planes are full, women end up in the center seats. And let me tell you, I do not like center seats," Wynne scoffed.

"So you're the marketing expert. Why is it they do that? Do they really not value women as customers?"

"In some businesses they do. Department stores, grocery stores, even the auto industry's finally coming around. But I think

72

it's different with the service industry—like the travel and dining business—because the service workers tend to be younger and they're generally more intimidated by men than they are women." She nodded her head in the direction of a clean table in the center now being occupied by two men. "If they had put us at that table, the men would have been seated over here, and they probably would have complained. I think the hostess was just trying to avoid that. It might be subconscious, or it might be policy, but we didn't complain, so it got reinforced."

"I'm going to start paying attention to what we do at the hotel. If we do something like that, it isn't intentional. But we go out of our way to address problems, and that usually means the complainer gets rewarded, like that man at the counter the night I checked you in. I'm really going to watch that from now on."

"It may just be that women really don't complain as much at the hotel. They know what it takes to clean a room and handle small details, and they're more willing to overlook lapses because some mistakes are easy to make."

"I'm going to start complaining," Paula announced sternly, pounding her fist lightly on the table. "But not tonight. Tonight, I'm just going to enjoy the company of my lovely companion." She enjoyed the smile her compliment elicited.

"I'm enjoying your company too." Wynne resigned herself to the truth of her words and had given up for the moment on trying to resist the attraction. She had decided earlier to open up tonight and talk a bit about how things were back in Baltimore. That would make it easier to manage their expectations about what they were getting into.

But as soon as the Miata had pulled into the circle, her resolve crumbled. Her time in Orlando was her only respite from all those obligations, and she didn't want to give it up. Her work here would be finished before long and it wouldn't matter anymore.

All through dinner, Paula told funny stories about things that had happened at the Weller Regent over the years, leaving Wynne in stitches at times. There were just so many things about her that were appealing, Wynne thought as she eyed her companion. She was witty, mature, ambitious—all things that Wynne found attractive, but had been unable to find in a lifetime of looking. Paula was also downright sexy . . . "I'm sorry, say that again."

"I said I know a place near Disney where we can get a pretty good look at the fireworks display if you're interested."

"That would be fun," she readily agreed.

"Where was your head just now?"

Wynne could feel her face turning red and she fumbled for a response. "I was just thinking about . . . how glad I am that I've gotten to know you. Honestly, I used to dread these trips, but having a chance to spend time with you has really changed all that." She gave in to what she wanted to do, reaching across the table for Paula's hand.

Paula took it and smiled. "You have no idea how much I look forward to your visits. Sometimes I go nuts thinking you're right there in my hotel and I can't—"

"Good evening, ladies." A distinguished gentleman and sharply dressed woman suddenly appeared beside their table, and Wynne immediately withdrew her hand.

"Mr. Markoff, hello," she stammered.

"Please, it's Ken. And this is my wife, Rachelle."

"Pleased to meet you. This is my friend, Paula McKenzie."

Paula leaned forward to shake the couple's outstretched hands. From her days managing the business meetings at the hotel, she recognized the CEO of the company where Wynne worked.

"You look familiar, Miss McKenzie." Realization dawned and he went on, "I remember. You run things at the Weller Regent."

"Well, I don't exactly run things, but sometimes it feels that way."

"We've always been pleased with your hotel. Oh, and Wynne, Cheryl stopped in today to show me a few of the slides you two prepared. Great job."

"Thank you."

"Ken, we should leave them to their dinner and get out of this aisle. It was very nice to meet you both," Rachelle offered sincerely.

"The pleasure was ours," Wynne answered, stunned to realize that her boss had happened upon her holding hands with her dinner companion. As they walked away, she turned to Paula and lowered her voice, which shook uncontrollably. "Maybe we should settle the check and go."

"You okay?"

Wynne shrugged. "I guess it's not all that big a deal. It's not like I'm going to be working there much longer anyway. I just hope it doesn't affect my reference."

"You know, they didn't act surprised or put off by anything. In fact, I'd say your boss was perfectly casual about it."

"He was, wasn't he?"

"Yes, and we were casual too. If that had been the CEO of Weller Regent, you'd be doing CPR right now."

Wynne sighed. "We do this to ourselves, don't we?"

"You mean act like we're doing something wrong?"

"Exactly." She pulled the gift certificate from her purse and tossed several bills onto the table for their waiter.

"Shall we go see the fireworks?"

"I'm not sure I'd be very good company. Maybe we should call it a night."

Chapter 8

The wall clock in Wynne's small office at Gone Tomorrow Tours read twenty after six, and the calm quiet from the cubicles outside her door told her she was probably the only one still here. Another typical workday. The days were getting longer now, but she had grown accustomed to working well past dark, irrespective of the time.

Wynne scooped up the papers from her desk and placed them back in their respective files. This might be her last big media buy for Gone Tomorrow Tours. The marketing plan she had been working on with Cheryl would consolidate advertising for all of the Eldon-Markoff subsidiaries under the direction of corporate staff. Right now, it looked as though the marketing managers who were terminated would get a six-month severance package.

There was a bright side to all of this, she had decided, besides the severance package. She had reached a ceiling at Gone Tomorrow, which, before it was acquired by Eldon-Markoff, was a small company. At least now she would be forced to hit the streets again, and maybe she could find something that would allow room for advancement. Ideally, she would go to work for a major corporation, with the chance to earn a high-ranking job like Cheryl's. Wynne was confident of her ability to move up. All she had to do was find the right opening.

Her stomach growled viciously as she eyed her inbox, which held a stack of files and letters that never seemed to get smaller. She remembered the frozen box dinners she always kept in the kitchen. One of those could keep her going another two or three hours.

What Wynne wanted as much as a great job was a reason to leave the work for tomorrow and go home at the end of the day. A woman like Paula McKenzie could get her mind off the office. But after that incident in the restaurant, they hadn't even made plans to see each other again on her next trip.

Just this once, Wynne wanted to forget about all the things that worried her and have fun. She had only two remaining trips to Orlando . . . only two more chances to enjoy Paula's company.

Slayer carefully eyed the distance between the small dining table and the bar at the kitchen, where the woman who lived here at his house was making pictures on a screen by clicking her fingers across its base. If he could get closer, he might persuade her to stop for a moment and scratch his head.

Thump.

"Hi, sweet boy." Paula's right hand automatically rose to do his bidding, her left hand manipulating the mouse to log on to her Internet connection. She had sent Wynne a cheery e-mail last Thursday, hoping to ease the angst she obviously felt about what had happened at dinner the other night. So far, she had received no reply.

Today, though, was different. Among her eleven new messages—including three that promised to make her penis longer and thicker—was a note from Wynne.

Hi Paula,

I'm sorry to be so slow getting back to you. As usual, there is a lot to do when I return to Baltimore, and again when I'm preparing to leave. This is the lull between those times, when only a 10-hour workday is required. <g>

I've confirmed with E-M that I have only two more trips to Orlando, this weekend and again two weeks later. If I'm invited to participate in the presentation of our plan, that will be in New York, but I'm not holding my breath.

So if you can overlook the fact that I became a total basket case the last time we went out, I'd love it if we could get together again next Tuesday. Since you mentioned the fireworks at Disney, I wonder if you'd be willing to consider an evening there. I sure hope so.

Wynne

Paula reread the note several times, not just to understand what it said, but to come to terms with what it didn't say. Two more visits and that would be it. Obviously, Wynne wasn't thinking past her work here in Orlando. In fact, that kiss they had shared seemed a long time ago, and Wynne hadn't made any kind of sign at all she wanted to go there again.

Disappointed, Paula shut down her computer. She had been nearly certain things had clicked for Wynne just as they had for her, especially after their kiss. Her practical side said it was probably just as well—not much you can do with a girlfriend in Baltimore when you live a thousand miles away and work at a job that gives you Tuesdays and Saturdays off. But her impulsive side was frustrated. She had hoped they might be able to work something out.

The good news was she had made a friend, perhaps even someone she would see again if Wynne held onto her job and made occasional trips down to the company's headquarters. But the idea of having Wynne Connelly as a friend wasn't as comforting as she hoped it would be.

Wynne settled into her favorite chair in the corner of the concierge lounge, balancing a small plate of peeled shrimp and fresh vegetables. The Sunshine State wasn't living up to its moniker and that would likely thwart her plans with Paula for an evening at Disney World, as the forecast for tomorrow was more rain.

Things had gone great at work today, where she and Cheryl finished the cost and revenue projections for all six scenarios of their marketing plan. They had only to rank-order their recommendations and finalize the slide presentation. On Wednesday afternoon, she and Cheryl would present them to Ken and Wendell, and Wynne would spend her final visit two weeks from now readying the presentation for the industry stock analysts.

"Nice day for ducks, huh?"

Wynne brightened at the familiar face. She had been lost in her thoughts and hadn't seen Paula come in. "Hi, stranger. I was wondering if I'd see you tonight."

"Yeah, it's kind of quiet tonight for a change. I was hoping I'd find you here."

"Thanks again for sending up that umbrella." Wynne found herself oddly nervous in Paula's presence.

"You're welcome. In fact, that's why I wanted to find you tonight. Not the umbrella, but the weather in general. We're supposed to get more of this tomorrow, so Disney might not be a good idea."

"Is there a Plan B?"

Paula hesitated while one of the hosts came to clear Wynne's plate. "You know, I like to cook," she said, keeping her voice low and trying her best to sound casual. "How would you like to come to my place for dinner?"

Wynne had wanted to get together, but going to Paula's house might be more temptation than she could handle. Her logic said no, but her mouth answered of its own accord. "I'd love to. That sounds wonderful."

"Great." Paula smiled, and all of a sudden, the air between them was electric. "Should I come pick you up at seven?"

"What if I just got a taxi? Wouldn't that be easier?"

"It would let me keep cooking, I guess. Are you sure?" Paula drew a pen and a business card from her pocket, looking over her shoulder to see if her employees were watching. She was clearly nervous about talking with Wynne for so long and hurriedly jotted her address. "Here you go. Come whenever you're ready."

"I can't wait." *You shouldn't do this.*

"Oh, I hope you don't mind a cat . . . although Slayer doesn't know he's a cat."

"Not at all, and I promise not to tell him." *Are you crazy?*

"Great. Then I'll see you tomorrow."

Paula watched from the living room window as Wynne paid the cabbie and started slowly in the rain toward the cover of the steps. Immediately, she ran out the door to offer a hand.

"Let me take that," she insisted, grabbing the umbrella and holding it high as Wynne struggled with the rail. "I'm so glad you're here."

"Me too. I've been looking forward to this all day."

"So have I. I hope you like chicken Marsala."

"That sounds great."

Paula walked slowly alongside as Wynne persevered. "I guess steps are the hardest, huh?"

"I'm just tired. It was a long day." They reached the second floor landing and stopped, the awning shielding them from the rain. "Paula, this is a lovely community," she said, turning back to take in the small lake, the tropical landscaping, and the neatly arranged condominium buildings.

"Thank you. There are developments like this all over Orlando. Each one is a little different, but the idea is the same. I like this one because the clubhouse has a nice fitness room and a pool, and there's a jogging trail around that golf course over there." She pointed past the parking lot to the path that led next door.

"It's also very nicely laid out. The places like this in Baltimore don't have all this pretty landscaping and the buildings are right on top of each other. I live in a townhouse, and we hardly have any of this common area, let alone something so pretty as a lake."

"Well, come on in. Let's see if you like the inside as much." Paula led her on a tour through the kitchen and living room, which were right inside the front door. Since she was on the second floor, she had a cathedral ceiling with skylights in the living room and dining area. In the hallway, they passed the door that led down to the garage, then the guest bedroom and bath, and finally, the master suite with a larger bath and walk-in closet. "But here's my favorite room." Paula opened the door off the master bedroom that led onto the sun porch, where Slayer lay curled on a cushioned chaise lounge.

"Hi there, handsome," Wynne cooed, stretching out a hand slowly to pet the indifferent orange beast.

But after a few strokes, he was fully on his back, apparently quite interested in these soft new hands that adored him so. This new person could stay.

"I'd say you have a new friend."

"He's adorable," Wynne offered, still stroking the white belly as Slayer lay in near-hypnotic bliss.

"Let's see if you say that when he tries to eat off your plate. I won't even tell you some of the other adorable things he does." But when coaxed, Paula did share a few of the cat's more colorful exploits, including his penchant for collecting lizards.

"Sounds to me like he's just doing his job," Wynne defended the cat, who had followed her back into the living room.

"Figures you'd take his side. You'd be singing a different tune if he dropped a squirming lizard in your bed."

Wynne chuckled softly, still scratching her new furry friend. "I really do like this place, Paula, everything about it. I bet you're very comfortable here."

"I am. I sort of wish I'd bought a three-bedroom so I'd have a little more room, but I don't get that much company. My mom comes over from Cocoa once in a while, and my best friend stayed with me when her place got tented for termites."

As she talked, Paula poured them each a glass of cabernet sauvignon to enjoy with crackers and cheese as their dinner simmered. Shaking her head in resignation, she watched as Wynne shared the cheese with Slayer, who was acting positively slutty.

The friendly cat was a welcome distraction for Wynne, who otherwise would have fumbled nervously for conversation. It was almost tormenting to be here in Paula's home, to witness her in such a casual, familiar way. She was barefoot, dressed in faded jeans with a tightly fitted long-sleeved top that crept up her muscular midriff each time she moved. Wynne had never before been so aware of another woman's sensuality. Coming here was not a good idea, she now realized. But she didn't want to be anywhere else.

"Dinner should be ready," Paula announced. "Go ahead and have a seat at—"

"Let me lend a hand," Wynne cut her off, following her into the kitchen.

"Why don't you pour more wine? I have white on the top rack of the refrigerator if you want it."

"The red is fine with me. You want the other?"

"No, I'm fine with this too."

Together, they carried dinner to the table. Paula noticed as they ate that Wynne gradually relaxed. She had seemed nervous when she first arrived, almost standoffish. She wondered if that was the residue from Wynne's discomfort after running into her CEO. "So how are things going at work?"

Wynne talked about how their presentation was shaping up. "Cheryl walked through it today in her office with Curt and me. He's the assistant VP for operations. Tomorrow, she'll give it again to Ken and the guy who handles the analysts."

"What do you do on your next visit?"

"Just wrap it all up, I guess. I suppose I'll work a couple of days with the human resources department to lay out how they might shift some of the talent around in the company. It would be a shame to lose some of these people just because their jobs are getting cut when there are others who are underperforming. I'm glad I don't have to make the final call on that one, though."

"Is your job really going to get cut?"

"Yeah, it looks that way," Wynne acknowledged.

"Do you think you'll be offered something else? I mean, surely, you're one of those people they'd hate to lose."

"I don't know, Paula," she said wistfully. "I'm not sure I want to move into just any slot. Eldon-Markoff's a great company, but someday I'd like to sit in one of the big chairs, like Cheryl's. The problem is she's only forty-seven years old, and she'll probably work at least another fifteen years. I'd like to move up before then, so I don't really see much chance of doing that here."

"Maybe you ought to think about the hotel industry," Paula suggested.

"Yeah, or one of the cruise lines, or even another travel company. I'm not limited to just tourism, but I feel like I know the market pretty well."

"I think whatever company hires you on is going to be awfully lucky."

"Thank you. Now, if you don't mind, can we talk about something a little less depressing? I'd hate to suddenly get the urge to slash my wrists with your cutlery."

Paula chuckled at what she hoped was a joke. "Oh, no, I wouldn't let you do that." More seriously, she added, "I hope you get your dream job someday, Wynne. I know we haven't known each other that long, but I can see how important it is to you. And I think you're one of those special people that deserves good things."

Both women looked at each other quietly, slowly pushing their hands together as they had in the restaurant.

"Thank you. I happen to think you're special too." Wynne was mesmerized by the calm brown eyes as she laced her fingers with Paula's. No one would walk by their table tonight. With a small tug, she urged Paula forward, leaning slightly herself until their faces almost touched. "Very special," she whispered, closing the distance to lightly touch the waiting lips with her own.

Again, they looked at one another, this time with dancing eyes. That kiss was the affirmation they were more than just friends. To Paula, it was a welcome signal, one she needed. But to Wynne, it was an alarm. After a long moment, she squeezed Paula's hand and released it, finally breaking the spell.

"So would you like more?"

"No, I'm stuffed. It was wonderful."

"How about coffee or dessert? I have lemon sherbet with raspberry sauce."

"Maybe later." Wynne was nearly overwhelmed by the sensations the tiny kiss had wrought. What she wanted next wasn't exactly on the menu.

Paula stood and picked up their plates. "Why don't you take your wine out to the porch and grab a chair. I'll be out in a minute." She knew Wynne had a long day coming up tomorrow, but she dreaded the signal that it was time for her to leave. They had finally taken another step in the direction she wanted to go, and she wanted to broach the subject of how they might keep their friendship going once Wynne's travels ended.

"Do you want some help?"

"No, I'm just going to set these in the sink and run some water on them."

Wynne started to do as she was directed, but the pull was too strong. She followed Paula to the kitchen, standing in the archway to watch her from behind. The sensations from earlier persisted, and before she knew it, she had crossed the tile floor to position herself directly behind Paula as she stood at the sink. Automatically, her hands went to Paula's waist as she lowered her mouth to the bare neck. "You're so lovely."

Paula shuddered as the hot breath tickled her ear. When the lips began to caress the sinewy muscle, her head fell back against Wynne's shoulder. She gasped as long fingers slid underneath her top to stroke her stomach.

Wynne was lost. She knew she had crossed the line, but she found herself unable to stop. Her right hand left the confines of the shirt to cover Paula's breast, which she squeezed softly, but with confidence.

Paula turned, her own hands beginning to caress the warm skin beneath Wynne's silk blouse. Their lips met fiercely, with a near animalistic fervor. Paula leaned back into the counter and pulled Wynne's hips closer, and soon both women were pushing against one another, aching for more contact.

"We shouldn't do this," Wynne murmured, burying her mouth in the soft flesh behind Paula's ear.

"We're both big girls, Wynne. We don't have to stop," Paula whispered boldly. Grasping the hand on her waist, she moved toward the door, flicking off the lights as they passed through the dining room. Moments later, they were standing together in the master bedroom, the queen-sized bed cast in a glow from the bed-side lamp.

The voice that had plagued Wynne since the first moment she had met Paula had finally relented, leaving her on her own. Hungry to know the treasures before her, she hooked both hands beneath Paula's top and lifted it smoothly over her head.

"Come lie with me," Paula urged, tugging Wynne's hand to the bedside, where with one jerk of the arm, she sent the spread and the top sheet to the foot of the bed. Before they sat, she made quick work of the buttons on Wynne's silk top, pushing it off her shoulders as they tumbled downward.

Both women ran their hands over newly exposed skin as they locked again in a heated kiss. Wynne's hand slipped around to caress Paula's back and pull her closer.

Paula reached behind the broad back and loosened the clasp on the bra, pulling the straps over the shoulders. Unencumbered, her hands slid across the smooth plane.

"I want to feel you next to me," Wynne whispered, releasing the clasp of Paula's bra with a simple twist of her hand. As she lifted up, she pulled Paula with her, leaning back as both removed their bras. Wynne suddenly stood and unfastened her slacks, sliding them off and tossing them over the bedside chair.

Paula eyed the beautiful woman standing before her in only a burgundy thong. Never in her life had she been so aroused. Now matching Wynne's moves, she pushed off her jeans, which dropped crumpled on the floor. Her eyes never left the hungry ones that watched her as she slipped her panties off as well. Reaching out, she hooked the thong with her index finger and lowered it to reveal a closely trimmed triangle of brown curls.

Wynne finished removing her thong, quivering with lust as Paula lay back on the bed in invitation. The scent of their passion hung in the air and she lowered herself until their skin fused from their breasts downward. Instinctively, her hips settled on a muscled thigh and she hooked her hands underneath Paula's shoulders as the rhythmic dance began.

Paula raised her knee, feeling Wynne's damp center against her skin.

Wynne responded to the move by pulling back and drawing alongside, but not giving up the contact of their skin. Burying her face into Paula's neck and shoulder, she raised a hand to stroke a breast, gently rolling the nipple between her thumb and forefinger.

Paula moaned at the tingling sensation, her hips writhing as she sought intimate contact with anything on Wynne's body. "Please."

Wynne fought the urge to rush this encounter. That wasn't right for this, not for the way she felt about Paula. Lowering her mouth, she engulfed one breast while her fingers teased the other. Both nipples were rock hard and it was all she could do not to bite down.

Pushing her fingers through Wynne's hair, Paula held her head close as her breast was devoured. The sight of the mouth encircling her nipple made her want to feel it everywhere.

"Gorgeous," Wynne murmured as her fingers now traced the curve of Paula's hip. When her fingertips brushed the curls at the apex of her legs, she was amazed to find them soft and fine and she couldn't resist lingering there for longer than Paula could stand.

"Please touch me," came the desperate plea.

Wynne's resolve to take things slowly crumbled as her fingers slipped through the warm wetness between Paula's legs. Paula cried out as she stroked two fingers inside and out, unrelenting as their hips rocked in rhythm. Wynne had been barely aware of the hand on her breast, but now her nipple was being pulled and pinched in tandem with her own movements. She wouldn't be able to take much more of this. With her thumb, she flicked the hardened clitoris until she felt the body underneath her grow still and rigid. "That's it. I want to feel you come."

Paula exploded at the simple command, feeling herself tighten and pulse around the hand that filled her. Wynne's eyes were boring into her soul as she rode the wave, and she felt herself climbing again before she ever stilled. Clutching Wynne's shoulders, she pushed her thigh between her legs again, astounded at the wet heat she found. It was enough to tip her over the edge once again, and it was no surprise that Wynne soon followed.

They rested, both bodies throbbing from release. Suddenly conscious that her entire weight rested on Paula, Wynne moved to pull away.

"No, stay another minute," Paula whispered her plea. The body that covered her gave her more than a physical sensation. She had never felt this close to a lover—not to Shauna, not to Susan, both women that she had loved. This connection with Wynne was as though they had known each other forever. "You feel so good."

Wynne answered her request with a deep kiss. She could still feel an occasional tremor from Paula's center as it gripped her fingers. Her lips traveled again to Paula's neck and shoulder. "I could just devour you."

"Oh no, you don't. It's my turn now." In a fluid move, Paula reversed their positions, reluctantly sliding off Wynne's fingers. At once she covered the tortured nipple with her mouth, licking and sucking. The gasps and hisses that followed drove her to try to kiss every inch of this beautiful body. She left the breast and moved lower, stopping when she found a fading scar on Wynne's left side.

"What's this from?"

"They had to take out my spleen," Wynne explained with apprehension, suddenly self-conscious. "I have . . . a lot of scars."

"They're beautiful."

Paula trailed her tongue along the red line, which ended near Wynne's navel. As her lips traveled lower, she inhaled a luscious scent. When she reached the dark triangle, Wynne parted her thighs to expose her glistening center. Paula shuddered and finally dipped her tongue into the wet folds.

Wynne rarely revealed herself this way to anyone. But she didn't feel vulnerable this time—she trusted Paula to share this intimacy. Reaching low, she grabbed Paula's hand, squeezing hard as the sensations began to build.

Paula recognized the response of Wynne's hips and narrowed her focus to the swollen clitoris, sucking it gently but rhythmically between her lips.

"Oh God!" Each flick of Paula's rigid tongue jolted Wynne's core until the sensations gathered deep within and erupted in a powerful climax. When the waves receded, she reached out, laying her hand on Paula's cheek. "Come up here and lie with me."

Reluctantly, Paula left her treasure and moved up for a deep kiss. "You're amazing . . . and so beautiful."

"You make me feel that way." Wynne pulled her directly on top. "Will you let me taste you like that?"

"You can do anything you want with me."

Chapter 9

Wynne resisted the temptation to brush her tongue into the sleeping woman's ear, knowing it would trigger anew an exhausting round of lovemaking that would leave her shattered before her workday even began. For three hours last night, they had quietly explored one another, Paula finding and kissing all of the visible scars from her accident three years ago. What Paula didn't know was that her touch had begun to heal some of the scars that couldn't be seen.

Slayer draped lethargically across Wynne's hip, his paws resting on the arm that wrapped around Paula's waist. The cat had tactfully granted them many hours alone last night, but it was now time to assert his domain.

Daylight bled through the blinds, prompting Wynne to look about for a clock. Beside Paula's head, the green digital display read 5:36 a.m. She had persuaded Paula to set the alarm for six, but it wouldn't be needed after all. Carefully, she resituated the big orange cat beside his mistress, and extricated herself from the covers. Scanning about, she gathered her clothes and found her way down the hall to the guest bathroom.

The face that greeted her from the mirror was oddly peaceful, given that she had broken a major rule last night. But like Paula had said, they were both big girls, and she would have to deal with it. She just couldn't gather enough guilt right this minute to feel regret.

Quickly, she washed and dressed, then slipped into the kitchen to use the phone. The card she had gotten from the taxi driver came in handy after all, she mused.

"Paula? Wake up, hon." Wynne sat on the edge of the bed, gently shaking the sleeping woman's shoulder. She could tell by the tiny smile that her voice was getting through. "Paula."

"What is it?"

"I need to go soon. I called a taxi."

Paula twisted her body in the bed so she could wrap her arms around Wynne's waist and lay her head in her lap. "Don't go. Last night was amazing," she mumbled, drifting off again.

"It was magnificent," Wynne agreed, meaning every word. "Paula? Did you go back to sleep?"

"No," the disheveled woman protested, still without opening her eyes.

"Listen to me." Wynne lowered her voice. "I really must say, you throw a hell of a dinner party."

Paula chuckled, finally sitting up.

"I have to go. Paula, last night was . . . it was just incredible. You are one amazing woman." In fact, as far as Wynne was concerned, it was the most enjoyable night she had ever spent. She pulled the drowsy face to hers and delivered the kiss that finally awoke the sleeping beauty.

"You'll be back in two weeks?"

"I will," she promised. She was already looking forward to doing this one more time.

❧

It took every ounce of concentration Wynne could muster to stay focused on Cheryl's presentation of their recommendations. Ken and Wendell were impressed with the logic and the many positive implications for their company's bottom line. The stockholders were going to love the new strategic plan for marketing.

All day, Wynne's thoughts wandered back to the night before, to the images on Paula's face as she shuddered her release, of brown eyes that watched her as she lowered her mouth to Paula's most private place, and of the sleeping innocent in her arms. She remembered so vividly the taste—

"Okay, we're done here, gentlemen. Thank you for your comments. We'll make those two little revisions, and polish it up for the analysts," Cheryl finished.

"Cheryl, now is good for me if you have a few minutes," Ken said as he exited the conference room to return to his office.

"I'll be right there," she called. "Wynne, what time is your plane?"

"It leaves at six. I suppose I should pack up my things and head out."

"Could you look into catching something a little later? I really need to talk with you, but I have to go over some things with Ken first."

Wynne's stomach knotted with anxiety. "I think there's another one around eight-thirty."

"Ask Denise to help you change it. I'll be happy to run you to the airport if we get pinched for time."

"Sure."

Wynne managed to get booked on the eight-thirty flight. Then she edited their slide show as discussed and began to put the final touches on it for the stockholders presentation. It was almost six o'clock before Cheryl returned to her office. "Wynne, would you join us for a few minutes, then I promise to let you go."

She followed her boss back into Ken Markoff's office, her heart beating faster as she realized that this meeting was about her. They sure didn't waste any time once the plan was finished, she groused to herself, readying herself for the axe.

91

At Cheryl's direction, she took a seat at a small round conference table directly across from the CEO. Cheryl sat down between them.

"Wynne, thank you for sticking around this afternoon," Markoff started formally. "In fact, thank you for everything. I want to let you know personally that I really appreciate your contribution to this project. Cheryl has kept me up to date throughout the process, and has always spoken highly of your work. And she told me what you said about working for what was best for the company and for the stockholders, and I have to say, that attitude is awfully impressive."

Wynne was starting to breathe a sigh of relief. It sounded like she was going to get a glowing recommendation from both Markoff and Cheryl Williams.

"Cheryl has been after me for a year to let her hire an assistant vice president who can manage the marketing aspects and let her concentrate more on the sales end, and we'd both like it very much if you'd accept that job. It will mean a move here to Orlando, of course, but we'll pay for all that. And I hear that assistant VPs make a little more than managers, isn't that right, Cheryl?"

"It's about double, maybe a little more."

Assistant vice president. Move to Orlando. Double the salary. Here was the opportunity Wynne had dreamed of.

"So will you accept?" Cheryl prodded.

"Of course I accept!" Wynne stood and extended her hand across the table to her CEO. "Thank you, Mr. Markoff."

"It's Ken, and welcome to the family."

"Cheryl, I don't know what to say."

The VP tossed out all formality and reached out to offer a warm hug. "I'm so glad to have you aboard, Wynne. It's going to be great working with you every day."

Paula wrapped up her inspection with a walk through the concierge lounge, where she automatically glanced toward the wingback chair in the corner. It was just after six, so Wynne was probably on her plane already.

All day, she had thought about their night together, her head fighting doubts. A simple phone call from Wynne today would have gone a long way to assure her it had meant something to both of them. Too bad she had forgotten to supply her home phone number, because Wynne probably would never call her at work, especially for something so personal.

A part of her was bursting with happiness, certain Wynne too had felt the emotional connection from their lovemaking that she had. The other part of her was in knots, desperately needing to know it hadn't been just a physical tryst.

Paula knew Wynne had a big day scheduled at work, and traveling back to Baltimore would keep her out of touch. Probably the earliest Wynne would have a chance to get in touch would be an e-mail from her office tomorrow.

Somehow, Paula would last that long.

It was almost midnight when the taxi pulled up in front of Wynne's townhouse, and she was dead on her feet. In the last twenty-four hours, her world had been totally rocked by all of the things that had brought her so much frustration over the last few weeks.

At Eldon-Markoff, she was being offered a new start, a chance to further her career at one of the top companies in the travel business. It was an opportunity she had only dreamed of, and Cheryl Williams had laid it at her feet.

Now was the time to shed the sense of duty and obligation that had plagued her life for so long. The move to Orlando would give her a clean break. She would sell the old townhouse and buy a home where she would be comfortable.

It would force her mother to take responsibility for her own well-being. Wynne would offer encouragement and advice, but ultimately, Kitty would have to rise to the occasion.

And then there was Paula.

As she more fully considered the ramifications of a move to Orlando, her thoughts of last night caused her sorrow to the point of a near physical pain. They were "big girls," Paula had said. Did that mean they were free to enjoy their sexual adventures without obligation? Or would they just deal with the consequences? Whatever it meant, Wynne knew that by spending the night in Paula's bed, she had probably ruined any chance to have a real future with her. It was one thing to have an out-of-town fling. It was altogether different to want something more serious. Those types of relationships were based on mutual trust, something she had violated with her secrecy before they even began. For that, she had regrets. Profound regrets.

But it was time to look forward now.

She fumbled with her key, finally getting it to work. It was too late to worry about unpacking, she thought, so she left her bags in the foyer and started arduously up the stairs to the second level, a nightlight guiding her path.

From the top drawer of her dresser, she removed a nightshirt and went into the bathroom to get ready for bed. A hot soak would feel great, but she was far too tired for that. Instead, she took three ibuprofen, brushed her teeth, and turned out the light.

Finally, she eased herself into bed, settling comfortably beneath the quilt. A warm arm snaked across her belly to pull her closer as a silky thigh nestled between her own.

"Did you have a good trip, sweetheart?"

"Just the usual." That would be her final lie, she vowed.

Chapter 10

Three Years Earlier

Wynne let out a deep sigh as she pulled out of the parking lot at East Oaks, a downscale apartment complex in Owings Mills. Her second date with Heather Bennett had been no more exciting than the first, and no matter what Heather did as a follow-up this time—she had sent a dozen roses to Wynne's office after their first date—Wynne would not answer with another invitation to go out.

She had met the twenty-four-year-old two weeks earlier at a party hosted by mutual friends. Heather was undeniably pretty, average height with long, curly black hair and large hazel eyes. Her hours at the gym were apparent from her trim figure. A sales clerk for women's clothing and accessories at a department store in Owings Mills, Heather anticipated a career in retail, hoping someday to take over as department head or buyer. She didn't want the headaches that came with an upper management job.

Wynne hated to admit even to herself that the only reason she had called Heather for a date after the party in the first place was because she hadn't had sex with anyone in almost two years. But the discovery that the young woman was utterly without ambition had been a total turnoff. Tonight they had seen a movie, and afterward shared a small kiss that, for Wynne, lacked any sort of spark at all. They clearly had no future, and this would be their last date.

She turned on her blinker and slowed, steering her Volvo sedan into the turn lane for the on-ramp to I-795. There wasn't much traffic for a Sunday night, she thought. The Ravens game on the west coast probably had everyone at home and glued to their—

The next few moments were a terrifying blur, as a force unseen came out of nowhere to ram into Wynne's left side, hurling her like a rag doll toward the passenger seat. The sudden crunch of glass and collapsing metal was deafening, as were the two exploding airbags that shielded her from the thrust of the door and steering column. Before she even realized she had been hit, her car slammed against the concrete overpass, deploying two more airbags on the passenger side. That was all that saved her from being crushed.

It was over in barely an instant.

Her first efforts to move were met with searing pain, as though a hot spear had pierced her from shoulder to knee on her right side, which was jammed against the console. From beneath the now-deflated airbags, she could make out flashes of blue as they painted the night. Voices grew louder and more distinct as a man and a woman approached.

"I see him. He's dead," the man's voice said.

"Can you see in the car?" the woman asked.

Wynne was vaguely aware of the car bouncing and she closed her eyes to shield them against a blinding flashlight.

"It looks like a woman. I think she's still alive. Get the EMTs."

As the voices moved farther away she took advantage of the quiet to rest. If she could sleep for just a little while, she would feel better.

"Stay with us!" the man shouted. "We'll get you out of there."
She wished he would go away for now. She was so sleepy . . .

Wynne remembered the exact moment she realized she was conscious. She was thinking about how outdoor media, like billboards on the freeways leading to major airports, would be the perfect vehicle for promoting the Yucatan tour. Winter was bearing down on the East Coast and a vibrant picture of the crystal blue waters off Tulum would have drivers pulling to the side of the road to make their reservations.

Then she recalled having purchased those ads months ago. The billboards were already in place and the tours were rapidly booking up.

She heard a steady beep and knew immediately it was her heartbeat because the same pulse pounded in her temples. With colossal effort, she blinked a few times until her eyes adjusted to the dim light. A woman sat beneath a reading light in the corner of the room. She was familiar but somehow out of place.

Wynne's mouth felt like it was filled with sand.

"Water," she breathed, the sound barely negligible.

"Wynne!" The woman left the chair and rushed to her bedside. "Oh my God, I'm so glad to see you. Try to stay awake, sweetheart. I'm going to get the nurse."

The woman was Heather Bennett.

"I . . . can't!" Wynne grunted, refusing to move her throbbing leg.

"Yes, you can. You have to." Heather stubbornly nudged the back of Wynne's calf until she strained to lift it one more time. "See? I knew you could do it."

Wynne dropped her leg and panted with exertion. She was drenched in sweat and her leg ached so badly she began to cry.

"I'm so sorry, baby," Heather cooed, wrapping her hands

around Wynne's head. "I know it hurts, and you're so brave to keep working."

Wynne tried to gather herself. Crying during physical therapy had become routine, but Heather was right. She had to do this if she was going to regain the use of her leg. And she probably wouldn't do it if Heather weren't here to push her.

"I don't know why you won't come home with me," Kitty said.

"I just want to be at my own house, Mom. I feel like I've been gone for ten years."

It had actually been only ten weeks since the accident, all of them spent at the University of Maryland Medical Center. During that time, Wynne endured two surgeries for her shattered pelvis and femur, abdominal surgery to repair internal injuries, and countless hours of physical therapy.

Wynne knew it was too much to ask of her mother to help take care of her after her release. It was obvious it had been very hard on Kitty to watch her daughter struggle for life, especially since she was only now coming to terms with her husband's sudden death a year earlier.

"But you have all those stairs."

"Heather lined up a hospital bed for the living room. It'll be fine for now, and I should be able to do the stairs in another week or two."

Wynne was dressed and waiting for the wheelchair that would take her to the front door. Her mother walked over and took a seat on the bed beside her. "Why didn't you tell me before the accident that you had someone special in your life?"

The truth—that she had no idea why Heather Bennett had rushed to her side—seemed disingenuous, considering all Heather had done. During the first two weeks of her recovery, Heather had taken a leave of absence from her job to keep a vigil in intensive care. When Wynne struggled with the grueling physical therapy regimen, Heather rearranged her work schedule to take part in the sessions, pushing Wynne to follow the ambitious plan. She was there twice a day for several hours to help with personal care, give comfort, and provide companionship.

"We hadn't been seeing each other that long." After weeks of what Wynne had to admit seemed like devoted care, she conceded to herself that she might have been wrong about Heather. She had first thought her immature and maybe even lazy. Heather was neither, and while it wasn't exactly love at second sight, Wynne had certainly come to appreciate her as a kind and generous soul.

"She seems to think you don't need your family right now." The bitterness in her mother's voice was not disguised.

"What do you mean?"

Kitty tossed her chin and looked away, a pouting look that Wynne had come to know very well. "When your sister came to see you the other night, Heather had the nerve to tell her not to stay long."

"She probably just thought I was tired."

"Janelle would have seen that for herself. And this business of getting a bed for your living room . . . Is she just going to move in there with you and take over everything?"

"It's only for a while, Mom, until I can manage on my own. I told her about Dad dying last year and how hard it was on everybody. I think she just wants to help."

"But I'm perfectly capable of taking care of you. I can make sure you eat right and drive you to your doctor's appointments."

"I know." Actually, Wynne didn't think her mother was up to it at all. It was obvious she wanted to help, but in only a matter of days, Kitty's own needs would begin to take precedence, and Wynne would find herself mired in helping her mother cope. She needed to focus on getting well, and Heather was facilitating that. "I just want to be at home."

Kitty sighed. "At least promise me that you'll let me come for a visit."

"Of course you can visit. You know you're always welcome in my home."

From the couch in the living room, Wynne could hear Heather on the kitchen phone.

"This isn't a good time, Kitty. We just did two hours of physical therapy and she can barely sit up."

That much was true, but Wynne hadn't talked to her mother in several days. "Let me talk to her," she called.

Heather returned to the living room without the phone and took a seat beside Wynne. "I explained to her that you were tired and still had a few things left to do."

"I should have said hello at least."

"Wynne, saying hello is never enough for Kitty. Next thing you know, she wants to whine about her light bulb being out or her checks bouncing. Every single time you hang up, you feel guilty because you can't help her."

"Sometimes all she needs is somebody to listen."

"But that isn't what you need. You need to be concentrating on yourself. I know you hate to hear this, Wynne, but your family isn't thinking about what's good for you. That's the way it is with people like us. Our families don't give a shit what happens, as long as we don't—"

"Mom isn't like that," Wynne argued. "I'll admit she's not crazy about me being a lesbian, but she still cares about me, especially now." Wynne knew exactly where all of Heather's anger was coming from. "It must have been really hard for you to have your parents turn their backs on you."

"I'm over it," Heather said bitterly. "But I learned that we have to take care of each other because nobody else is going to do it."

"I should at least let her know that I'm doing okay."

"I told her that. But if you still want to talk to her, go ahead and call her back. I'm going upstairs. Call me when you're ready to come up."

Wynne blew out a breath of resignation as she watched Heather head up the stairs. She didn't blame her for her distrust of

100

family, and it was true that Kitty usually managed to make all of their conversations about things that were going wrong with the house, the car, or her finances. And lately, Janelle being eight months pregnant and unmarried was at the top of her list of gripes. It was no wonder Heather was so protective.

Having Heather around these past few months had been a godsend. She had moved into the spare bedroom across the hall from Wynne's and took care of practically everything around the house. Even Wynne's temper tantrums and prolonged depression hadn't scared her off. Friends that loyal were hard to come by.

And friends is exactly what they were, as far as Wynne was concerned. She was pretty certain Heather would welcome something more romantic, more intimate, but Wynne had never felt that sort of chemistry between them.

"Fuck it! I'm not going to go through this again." Wynne could feel her frustration mount and knew at any moment she would begin to cry. They had just seen her doctor, who advised a third surgery to bond the bones in her hip.

Heather helped her up the stairs to the front door, then used her key to open it. "I know it's hard, but you have to think about the long haul, Wynne. The sooner you get this done, the sooner you can get back to a normal life."

"I just started back to work. I'd miss two weeks right off the bat, and who knows how many more hours for physical therapy."

"But then you'll be able to walk without shooting pains in your hip. Isn't that worth it, Wynne?"

"And then what if my leg doesn't heal? I'll have to go back and do it all again."

"So what? We'll get through it."

"It's easy for you to say. It's not your leg they're cutting on."

"Do you think it's been easy for me, Wynne?" Heather's voice held a sharpness Wynne hadn't heard before.

"Of course not." She slumped onto the couch exhausted, feeling ashamed of her whining. She offered the seat beside her and draped her arm around Heather's shoulder. "I'm sorry. You've done everything. I couldn't have made it this far without you."

Heather fell into the embrace and laid her arm across Wynne's lap. "I need to talk to you about something."

Wynne leaned back so she could see Heather's face. "What is it?"

"My lease is up at the end of the month. Either I need to give them notice that I'm moving or I have to renew it . . . and my rent's going up a hundred dollars. I don't think I can afford that much, especially after cutting back so much on my hours."

"I can help you with your rent, Heather. God, after all you've done for me, you can't think I wouldn't give you whatever you need."

That must have been the wrong thing to say because Heather suddenly began to cry.

"What is it?" Heather covered her face with her hands and shook her head. That's when Wynne realized what Heather wanted. "If . . . you want to move in here . . ."

"Really?"

"Sure." Wynne swallowed hard with the recognition of what she was agreeing to. "I just thought you were probably sick of me by now and ready to get your life back."

Heather turned and cradled Wynne's face with her palm. "Don't you know? You are my life."

Wynne eased her slender frame into the steamy tub. An hour-long soak was the best relief for her aching leg, and the only sure guarantee she would sleep. She had submitted to the hip surgery, but now her doctor wanted her to go through one last operation to bond the splintered bones in her femur near the knee. She would rather endure the constant pain than be cooped up at home, dependent again on Heather for her recovery.

The nightly bath also served another purpose, one she kept to herself. It was her strategy for avoiding intimacy with Heather, just like the long hours she was putting in at her office and the extended visits with her mother on the weekends.

Wynne had no one else to blame for this mess. Accepting all the attention and care Heather had given during her recovery had left her beholden, but Wynne should have paid her debt with friendship and financial support to offset what Heather had sacrificed. Instead, she had succumbed to the pressures of what Heather wanted in return, which was romantic love and intimacy.

Almost from the beginning, Wynne knew it was a mistake. She genuinely loved Heather, but not the way she wanted to love a life partner. She had hoped her feelings would grow in that direction once they became lovers, but after more than a year, she still didn't feel the kind of passion and hunger she wanted, or that Heather seemed to have for her.

Even with the bathroom door closed, Wynne could hear the television in their bedroom. She hated the mindless fare that Heather seemed to watch for hours on end—sitcoms and those dreadful reality shows. They never talked about anything of substance. Heather rarely read the news, since she had little interest in politics, sports, or business. She liked going to parties and clubs, something Wynne did only once in a blue moon.

Wynne knew she was making things worse by dwelling on the negative aspects of their relationship. But she didn't have the guts to sit Heather down and tell her this wasn't working. That seemed so cold and selfish after all they had been through. So she would have to try harder to enjoy Heather's favorite pastimes and connect with her on an emotional level. And she would have to find a way to awaken her sexual interest.

She slinked lower in the tub, wishing she could pull the stopper and follow the water down the drain.

Chapter 11

Present Day

"I was beginning to wonder if you were planning on coming home tonight." Heather met her at the door, taking both the black leather briefcase and the flannel-lined raincoat.

"Sorry, my inbox was stuffed. Dinner smells good."

"It was very good when it was hot," Heather chided. "But I saved you some."

"Thanks." Wynne didn't miss the admonition. She rarely came home in time to eat dinner with Heather, seeking solace instead in her office or at her mother's house. It was almost unbearable to listen to the drone of the television in the background, but attempts to make meaningful conversation instead had failed miserably.

Heather followed Wynne into the small kitchen and quickly went about warming dinner in the microwave.

"I can get that, Heather. You don't have to wait on me."

"I don't mind. Go ahead and have a seat."

Wynne did as she was told, sitting on a stool at the two-person counter while her meal was prepared.

"Did you get a feel for what's going to happen to your job?"

"Yeah, I talked about it with Cheryl and Ken. I don't think they're going to let me go." Wynne wasn't ready to share her news, especially now that she was on the precipice of making some big changes in her life. Heather Bennett would be one of those changes.

"That's great, honey." The phone interrupted their chat. "Oh, your mom called about three times. She said you didn't answer your cell phone."

Wynne almost snapped at her for not simply suggesting that her mother try the work number. It was no secret Heather was jealous of the time she gave to her family. She barely spoke to the Connelly woman, and vice versa. In Heather's mind, Wynne's constant catering to her mother took her away from what should be her primary relationship.

"Hello . . . Yeah, I just walked in the door. Heather told me you'd called," Wynne said, covering for Heather's indifference. "That's a good idea, Mom, but I think you ought to get more than one estimate. That seems like a lot of money." She had advised her mother to have the exterior of her Tudor home painted. "Sure, I'll come on Saturday and meet with them."

Heather slammed her glass down on the counter, clearly angry at Wynne's easy acquiescence, and left the room in disgust.

"Okay, I'll see you about ten-thirty. Bye."

Wynne knew Heather was steamed, but she didn't have the energy to deal with it. Besides, it would never be resolved to Heather's satisfaction unless she severed all contact with her mother and sister, as Heather had with her own family. Wynne had given up trying to placate her, no longer defending her desire to be with her family.

The microwave beeped and she retrieved her meal, a bowl of

chicken stew. Briefly, she considered taking it into the living room where Heather no doubt was already absorbed in something on television, but Wynne didn't want to deal with either the noise or Heather's foul mood. Not tonight . . . not again.

If possible, things between them had taken a turn for the worse, or at least they had for Wynne. The more her mother called on her, the more Heather seemed to resent it, now to the point that she objected each time Kitty asked for help with something, or even whenever she wanted to stop by the townhouse. Wynne managed the strain by keeping the parties apart, but the stress of putting up with Heather's constant disapproval was wearing on her nerves.

"Why don't you come watch this show with me?" Heather called from the living room.

Wynne rinsed her bowl and placed it in the dishwasher. "I'm going up to bed. I'm really tired."

"Yeah, what was with that late flight last night?"

"Just a late meeting. I missed the earlier one."

"Why don't you come sit with me and I'll rub your neck?"

"Thanks, but I think I'll soak in the tub for a while then go on to bed." Without waiting for a reply, Wynne labored up the staircase to the second floor. Ten minutes later, she was lowering herself in a steaming bubble bath when Heather appeared in the doorway.

"Got room for me in there?"

Wynne couldn't hide her grimace at the intimate suggestion. "I'm tired, Heather. I just want to soak awhile until my leg feels better then get some sleep."

Heather's shoulders slumped at the rejection. "I'm just trying to meet you halfway, Wynne. I know you hate the TV, so I turned it off. What else would you have me do?"

Wynne didn't want to play this game. "I just want to rest. I don't care if you watch TV."

"You act like you don't care what I do at all. You've barely said hello since you got back last night. Why is it so hard to accept that

I might want to spend a little time with you tonight? You've been away from me for the last four days. Surely you don't need more time to yourself."

That's exactly what she needed, Wynne thought. "Heather, look . . . I'm sorry but my leg is sore and I'm tired. I have another long day tomorrow and I need to be ready for it."

"Yeah, and I heard you're not going to be around on Saturday either." Now angry, Heather shut the door loudly in retreat, leaving Wynne to sigh deeply and slip lower into the mass of bubbles.

". . . Forty-nine . . . fifty!" Paula collapsed on the mat, exhausted from her sit-ups.

"So have you seen The Beautiful Woman from Baltimore?" That's the name Val had assigned Paula's new romantic interest.

"Yeah, she came over for dinner Tuesday night." Paula wasn't ready to share the details of her night with Wynne Connelly. She could hardly believe it herself. They had spent a wonderful . . . erotic . . . passion-filled night together and had seemed to connect at every turn. But that was four nights ago and she hadn't yet heard from Wynne.

"How many more trips down here does she have?" Both women stood before the mirror doing curls.

"Just one for sure. If they keep her on, I guess she'll get a chance to come down every now and then."

"I take it that means you two aren't going to pursue anything serious."

The question prompted a surprising rush of feelings—none of them very comforting. "I don't know. I guess realistically, the answer is no. But if there was a way we could work it out, I'd be willing to give it a try."

"How do you think she feels?"

"I'm not sure." Paula was pretty certain Wynne had feelings for her, but the scope of those feelings was unclear. There was definitely something there, but outside of the utterances that poured forth during the heat of their passion, neither woman had said much of anything beyond letting the other know she was special.

"So maybe next week you should raise the stakes a little," Val suggested mischievously. "You know, soft music, candlelight . . . a little massage oil."

Paula blushed, now feeling guilty at holding out on her friend. She was dying to talk to somebody, and Val was really the only one she could safely say anything to. "We uh, already sort of did that."

"What!" Val looked at her with both shock and thrill. "You mean you two already . . . ?" She made a finger-through-the-circle motion with her hands.

"You're so crude," Paula said, feigning disgust. "But yes, we"— Paula mimicked the gesture, adding—"among other things."

On that note, Val now sported a small blush of her own. "Let's not overshare."

"You're the one that asked."

"So the two of you had sex and you still don't know how she feels?"

Paula found herself a little embarrassed at her friend's frank implication, but there was really no dodging it. "I don't know how to explain it. It's like there's something there, but we both know that a real relationship probably isn't feasible, so we just sort of took a shortcut. I know she likes me. But the sex thing just happened. It really wasn't about expressing any feelings." At least it probably wasn't about feelings as far as Wynne was concerned. Paula noted the look of doubt on her friend's face. "Don't you ever get carried away with somebody who's really hot?"

"Maybe once or twice," she conceded. "So how was it?"

Paula returned the dumbbells to the rack, contemplating her response. "I think I'm ruined for anyone else."

"Uh-oh."

"Uh-oh is right."

"What do you mean moving?" Janelle's brown eyes were wide with panic.

108

"Shhhh! I haven't told Mom yet." Wynne guided her younger sister into their father's old study and shut the door. "Janelle, this is an opportunity I've wanted for a long time. It's always been my dream to achieve something like this at work. You know that. I have to take it."

"Who's going to take care of things for Mom? I can't handle that. I've already got enough on my plate with school and Sophie."

"It isn't our responsibility to take care of her. She's a grown woman. She should start taking care of herself. Maybe she'll do that if I'm not here to handle every little problem."

"That sounds like something Heather would say."

The truth of that was inescapable.

Janelle went on, "I bet she's thrilled with all of this. Now she gets you all to herself."

"I haven't told her about the job yet. I . . . I'm not going to ask her to come with me."

"What?"

"I just think this is a good time to end things. We're just not all that good together."

"I can't imagine Miss Congeniality would be good with anybody."

"Janelle, that's not fair. Heather was very kind to me when I really needed it. I don't know how I would have made it through all that without her help."

"I can answer that, Wynne. Mom would have been there for you and you know it. Maybe if you had given her a chance, she would have figured out that she wasn't so helpless after all."

"I didn't think she could handle it. I couldn't afford to put myself in her hands and have her fall apart."

"Maybe not, but when you did get better, you let that woman take over your life," Janelle complained. "Do you have any idea how many times Heather told us not to come by because you were resting, or because you needed to focus on your therapy, or because the two of you were . . . busy, whatever busy meant."

Wynne's face reddened at the obvious sexual innuendo. She hated to think that Heather would have given away the privacy of

109

that aspect of their life. Her mother had had enough difficulty with her lifestyle without having it thrown in her face.

"Mommy?" The little voice came from beyond the door, Sophie obviously scurrying from room to room in her search.

"In here, sweetie." Janelle opened the study door to welcome her daughter.

Wynne was grateful for the diversion, her head spinning from her sister's reaction. If Janelle was this bad about her moving to Orlando, how was her mother going to take the news?

But the real fireworks would come when she told Heather.

Wynne was glad to be back at her desk on Monday morning. She had planned on talking with her mother on Saturday after-noon and with Heather on Sunday, but after Janelle's response, she lost her nerve. Things were so tense at home yesterday that she and Heather had barely spoken.

Cheryl Williams had obviously been working over the week-end, Wynne noted, as her e-mail box was filled with a series of messages on the new job and the upcoming presentation.

CWilliams Presentation—final copy

Wynne downloaded this one to study later.

CWilliams New York

This was an unexpected but very welcome invitation to come to New York with Eldon-Markoff's officers for the presentation to the stock analysts in three weeks.

CWilliams Contract

This time, Wynne went straight to the downloaded document. It was a detailed job description, packed with the kinds of tasks in which she reveled. The new job would require travel, estimated at once or twice a month at first, perhaps more later as Eldon-Markoff expanded or acquired new companies.

In addition to the contract was a draft of the official offer, which almost took her breath away. Her new base salary would be—*holy shit!* And she was eligible for an annual bonus worth up to half her salary if corporate and department goals were met. She would also receive stock options each year.

Eldon-Markoff would pay all of her moving expenses, including real estate commissions and closing costs. She was expected to start full time in Orlando six weeks from today.

That last part lit a fire under her. She needed to contact a real estate agent to put her townhouse on the market, so she couldn't postpone her talk with Heather any longer. Tonight . . . she would talk to Heather tonight.

PMcKenzie Your next visit

A knot formed in Wynne's stomach as she hovered the mouse over the subject line. There hadn't been a waking hour in the week since she had been home that she hadn't thought at least once about Paula and the exciting things they had done, or the wonderful things she had felt. Each time, the guilt grabbed her and pulled her back down to earth.

Hi Wynne,

Well, this is my usual mid-visit note—you know, the one where I say that I had a great time seeing you on your last trip and that I hope we can get together again next time to do something fun. The words are certainly true again, but somehow they just don't seem to say enough this time.

I don't really know how to say this, so I'll just blurt it out. I'm really looking forward to seeing you again, but I don't want to be presumptuous. I'm open for anything you'd like to do.

Paula

Wynne felt the tears well up. She had played it so terribly wrong. In six weeks, she would be moving to Orlando. And she would be single. Paula was someone she might have had a future with had she not gotten carried away last week. If she had kept her distance and told the truth, things may have worked out for them. But hiding her relationship with Heather was wrong.

Her best bet was to come clean and try to salvage a friendship. Maybe in time, they could start over. But she couldn't deal with Paula before talking to Heather. She had to start putting her life in order.

Paula clipped her nametag above the pocket of her navy suit and stepped into her shoes. Careful not to collect the orange cat's pervasive fur, she stretched her fingers out to scratch behind his ears.

"You be a good boy, and don't answer the door or the phone." As if on cue, the phone rang at that moment. "I'll get that."

Slayer turned around in circles several times before settling in his favorite chair, which also happened to be Paula's favorite chair.

"Hello . . . Oh, hi, Dad." It was rare for her father to call, since he was at work when she was at home and vice versa. "What's up? Is everything okay?" Paula brushed a lint roller along her skirt as she talked. "Oh, right. Would it be all right if I brought a friend? I know, you need a full name and social security number." The shuttle Discovery was launching on Saturday morning and her father was offering a pass to the press site. "Can I let you know tomorrow? I'll call you . . . Thanks, Dad. Bye."

This was good. She wouldn't have to wait for Wynne to find time to answer her e-mail. Now she had an excuse to call, and that would ease any awkwardness either might feel about their intimate encounter. But the business card Wynne had given her was in her desk drawer at the WR, so she would have to call from there.

"You look awful, Jolene." Paula took in the sight of her red-eyed desk clerk. The African-American woman shone with sweat, clearly the product of a fever. "You should go on home."

"I hate to leave you to do this by yourself." Matthew had called in sick tonight as well, so Paula and Rusty would have to man the front desk. It wouldn't be so bad if they took turns, since they weren't expecting a lot of new arrivals tonight.

"I'll be all right. It'll be like the old days, when I was young and carefree," Paula said with a small chuckle. "Go on. Go home and take something and fall into bed. And if you still have a fever in the morning, call in and ask them to schedule someone else."

"Thanks, Paula."

"Take care of yourself." She immediately took over the front desk duties, which consisted mostly of answering the phone and checking in the occasional guest.

It was seven-thirty before she remembered her father's invitation. Pulling up the database, she quickly found Wynne's record, which listed an Orlando number for work, and a Baltimore number for home. She could call Rusty down and run up to her desk to retrieve the work number in Baltimore, but at this hour it wasn't likely Wynne was still in her office.

Paula debated about what to do. On the one hand, it was technically an abuse of her access to information to look up a home phone number for personal reasons. On the other hand, she and Wynne had slept together and you couldn't get much more personal than that. Besides, if there was a chance that Wynne could make it down for a launch at the press site, she probably would be sorry she missed it just because Paula thought it improper to call her at home.

Using her cell phone, she placed the call. After four rings, she was mentally preparing to leave a callback message, when an unfamiliar female voice picked up.

Momentarily startled, Paula debated for a split second about hanging up. "Uh, hi. May I please speak to Wynne Connelly?"

The woman said she wasn't home, but that she would take a message.

"Uh, sure . . . Would you tell her that Paula called?"

She waited while the woman read back the number on her caller ID.

"Yes, that's it . . . Thank you."

Paula was surprised to find herself shaking. Who was the woman who had answered the phone? Wynne had told her about a sister, but she hadn't said that they lived together. She had never mentioned a roommate. A sick feeling crept into her gut.

⊷⊶

113

Wynne fumbled for her front door key, dreading the night ahead. She had dragged out her workday, even buying a dinner of snack crackers and soda from the vending machine to postpone the imminent conversation with Heather. It was nearly nine o'clock when she entered her home.

"Boy, you really must have a mountain of work to stay there so late," Heather said in greeting.

"Yeah, but I'm making progress." Wynne tried to smile. This was going to be a difficult night, and she didn't want it to escalate to a confrontation. If she could stay calm, they could talk it all out. Still, she knew she couldn't simply will away Heather's emotional response.

"Somebody from Orlando called about a half hour ago. I guess they all work late down there too."

"Was it Cheryl?" Wynne had called her boss at home about an hour earlier to suggest one last change in the presentation.

"No, she said her name was Paula. She left a number."

Wynne felt her chest constrict as the anxiety rose inside her. So Paula had called her at home and now knew about Heather.

"I'll . . . call her tomorrow. It's late."

"Well, it was only a half hour ago. I started to tell her just to call you at work. What are you guys working on?"

It wasn't like Heather to ask about her work. For whatever reason, it was the segue she needed. "Sort of a reorganization. Why don't I put this away and we can talk about it."

"Or we can talk about something else if you'd rather not think about work any more. You must be sick of it. You want something to eat?"

"No, I had a bite at my desk. I'm not hungry. And I really do need to talk to you about things at work." She noted just the barest hint of a shake in her voice, and hoped she could keep it from getting worse. The hardest part of this conversation would be sticking to her resolve in the face of tremendous pressure, and she couldn't show any sign of weakness.

Wynne hung her coat in the closet and stowed her briefcase. Heather had taken a seat on the couch in the living room, muting

114

the television. Wynne walked in front of the set and turned it off, taking a chair on the other side of the small room.

"What is it, honey?"

Wynne leaned forward and folded her hands, forcing herself to look Heather in the eye. Slowly, she began. "This is going to be a very tough conversation."

The younger woman shifted uncomfortably on the couch, obviously anxious to hear what the reorganization at Eldon-Markoff had to do with her.

"Heather, I don't think it's much of a secret that you and I haven't been connecting very well lately. In fact, it's been like this for a long time, at least for me."

"Well, you've been working long hours, and you've been gone a lot. I'm sure things will smooth out when things calm down at work," she offered nervously.

"I'm not as sure about that as you. I've been thinking—for quite a while, actually—that maybe we should both . . . move on. I look back over the last couple of years, and I can honestly say that I have never felt more loved by anyone, and I owe you more than I can ever repay for all the things you did for me after my accident." It was taking everything Wynne had to keep her voice and gaze steady as she said her piece, taking in the stunned look on the younger woman's face.

"Don't do this, Wynne."

Wynne shook her head in resignation. "But I can't be what you need . . . what you deserve. I've tried, Heather, for a very long time, and I just can't do it."

"In other words, you don't love me like I love you," Heather said sharply.

Wynne sighed deeply and leaned back in the chair. The summation was cold, but accurate. "I'm sorry."

Tears started to pool in Heather's eyes, and her voice grew small. "You know, Wynne, maybe we should go away together and take some time to enjoy each other. I don't want to just throw away the last two years without feeling like we tried to fix it."

"Heather, it's not . . . How do I explain this? It's not like anything is broken. It's that it never really fit to begin with. We had a wonderful friendship, but it was a mistake on my part to try to make more of it than that, because my love for you was never the deep, passionate love that both of us deserve to feel. I've really tried to love you that way, but I just can't."

"So the last two years have been a lie for you. Is that what you're saying?" The tone of Heather's voice had taken on an edge.

"I haven't intentionally misled you. But I can't manufacture the feelings you need."

"Why do you keep talking about what I need and what I deserve?" she wailed. "I have what I need. I'm happy with you."

"But I'm not."

"So now that you're all better, you're just going to toss me out like yesterday's trash? I gave up my home, Wynne. And I got rid of nearly all of my stuff because there wasn't room for it here. What am I supposed to do now?"

"I'll help you with whatever you need. You can take things from here . . . furniture, linens, dishes, whatever you need." She recalled that most of Heather's furniture was second-hand, and that many of her dishes and linens were mismatched sets, things collected at yard sales. Wynne was willing to part with almost anything in her house—not her grandmother's china or the antique brass bed—but as far as she was concerned, Heather could have the rest if she wanted it.

"Can we please give this some time, Wynne?"

"I'm taking a new job in Orlando. It starts in six weeks, so I need to put the house on the market this week."

"So you're moving to Orlando. That's what this is about."

"No. It's about us, and the fact that this isn't working for me. I wasn't about to uproot you from your job and your friends when I knew in my heart that we weren't going to make it."

The two women sat quietly for long minutes before Heather finally stood. "I can't talk about this any more tonight. I'm going for a drive."

"Heather, please. You shouldn't drive if you're upset," Wynne pleaded. "I'll . . . I'll go over to Mom's if you need to be by your-self."

"In other words, you're not too upset to drive, right?" The cork that had held the young woman's emotions in check up to now had come undone. "And the reason you're not upset, Wynne, is because you've gotten everything you needed from me. And now that you don't need anything else, you're moving on. It doesn't matter to you that I still need you."

"Knowing that I'm hurting you breaks my heart, and I'm so sorry. But it would be wrong of me to let you give up even more for me feeling the way I do about our future."

"What, did you get a promotion?"

"Yes," Wynne answered simply.

"So now you have a fancy job at corporate, and I'm not the right accessory. Is that it? Don't tell me, let me guess—they don't even know you're gay."

Actually, Ken Markoff probably did, Wynne realized, but she certainly wasn't about to volunteer that and have to explain how he came to know. "It's not about that at all. I don't know what they know, but I don't intend to live my life in the closet. And I would never consider a partner as an accessory to my work. Both of us deserve better than that."

"Don't keep patronizing me with your opinion about what I deserve!" Heather shouted, angry tears streaming down her face as she grabbed her purse and stormed toward the door. "I'll get out of here as soon as I can. Believe me, now that I know how you really feel about me, I don't want to be here any more than you want me here."

Wynne winced as the door slammed and rattled the pictures on the walls. It was about as ugly a scene as she had imagined it would be, but all she felt right now was relief that it was over. She knew it was only Round One, as Heather would be back, and would prob-ably make a calmer plea for her to rethink her decision. Wynne had given no ground thus far, but Heather would no doubt increase the pressure for her to relent.

Saddened that things would be ending on such a hurtful note, Wynne resolved to try to make the transition as friendly and peaceful as possible. She had a healthy savings account and would gladly help Heather get set up in a new place. It would probably be difficult for them for a while, but surely their friendship was solid enough to weather this. As long as she had family in Baltimore, Wynne knew she would be coming back to visit. It would be nice to think she and Heather could salvage something from their time together.

Walking into the kitchen for a bottle of water, Wynne saw the note on the counter, the number for Paula. A new wave of nausea passed through her as she wadded the paper and dropped it in the trash. What would she say? Paula had the whole picture now.

Chapter 12

"I'm going to do my hall inspection," Paula said as Rusty settled into his chair to begin his Sunday night paperwork routine. She didn't want to watch the video this week, since Rusty would likely comment on the fact that the woman from Baltimore hadn't checked in tonight. She had monitored reservations all week, noting that K. Wynne Connelly was not among their expected guests.

Wynne had neither answered her e-mail nor returned her call. In fact, Paula hadn't heard one word since the morning they had kissed goodbye in her bed. Though she didn't want to accept it, she knew she had stumbled onto Wynne's little secret—she was unavailable.

Paula had to laugh at herself for all the time she had spent worrying about how hard it would be to overcome living in two different cities. To think that she had even found herself perusing the job listings in the DC area, only a few miles from Baltimore.

She hated to admit it, but she had been played for a fool. She wanted to be angry, but right now she felt only sorrow, hurt, and embarrassment. How could she have misjudged the connection she had with Wynne when it had seemed so strong?

When she reached the concierge floor, she inspected the dessert display and proceeded to the small office area that linked the lounge with a service elevator. The hostess was out serving drinks, so she took advantage of a few moments of privacy. Rummaging through the bottom desk drawer she located a telephone directory.

Wynne stretched out on the bed, propping up her sore knee with the extra pillow. She was back at the Hyatt, too embarrassed to return to the Weller Regent to face Paula. As she settled in to read her notes for the next morning's meeting, she was startled by the phone.

"Hello."

"So . . . did the Hyatt give you a better rate?"

It took only a split second for the voice on the phone to register. "Paula. I . . . I wanted to call you, but I just didn't know what to say."

"Well, for starters, why don't you tell me how we got this far apart in just twelve days?"

"I . . . I haven't been honest with you. I . . . ."

"Yeah, I got that part when that woman answered your phone."

"Paula, I didn't mean for you to find out that way."

"I'd say you didn't mean for me to find out at all. But it doesn't matter, Wynne. I was just calling to tell you that I'm sorry if I led you into something you didn't mean to do."

Wynne stared at the phone in her hand as the line went dead.

The agent pulled into a wooded cul de sac, stopping at the first house on the circle. Cheryl had canceled Wynne's meetings for the afternoon, hooking her up with a realtor who would show her properties in some of Orlando's best neighborhoods.

"This is my favorite of the houses we'll see today," the agent remarked. "It's four bedrooms, three and a half baths, a formal living room and dining room, an eat-in kitchen, and a screened-in patio." The house, an older Mediterranean bungalow, yellow with a white tile roof, definitely had curb appeal. Wynne especially liked that it was a single story.

"This is very nice, but it's really more than I need," she said when they had finished the tour. It would cost her thirty or forty thousand dollars to tastefully furnish a place this large. Heather had taken her up on her offer and already laid claim to the living room furniture, entertainment center, and the suite in the guest bedroom, where she had been sleeping for the past week.

"Maybe it seems that way now, but things can change. It's a great house for children, and this is a top school district."

Wynne smiled as she recalled with irony that the real estate agent who had sold her the townhouse in Baltimore had said practically the same thing. She figured it was a standard line they learned in real estate classes. The children arguments meant nothing to her, but one of the bedrooms would make a nice office and it would be handy to have two spares if the Connelly women came to visit.

They had done the paperwork before leaving the realty office, so both women knew Wynne could afford this house if she wanted it. She also had a loan letter in hand from Eldon-Markoff, guaranteeing the purchase of her house in Baltimore, so the contingency wouldn't be a problem.

This house was the most expensive of the ones she had seen, but it was head and shoulders above the rest. It was also in turn-key condition and in an older, established neighborhood. And it wasn't far, she noted, from that nice condominium community where Paula lived.

"Okay, let's do it."

❦

121

"You're in early," Stephanie remarked. Stephanie Anderson was the director of the Weller Regent, the Orlando hotel's top dog. She was a vibrant woman of fifty-seven, and a good administrator. In her thirty-plus years with Weller Regent, Stephanie had mentored scores of people, many of whom had gone on to manage their own hotels or to work in the company's New York headquarters. Paula had always been one of her favorites.

"Yeah, I'm . . . uh . . . ."

"Looking at the job openings?"

Paula was stunned at her boss's perceptive abilities. "How did you know?"

"Actually, it was just a guess, but thank you for confirming it." She grinned wryly as she pulled up a chair next to Paula's at the computer. "Did you see the job in Denver?"

Paula nodded. Their newest hotel was looking for a senior shift manager, the equivalent of Rusty's position. It was a plum job in the system, and would probably go to someone with more seniority than she.

"I think you'd be perfect for it. Mind you, I wouldn't be excited about losing one of the best managers I've ever had working for me, but I'd like to see you venture out of Orlando and earn your wings. I'm not going anywhere for a few more years, but when I do it would be nice if you had some senior management experience under your belt."

Paula was awed by the praise. Stephanie was practically telling her that she had a chance to succeed her in a few years at this hotel, but only if she seized the opportunity now to gain experience at an advanced level.

"Do you really think I'd have a shot at this job in Denver?"

"I think you're a shoo-in."

"I think she wants that over there," Wynne said, pointing to the empty space beneath the window. It was moving day for Heather, and though Wynne had returned from New York last night at midnight, she had set aside the day to help however she could.

Things were happening very quickly on the relocation to Orlando. Wynne already had a contract on her townhouse, and Heather's move to this new apartment meant she could send the rest of her things to Florida right away.

Her most important preparation was scheduled for Thursday— one last surgery to reinforce her injured leg. She planned to recuperate at her mother's home for three weeks before heading to Orlando to begin her work at Eldon-Markoff.

Heather came through the front door carrying an armload of hanging clothes.

"You need any more help?"

"No, this is it." She disappeared into the bedroom to deposit her load.

Their last few days had been calm, less confrontational, as Heather began to accept the finality of Wynne's decision. Wynne felt guilty at knowing that, for her, the whole episode would be closed when she left the apartment today. For Heather, it could be years before the hurt and anger ran their course. Wynne knew it would have mitigated her guilt if they had managed to stay friends, but Heather said she didn't need friends like Wynne, and had no interest in having any sort of contact after today.

Wynne absorbed the bitterness and took it to heart. The way she saw it, it was part of her penance, since her stupid, selfish decisions had caused all this pain.

"Who's going to sign this?" the moving supervisor asked, waving his clipboard.

"She will," Heather said flatly as she returned to the living room.

Wynne took the clipboard and fixed her signature to the bottom of the page. "You have my credit card on file?"

"Right-o," the man said, picking up the last of the protective blankets as he exited.

Heather dusted off her hands as she watched the crew load up and leave. "That's it, Wynne. All I need is the check."

Wynne reached into her pocket and pulled out a personal check for several thousand dollars, money she had offered so Heather could buy new things for her kitchen and bath, and put deposits on her utilities. Wynne had already paid the first six months rent on the apartment. Guilt money, but she didn't care. She wanted this part of her life behind her.

They stood quietly amid the boxes that lined the room, both choking back tears.

"Take care of yourself, Heather." Wynne tentatively held out her arms, hoping they might share one last hug.

"You too."

Heather was obviously fighting her emotions, but she finally gave in to the embrace. They held each other tightly for over a minute, both crying freely.

"Drop me a line when you get settled in Florida. I can't promise I'll answer back, but I always want to know how you're doing."

Wynne nodded, reluctant to offer more. It was time to move on.

"Would I be a shitty friend if I wished you bad luck?" Val asked. She was dropping Paula at the airport for her flight to Denver.

"It'll work out if it's meant to. Stephanie thinks I have a good chance, but it all depends on who the other candidates are."

"Are you nervous?"

"A little. It's been a long time since I interviewed for a job, but Stephanie grilled me yesterday for about two hours. I'm as ready as I'll ever be."

Val signaled for the exit off the Beeline Expressway. "You sure you want to do this?"

"I think it's time for a change." Promotions weren't going to fall in her lap while she lolled in Orlando. The Denver job was the right step career-wise, and that's where she needed to focus her energies.

"Does this have anything to with that woman from Baltimore?"

Paula blew out a ragged breath. "Maybe some. I figure if I'm

124

not ever going to have a life outside of work I might as well have the best job I can get."

"You can't let one bad experience with a lying bitch turn you into a cynic, Paula."

"No, but every time you get burned you have to step back and regroup. Seems like a pretty good time to concentrate on work."

Val followed the signs to the departure lane as Paula reached through the console to grab her overnight bag.

"Break a leg, you hear?"

When they pulled to the curb, Paula leaned over and gave her friend a warm hug. "Thanks. If I get this job, you want to come run my restaurant?"

"I don't think so. Cold weather and I don't get along."

"It gets cold there?" Paula asked with a wink.

"I'm sure it's just a rumor."

The pain had lessened since the surgery, but Wynne still had trouble with her stamina. She was already looking forward to her first night at her new home in Orlando.

"I don't know how we're going to manage all these bags," Kitty said, taking her seat next to Wynne in the first class cabin.

"Eldon-Markoff is sending a car, Mom. We'll get a skycap to help with the bags at the airport, and the driver can bring them in when we get to the house."

"I'll need to go to the grocery as soon as we get there."

"You don't have to do that. You'll be tired. We can order out."

"And what about breakfast? There won't be anything there and we're not going to start the day like that."

Wynne looked out the window, smiling to herself. The transformation in her mother had been nothing short of a miracle. Just as Janelle had predicted, the Connelly women had risen to the occasion when called on to help.

A week ago, Kitty had left Wynne in her sister's care to fly to

Orlando on her own. She met the movers and unpacked the boxes for the kitchen and baths, then purchased a bedroom suite for the guest room to replace the one Heather had taken. She and Wynne would shop together for living room and dining room furniture, but not until Wynne was mobile.

"I appreciate all you're doing, Mom."

Kitty squeezed her daughter's arm. "It's time I started paying you back for all you've done for me. I'm so proud of you, Wynne. I wish your father could have seen you get a promotion like this. He always said you were going to make something of yourself."

"I wish Dad were here too. But I'm glad to be sharing this with you."

Vince Tolliver couldn't believe his luck. Across from him sat the fourth applicant for the senior manager position, a Stephanie Anderson product like himself who, in addition to her other skills, spoke Spanish. On paper, they didn't get any better than this.

"Is there a part of your current job that you don't like, Miss McKenzie? For example, the paperwork, the supervision, dealing with the public?"

Paula thought for a moment about how best to answer the hotel director's question. "I suppose I'm like everyone else. I hate to have to discipline a worker, but the positive interactions with staff overwhelmingly outweigh the negative ones. It's the same way with troublesome guests." That was a good answer, she thought, but Tolliver waited for more. "Okay, the paperwork is a pain," she admitted with a chuckle.

Tolliver laughed. He liked a manager with a sense of humor, knowing that someone like that usually worked well under stress. He had it on Stephanie's authority that Paula had a real talent for handling problems without letting things escalate. And he also knew Stephanie wouldn't have kept a staffer for nine years if she couldn't handle paperwork.

"You know, our weather's a little different here," he cautioned.

"I'm looking for a change," she answered simply.

126

"Thanks, Mom. I really appreciate this." Wynne pulled her crutches from the back seat and leaned them against the car door.

"Are you sure you don't want me to come up with you?"

"No, that's okay. I can hang this strap on my shoulder—"

"Wynne!" An excited Cheryl Williams rushed to meet her. "I'm so glad to finally see you here."

"Hi, Cheryl. This is my mother, Kitty Connelly."

Kitty leaned across the passenger seat of Wynne's Volvo to say hello.

Cheryl pushed her hand inside the car in greeting. "Really pleased to meet you. We think the world of your daughter."

Wynne blushed like a schoolgirl on a date. Carefully, she pulled herself up and positioned the crutches beneath her arms.

"Let me take that," Cheryl said, grabbing for the heavy brief-case. "Thanks for the delivery. I can take it from here." She waved to Kitty as she steered Wynne toward the entrance.

"Thanks for your help."

"You're welcome. Are you sure you're up for this already?"

"I'm sure that I'm about to go insane. Please let me stay today, even if you change your mind and fire me," she quipped. Wynne loved her mother dearly, but they had spent nearly every waking hour together for the past three weeks.

"Okay, but we've decided not to pay you."

"Fine."

". . . and that your new office will be beside the copy machine."

"Perfect."

". . . and that Denise will be your secretary."

"You're cruel, Cheryl Williams."

"I know, but two of those aren't true."

"Denise," Wynne sighed.

"She can handle your needs for now. You can pick out some seminars and send her on company time if you want. If things don't work out, come see me."

127

Wynne knew that she would make things work out. Denise was deficient, but she was dedicated and willing to learn.

The elevator deposited the pair on the top floor, where Wynne followed her boss to the west end of the building. Three slots in from the corner was a small office, its outside wall solid glass. An executive desk with a return for her computer faced the door. A bookcase, work table and three chairs packed the room.

"I know it's not the Taj Mahal, but it's your very own space. If you want to move things around, just buzz Denise and she'll find some muscles."

"It's great. I'm going to love it."

"After you've been here a while, you'll move up in the pecking order. In a year or two, you can move to a side that doesn't get the afternoon sun. That's when you'll know you've hit the big time."

"You're forgetting I'm from Baltimore. It will take me a while to complain about being too warm."

"I'll remind you of that."

On that note, Cheryl departed for her own corner office and Wynne struggled to her chair. Already, a stack of folders filled her inbox. Settling in, she reached for the first one. She was thrilled to be here.

"Wow, Paula! If you think I'm going to say no to that, you're out of your mind." Kevin Ross was ecstatic at his new boss's offer. She would take Tuesday and Wednesday off each week and he would have both Friday and Saturday. A person could practically have a life with the weekend free.

"Not that it's permanent, mind you. But I'd like to be here on the busy days until I get acclimated to the hotel and the staff."

"You'll get no argument from me," the young man said happily. "Take all the time you need."

Paula liked her new charge quite a bit. He had spent the last two years running the business services center, and had also done his time in catering. He had been on the job as shift manager for only two months when her predecessor left to take a job with Ritz-

Carlton, so he wasn't yet ready to move up. That's why Vince Tolliver had looked elsewhere within the Weller Regent system for a new senior shift manager.

"So what do you do for fun in a place like Denver?" she asked.

"I don't know. I'm married. I don't ever get to have any fun."

That caused them both to laugh.

"So I've just granted you weekends off and you're going to waste them?"

"No, are you kidding? It means that Pam and I can actually go out of town once in awhile, skiing, or camping, or up to Estes Park. Of course, that also means I can't get out of going to spend time with my mother-in-law in Pueblo."

"You can always tell her that you're on call."

"I like the way you think, Paula."

"I'll handle the room inspections today. I need to get a feel for how everybody works."

"Knock yourself out. You want me to start the inventory?" Kevin was eager for the chance to do more of the management tasks.

"No, I'll do that when I get finished. Why don't you monitor the front desk and maybe pop in on the valet staff a little later?"

"Whatever you need."

Paula started her inspection on the third floor, one floor above their meeting rooms. By the time she reached the concierge floor, she was satisfied that the housekeeping staff was solid, and was glad to know that her first shift counterpart ran a tight ship. That always made the night shift easier.

The concierge lounge hosts were setting up for happy hour, much as they did in Orlando and throughout the Weller Regent chain. The hotels were unique in décor, but the major amenities were designed to be consistent from one hotel to the next. The Denver WR featured a Southwestern theme, the furnishings rustic but comfortable. Here in the lounge, the windows opened onto a spectacular view of the snow-capped Rockies, quite a contrast to the flat cypress expanse of Orlando.

The cozy arrangement of chairs in the corner conjured for

129

Paula an unwelcome image of Wynne Connelly. In fact, Wynne had become an irritating staple of her thoughts of late, especially on the long drive with Slayer to their new home almost two thousand miles away.

There was no denying the hurt when she learned she was no more than a dalliance.

"I don't know what to say." Wynne's words replayed bitterly in her head. There really was nothing to say, unless there was some other explanation than the obvious. And clearly, that wasn't the case or it would have been put forth. But Wynne had played the game so well that Paula had been nothing short of stunned by the other woman who answered the phone. The hardest part was Paula had been convinced Wynne shared her feelings. That left her uneasy that she couldn't protect herself from being taken for a fool in the future.

Unless she just kept to herself.

And that's what the move to Denver was all about. It wasn't a new start. It wasn't really even the job, though that part was a means to an end. For Paula, it was more about moving to a place where she didn't know anyone, and where she didn't want to know anyone. If she focused on doing a good job, she could soon move up to an operations post—if not here, then somewhere else.

"If you want, you can start sleeping on the sofa in my office. Just keep your PJs in the bottom drawer of my desk."

Wynne looked up to find Cheryl standing in her doorway on Tuesday evening, briefcase in hand.

"Really, Wynne, the rest of us go home by this time, sometimes a little sooner even. Have we given you too much to do or are you just slow?" The last bit was meant to be teasing, but the executive could tell right away that her joke had fallen flat.

"No, I . . . You were just kidding, right?"

"Right," Cheryl assured, dropping her briefcase to take a seat across from her assistant VP's desk. "I'm going to have to tell my husband about you. He won't believe there's someone who gets here before I do and stays until after I'm gone."

"I'm in the middle of drawing up this branding campaign. Do you think we might have a few thousand in the budget for a couple of focus groups?"

"Sure, we can move it out of advertising if you think we need it."

"I do. I'd feel better if we had some sort of disaster check before we launched this."

"That's a good idea. Now go home."

"I just want to finish this—"

"I'm waiting. We're going to walk out together so I can verify that you're leaving." Her boss was serious.

"Okay." Wynne sighed, closing her folder.

"And no taking it home to work on," the executive chided as she watched her protégé move to place the folder in her briefcase. "That would defeat the purpose of pushing you out of here."

"Yes, ma'am."

She followed Cheryl to the elevator where they waited.

"How's your leg?" The limp wasn't nearly so pronounced as it had been before the surgery, but it was still there.

"It's a lot better. I'm still doing physical therapy, but they're starting to think I've reached the ceiling."

"Does it hurt much?"

"Not like it did, but I doubt I'll ever be pain free."

"That's too bad." Wynne had told Cheryl the awful story of the accident.

"I've gotten used to it." They exited the building and walked casually to the parking lot. "Look, I said I'd go. You don't have to escort me, you know."

Cheryl chuckled. "Seriously, Wynne, I don't want to see you burn yourself out. I know there's a lot to do, but no one expects you to get it all done the first year you're on board. If you plan on being in this for the long haul, you need to get out and build a whole life here in Orlando, not just a work life."

"I know, Cheryl. I will." Actually, the idea of venturing out to explore the social scene in Orlando always led her to thoughts of Paula McKenzie, and that triggered feelings of guilt and sadness. She had been thinking a lot lately of how badly she had behaved, and wasn't at all interested in the idea of meeting someone new. "Believe it or not, I'm having a lot of fun at work right now."

"I can tell, and I appreciate all you're doing. But take it from an old pro. Save the best of yourself for your personal life, not your job."

Wynne nodded in understanding.

"You know, Wynne, we're a family here at Eldon-Markoff. Now I don't mean to be nosy, but if you aren't seeing anyone special, I'd be happy to host a couple of dinner parties to give you a chance to meet some single men, you know, professional men."

Wynne forced a smile and looked away. She had wondered if Ken Markoff had already shared the tale of seeing her with Paula, holding hands in the restaurant. Apparently he hadn't, or she wouldn't be facing this awkward moment.

"Cheryl, thanks but . . . I'm really not interested in meeting . . . men."

"But you . . . oh. Women?"

Wynne nodded nervously. "But to tell you the truth, I'm really not interested in meeting anyone at all right now. I'm still sort of coming out of a relationship that didn't end well. I'd just like some time."

"I understand. But if I come across any interesting women— I'm not sure where, but you never know—I'll probably mention it, whether you're ready or not."

"Fair enough," Wynne agreed as she opened her car door.

"Okay, this is as far as I go. I expect you to drive off, not just circle the lot until I'm out of sight so you can sneak back in."

"Scout's honor. See you tomorrow." Wynne started up her Volvo and backed out of her assigned space.

Instead of turning toward her own house, she continued a quarter-mile ahead to the condominium community where Paula lived.

She had given into temptation and driven through the neighborhood three times since moving to Orlando, but had never glimpsed Paula at home. Today was Tuesday, Paula's day off, and the thought of getting a peek of her from afar was tantalizing. It wasn't exactly stalking—it was more like . . . unobtrusive observation, just checking up.

Slowly, the Volvo wound past the small lake, turning left toward the buildings that overlooked the neighboring golf course. Wynne's breath caught at once as she realized the garage door directly beneath Paula's end unit condo was open. But the car inside was not the dark green Miata. It was a red sedan of some sort. Quickly, she scanned the parking lot for the familiar sports car, continuing until the road ended.

Wynne turned around and proceeded back the way she had come, slowing dramatically in front of Paula's place. She watched in confusion as the car began to back out, its passengers a young couple, and with a child's car seat plainly visible in the back.

She pulled over to get her bearings, double-checking in her mind the details of her one visit to Paula's home. This was the location she remembered, and the number on the side of the building was the one she recalled giving the taxi driver.

Wynne returned to the condominium complex the following day, as well as the next, both on the way to work and on the way home. When the weekend came, she paid one final visit, again spotting the family in the sedan.

Paula McKenzie didn't seem to live here anymore.

Chapter 13

"It figures my first winter here would be the worst on record," Paula grumbled as she traded her knee-high boots for the low black heels that accompanied her uniform. The eight blocks from her downtown apartment were brutal in the cold weather, but not as bad when the wind wasn't blowing.

"We ordered this up just for you," Kevin said with a chuckle she was unable to appreciate.

"Fine, Kevin. I can understand January and February, but this is April. Give me a break already."

"And the best part is this might not even be the last of it."

"Oh yeah, that's the best part, all right."

The phone on Paula's desk buzzed, signaling a direct patch from security.

"Paula McKenzie," she answered crisply. "Great . . . twelfth floor . . . Okay, one of us will be right there."

"What have we got?"

"Some guy's smoking a cigar by the elevator on the twelfth floor. Says his wife won't let him smoke in the room."

Kevin stood and pulled a quarter from his pocket. "Winner chooses?" he asked hopefully, knowing full well that his boss could simply order him to deal with it.

"Heads."

The coin sailed into the air, turning over and over until he caught it and slapped it on the back of his other hand. "Heads it is."

"I'll take care of the cigar. You get the front desk. They're about to get slammed." Paula gestured over her shoulder at the video, which showed a large group of guests lining up for registration.

"That was sneaky."

"I'm clairvoyant."

"I can't believe you've never been to one of these travel and tourism conventions. You should get out and meet people, but don't talk much, okay? I'm afraid you'll get recruited and then I'd have to kill somebody," Cheryl said, only half-joking.

"Don't worry. I can't imagine I'd be as happy working for anybody else. But it's nice to know you're not taking me for granted." Wynne had been on the job in Orlando for nearly a year, and had continued to impress her boss, as well as her CEO. More every day, she felt at home in the company, and her responsibilities had grown as she proved herself again and again. Already, she had moved to an office on the building's south side.

"Believe me, I would never take you for granted." Leaning forward in the seat, Cheryl asked the cabbie, "Does it always snow like this in April?"

"I don't think this winter's ever going to end. We've had one storm after another since the first week in October . . . more snow than we've ever had before. At least today it's not in the single digits like it has been."

"Thank God for small favors," she groused. "Look at you,

135

Wynne. All bundled up nice and warm. You're used to this from your days in Baltimore, I bet."

"Yeah, like he said, it's not so bad when it's in the twenties. Unless of course the wind is blowing."

"Do you miss Baltimore?"

"Baltimore, no. I was homesick at first, but once my mom moved down, I didn't give it another thought." Wynne had returned to Maryland for a few days at Christmas. During her time at home, a water pipe in the old house ruptured and the furnace drew its last breath. That was enough for Kitty, who proposed that she give up the house for good and move south. Wynne's realtor found her a first-floor two-bedroom unit with a garage in the nice complex where Paula used to live. Wynne was pleasantly surprised at how glad she was to have her mother close again. She and Janelle should have encouraged the move to a condo years ago.

The cab wound through the maze of one-way streets in downtown Denver, finally pulling into the circle in front of the Weller Regent. They were immediately met by a valet in a down jacket and gloves with a wool cap pulled over his ears.

"Welcome to the Weller Regent, ladies. Sorry about the weather, but we'll do everything we can to make your visit as comfortable as possible." The young man smiled sincerely and collected their bags from the taxi's trunk, loading them onto a cart that was whisked indoors with the bundled women close behind.

"Warmth!" Cheryl exclaimed. "How do people live in this climate?"

"They say the same thing about us in August, don't they?" Wynne followed her boss to the registration desk. In her frequent travels, she often stayed in the Weller Regent, and each time she entered the reception area, she thought of Paula McKenzie. She had learned after finally getting up the nerve to call the Orlando hotel last fall that Paula was no longer working at the WR, but the employee she spoke with couldn't give out further information.

"I'm supposed to meet a couple of old friends for dinner. You're welcome to join us if you'd like."

136

Wynne knew Cheryl well enough by now to know the invitation was sincere, even though she would only be tagging along.

"I don't think so. I'm probably just going to grab something upstairs in the lounge a little later and go to bed early. But I really appreciate the offer."

"Yeah, you're the smart one. With the two-hour time change, you're going to be rested tomorrow and I'll be walking around like a zombie. Don't let me give away any of our trade secrets, okay?"

Cheryl stepped forward to the reservation counter, looking back at her assistant VP who waited patiently for the next available clerk. It was a lucky day for Eldon-Markoff when they brought Wynne Connelly on board in the corporate office. The woman was a workhorse, not to mention smart and innovative. Best of all, she had a presence about her, a demeanor that practically demanded attention. In only a year, Wynne had taken the position to a higher level than either she or Ken Markoff had envisioned, and was already sprinkling her ideas and initiatives into their sales department. No way were they going to let Wynne Connelly go to work for the competition.

When Wynne walked up to the busy counter to check in, she couldn't help but notice that the clerk who assisted her wore a nametag indentifying him as a shift manager. Checking her watch, she confirmed his was the second shift . . . Paula's shift. So this man had the same job here in Denver as Paula had held in Orlando.

"Wynne Connelly," she announced, handing over her credit card.

"Yes, Ms. Connelly. I have you for two nights on our concierge floor, king-sized, non-smoking."

"That's right."

Kevin worked efficiently to complete the check-in process. He used to hate the times when he had to fill in at the front desk, but over the last year, his new boss had helped him appreciate the opportunity to interact with both staff and guests. The front desk got most of the problems and complaints and he had learned more about dealing with them by exercising his newfound authority.

Best of all, Paula had said, his example would help the younger clerks do a better job, and that paid off when they learned to handle difficult requests on their own.

"Here you are, Ms. Connelly." Sliding the key card across the counter, Ross directed her to the elevators and informed her of the perks she would receive with her upgrade. "I hope you have a nice stay, and if you have any problem at all, please let someone know and we'll do our best to take care of it."

Wynne smiled and nodded, thinking back to the way Paula had handed her a business card, pointing out the direct extension. Flirting.

Paula hated situations like the one she was walking into. The fact that security was already involved and had called her indicated they hadn't been able to diffuse the situation with just their presence.

Exiting the elevator, she was met by one of the guards. "Do you have the gentleman's name yet?" she asked, all business.

"No, and this guy is not exactly a gentleman, if you know what I mean. If I had to guess, I'd say he likes his Johnny Walker straight up."

"It's four o'clock in the afternoon, for crying out loud." Paula turned from the guard to appraise the uncooperative guest, who sat in an armchair by a potted plant—his ashtray, she observed—holding a drink in one hand and a cigar in the other. He was a large, barrel-chested man, his tie knotted loosely but still obscuring his neck. His bulbous face was red and his eyes had that unfocused look that indeed said, "I'm drunk as hell."

"Hello, I'm Paula McKenzie. I'm the manager here. They tell me your wife won't let you smoke that cigar in your room. Is that right?"

"Goddamn right!" he barked.

"That's too bad, Mr. . . ." She waited a moment, but he didn't take the bait. "But I'm afraid the city of Denver has an ordinance

138

that prohibits smoking in the common areas of all public buildings, so your choices are pretty limited. You either have to stay in your room, or you can go to the smoking area on the second floor. Unfortunately, that's on an outside balcony."

"Or I can sit right here," he answered belligerently.

"No, that isn't one of your choices, unless you put out the cigar. I think it would be best if you returned to your room. I'd be happy to explain the rules to your wife. Maybe she'd change her mind." Her voice was calm and steady, and her face bore just a hint of an encouraging smile.

"Can I smoke in the bar?"

"I'm afraid not."

"Then I'm going to sit right here until I finish." Extracting his lighter, he relit the smelly cigar.

Paula sighed. "Look, as the manager, I have to enforce the smoking rules or I'll get in trouble with the hotel director. If that happens, I could lose my job. And if I lose my job, they might take my children away from me. I'm working so hard to keep my family together. Please help me here. All you have to do is put out the cigar and go back to your room."

The man looked at his drink, then at his cigar. "You mean you might get fired if I don't put this out?"

Paula nodded with a pleading look.

"How many kids you got?"

"Two," she lied, immediately thinking of her niece and nephew. "Josh and Jordan."

"Well, I don't want you to lose your kids on account of me," he finally acquiesced, turning to stub out the cigar in the plant.

"Why don't you let me take that?" Paula intercepted the smoking object, dousing it immediately in what was left of the man's drink. "I really appreciate you helping me out on this one. Why don't you stop by the front desk when I'm working tomorrow and I'll see that you get a coupon for a free drink in the bar?"

"Okay, thanks."

Paula turned back to her two security guards who were waiting at the ready in case the situation had escalated. "Will you see that this gentleman gets back to his room okay?"

"Yes, ma'am."

From the corner of her eye, Paula glimpsed the elevator door opening to allow a businessman to exit. The lighted arrow pointed upward, and she was vaguely aware of two women who remained in the car. As the doors began to close, her eyes met those of Wynne Connelly and she froze.

Wynne's heart pounded the very instant she recognized Paula McKenzie. The sensations were almost overwhelming—the tightened stomach, the shaking hands, the rapid breathing.

"Are you okay?" Cheryl noticed her companion had fallen back against the side of the elevator, gripping the rail for support.

"Yes, I'm fine. I just got . . . queasy all of a sudden."

"You better not be getting sick. Being sick at a hotel is one of the worst experiences there is."

"No, I'm fine, really," she assured, though her voice shook in response to the adrenaline rush. So Paula had moved to Denver.

The door opened on the top floor and both women stepped out, checking the placard to locate their rooms.

"I'm in 2116. Call me if you start feeling sick. If I'm not in, call my cell phone." Cheryl knew she was mothering her protégé, but after raising three children, it was her nature to worry about other people.

"I'm okay, honest. It was just . . . nothing."

"All right, but call me if you need anything."

"I will. You go out and have a good time with your friends. Don't worry, okay?"

"If you say so."

"I say so. I'll see you in the morning. Watch the margaritas."

"Spoilsport."

Wynne pushed her card into the slot across the hall from her boss and stepped inside, leaning her back against the door as it

140

closed. Coming face to face with Paula had completely unnerved her. An array of emotions had surfaced all at once—surprise, guilt, apprehension. And excitement.

Paula returned quickly to her desk, her fingers fumbling anxiously as she called up the guest register on her terminal. Scanning the details, she confirmed that her imagination wasn't at play.

K. Wynne Connelly, two-nights. Room 2117, billed to Eldon-Markoff.

So she hung onto her job after all, Paula thought. "And of all the hotels in Denver, she had to walk into mine," she murmured, understanding how Rick Blaine must have felt when Ilsa entered his club in Morocco.

There had been whole days of late when Paula hadn't thought of Wynne, but it didn't take much to conjure the image. Anytime she saw an elegant woman traveling alone, she remembered. And if one of those women spoke to her in a friendly way, she automatically invoked her most professional demeanor, a wall of resistance to familiarity. Even after almost a year, the wariness lingered, leaving her more isolated than she had ever felt. The fresh start she had hoped for in Denver had never panned out. Thank goodness she had a job that she loved.

And tonight, Wynne Connelly was staying in her hotel.

Like a moth to the flame, she needed to see her, to talk to her again, if only to let her know that she had risen above it. People shouldn't be allowed to treat others like that and get off scot-free. She wanted Wynne to know she was over it . . . even if her own shaking hands were telling her otherwise.

Wynne turned back to her notes for tomorrow's session on affinity partnerships, reading the paragraph for the fourth or fifth time, still not comprehending the words. She was situated in the corner of the concierge lounge, looking up from time to time to admire the sunset over the Rockies. She had held this vigil for over two hours, hoping—but doubting—Paula would stop by to say hello.

It was almost nine as she finished her second glass of red wine. Paula would know where to find her, if she would even consider speaking to her. Her last words—on the phone at the Hyatt—hadn't been harsh, but there was definitely finality in her tone.

There was so much Wynne wanted to say about what had happened. She needed to apologize not only for what she had done, but for the way she had run away from the mess she had made. Mostly, she wanted to tell Paula that her feelings had been real.

Suddenly, she felt more than saw the familiar face coming her way, a fixed expression not giving away Paula's mood. As it had in the elevator, Wynne's heart rate increased and her stomach fluttered in anticipation.

"Hello, Wynne," she said formally.

"Paula . . . It's good to see you." She looked fabulous.

"I'm glad to see things worked out for you with Eldon-Markoff." The kind words weren't exactly delivered in a friendly tone.

"Thank you," Wynne answered meekly. It was difficult not to feel as though she was under judgment. Spotting the nametag above the pocket of the black blazer, she returned the sentiment. "And I see you've made senior shift manager. Congratulations."

"Yeah, I decided I was ready to relocate."

"It must have been a difficult decision, leaving your family and a hotel you liked so much."

"I like this hotel, and I'm enjoying the new job. How about you?"

"Things are good. I . . ." She decided against telling Paula that she too had relocated. It wasn't important now that Paula was no longer there, and Wynne really didn't want to underscore the irony. "I really like what I'm doing now. They keep me pretty busy."

"Well, I hope things keep working out for you."

"Have dinner with me," Wynne suddenly blurted.

"You've got to be kidding." Paula looked around awkwardly to see if others were within earshot.

"I'm not. I have so many things I want to tell you. Please."

"No," she answered adamantly. "It isn't necessary, Wynne. It wasn't a big deal. We got carried away and did something we shouldn't have. End of story."

Despite the words of denial, Wynne could feel the anger and hurt emanating from the woman before her. She looked away and shook her head sadly. Turning back, she held Paula's eyes with her own. "Would it help at all to tell you that I'm sorry?"

"There's nothing to be sorry for. I didn't have any expectations. When people let things happen too fast, it's easy to make mistakes."

To Wynne, the words sounded cold and calculated, but who was she to argue that it had been more than just getting carried away? The voice that started in her head the moment she met Paula at the hotel had warned her not to let it happen, but she had chosen to ignore it and, like Paula said, she made a mistake. And perhaps the woman standing before her was the price of her poor judgment, and Wynne just had to let her know she realized that.

"Paula, it was my mistake, not yours," she offered, "and what I regret most is that I screwed things up with you."

"That you did." It had been said flippantly, but Wynne thought she saw a hint of sadness and regret in Paula's face. "Look, I need to go. It was good to see you again."

"Thanks for coming by."

When Paula left, Wynne retreated to her room, still wound up about their encounter, and deeply saddened at where they had left things. Despite everything that had transpired, she knew without a doubt if Paula were still in Orlando, she would want to be with her. No one had ever made her feel this way.

In her office on the second floor, Paula pushed her hands

through her hair. The encounter had left her nearly drained. That woman upstairs made her feel things, and after all this time, it still hurt. She had seen the sadness for herself in the shining aqua eyes, but she was determined not to respond to it. It didn't matter now anyway, and there was no way she was going to show how naïve she had been.

Chapter 14

"Paula, over here!" Maxine McKenzie shouted as she spotted her daughter coming through the terminal exit.

"Mom!" Rushing the final few steps, Paula dropped her shoulder bag and wrapped her mother in a hug. "I've missed you guys so much."

"We've missed you too. Josh and Jordan talked about you all through breakfast."

"Are they here?"

"No, I left everyone at home. I was being selfish because I wanted you all to myself for an hour."

"Fine by me." The two women lingered in baggage claim as they waited for the carousel to deposit her luggage.

"Are you still enjoying Denver, honey?"

"I'm not sure I ever actually said that I enjoyed Denver, but I really love my hotel."

"You don't like living there?"

"It's okay, I guess. It was awfully cold all winter. And those two blizzards we got in April didn't help matters. But it's actually quite pleasant right now."

"Have you had a chance to get out much?" Once again, Maxine found herself worrying about her daughter, knowing she was giving too much of herself to the Weller Regent at the expense of finding even a modicum of personal happiness.

"A little. The Rockies are gorgeous and I've taken a few drives."

"By yourself, I suppose."

Paula shrugged. "Yeah, it's hard to find someone who's free to do something on a Tuesday or Wednesday." The red rollerboard appeared on the carousel. "Here's my bag."

Moments later, they were getting into Maxine's white Accord, bound for Cocoa Beach. Paula reveled in the warm humidity of Orlando in June.

"Can I ask you a question, sweetheart?"

"Of course," Paula answered tentatively. She and her mom rarely talked about personal matters, but the tone of her mother's voice suggested it was going to be that kind of question.

"Do you . . . date anyone? I don't mean to pry, and you can tell me that it's none of my business if you want, but honey, sometimes I just can't bear to think about you being alone all the time."

"Actually, there was someone not too long ago, but things didn't work out."

"Oh? Someone in Denver?"

"No, it was here in Orlando, just before I left. I met her at the hotel. She was a guest."

This revelation surprised Maxine, not only because Paula had never mentioned it to anyone, but also because it was important enough to her to bring it up here and now, over a year later. "Was it serious?"

"It could have been, at least to me," she answered honestly.

"What happened?"

"It turned out she wasn't single. She had a girlfriend back home

146

in Baltimore . . . one she forgot to mention." Paula surprised herself by getting misty-eyed at the memory.

"Oh, Paula, I'm so sorry. Why didn't you talk to us about it?" Maxine already knew the answer to that. Ever since that day Paula left for Europe fifteen years ago, the subject of her love life was one they all avoided. Paula had been so quiet when she brought that one girlfriend around—Susan something or other, and Maxine and Ray took that to mean their daughter wasn't comfortable sharing her personal life.

"I just had to deal with it on my own, I guess."

"Is that why you took the job in Denver?"

"Maybe a little. It seemed like a good time to put some distance between myself and this place. But the main reason was the job. Of course, if I had known the one here was going to open up . . ."

Approaching the ramp to the Beeline Expressway, Maxine briefly changed the subject. "Do you want to go check on your place?" Paula had turned her condo over to a management company to rent, hoping that someday she would find her way back to Orlando. Her tenants' lease had expired in May and the agency was doubtful they would get another renter until fall.

"Sure, we can do that. No one's living there right now, so I doubt the lights are even on." Paula started groping in her purse for the key.

Maxine turned northwest toward her daughter's condo. "Do you want to talk about that woman some more?" Whoever this woman from Baltimore was, she obviously meant a lot to Paula, or it wouldn't still prompt the tears in her daughter's eyes.

"Not really." The last thing Paula wanted to do was waste her weekend in Florida with sad thoughts. "Tell me about Josh and Jordan, and what's new with Dad?"

"So what do you think? Are people going to hide their eyes when they see this?" Kitty Connelly stopped and turned to model

147

her dark blue swimsuit. At sixty-two years old, she bore the slightly plump physique of one who had lived a sedentary life after having two children.

"I don't think anyone will run screaming, but they may have to reach for their sunglasses." Kitty's alabaster legs hadn't seen the sun in over thirty years.

"Very funny," the elder woman scoffed. "I'm giving myself a half-hour, then it's under the umbrella."

"I think that's a good idea." Wynne, on the other hand, was eager to work on her tan, which made the scars on her legs and abdomen less visible. She had been out a few times in her back yard and was already sporting a golden glow. With a darker tan, her eyes seemed brighter and her hair shone with bright auburn highlights. She absolutely loved the feel of the sun on her skin.

The Connellys walked to the fenced-in pool area, already crowded with others who had the same idea for escaping the summer heat. Spotting two chaise lounges in the corner by an umbrella, Wynne spread their towels as she and her mom settled in. It was fun being able to spend time with her mom just relaxing together. The move to Orlando had turned out to be good for both of them, and Janelle was already talking about coming to Florida one of these days.

"Did I tell you I'm having dinner tonight with the Shumachers and one of their friends from New York? They're such nice people. She used to be a . . ."

Wynne was already absorbed in her book, stretched out on her stomach with the clasp of her top hanging unfastened at her sides. As she became more aware of her mother speaking, she rose up to listen. A white sedan in the distance stole her attention as it pulled to a stop in front of the unit that used to belong to Paula McKenzie. She watched in utter amazement as two women exited and disappeared inside the upstairs condo. They were more than fifty yards away, but she was almost certain one of those women was Paula.

"Uh, hello there," Kitty spoke up anxiously to get her daughter's attention. Wynne seemed completely oblivious to the fact that she had lifted up so far her bare breasts were now visible to anyone who cared to look.

"Oops!" Wynne lowered herself and snapped her top into place. Now sitting up, she stared at the end unit to confirm what she had seen. After only a few minutes, the two women came out and returned to the car. The blonde definitely looked like Paula, but Wynne couldn't make out the features of the other woman from this distance. Whoever she was, she and Paula were certainly familiar, apparent from the casual way their arms hooked together.

The uncomfortable feeling of watching Paula McKenzie walking arm in arm with another woman gave way to curiosity. Why would Paula be in Orlando? And why was she here at her former home? Did she still own the place? And more important, was she moving back to Florida?

" . . . so anyway, after dinner, we're going to play a few hands of bridge and see if we all hit it off. It might become a regular thing."

"That's nice, Mom."

"Paula, you look fabulous." Jolene gushed as she eyed her former boss, decked out today in a light blue sleeveless cocktail dress with ivory shoes.

"Wow, so do you." She beamed at her protégé, excited to see a familiar face.

"We miss you so much. I mean, Belinda's okay, but she's sort of . . . I don't know . . . unbending, if you know what I mean. Stephanie had to pull rank so we could all get the day off today."

"It's a tough job sometimes, Jolene. I'm sure she's trying to do what's best for the hotel," Paula cajoled. "Speaking of Stephanie, is she here?"

"I haven't seen her yet, but I'm sure she's coming."

No one who knew Rusty Wilburn would miss this day, the day Juliana became his bride. Following their honeymoon, the couple would hastily pack for a move to Philadelphia, where Rusty would take over as the manager of operations for the day shift—a great job in the Weller Regent chain, and one he roundly deserved, Paula thought.

She had read in the WR newsletter about her friend's promotion and couldn't help but feel a pang of regret about her move to Denver, especially since Rusty's job of senior manager for the night shift—the same post she now held in Denver—was temporarily empty. Though she was tempted to ask Stephanie about it, a parallel move in the company after such a short stint wouldn't look good for future considerations. She was happy for Rusty, but envious of the one who would fill his vacant slot.

"Well, if it isn't the Prodigal Daughter."

Paula immediately turned to the familiar voice and reached out to hug her mentor. "Stephanie!"

"How are you, hon? I've been hearing great things about you in Denver. Did I ever tell you that Vince Tolliver sent me flowers a month after you got there?"

"You're kidding." Paula laughed. She knew Vince liked her work, but this information was pretty good leverage for the next time she wanted something from her hotel director.

"No, he's crazy about you."

"Well, I'm pretty happy there. It's a great hotel, and the people are wonderful."

"Happier than you were here?" the director asked.

Not even close, Paula thought, but Stephanie didn't want to hear that. "It's different. You know how much I love the WR here, and how much I enjoyed all the people that work here . . . and how much I respected my boss." She giggled at that last remark.

"I figured as much. When Rusty told me he got the Philly job, I almost picked up the phone then to ask you to come back, but pulling you out of Denver so soon like that wouldn't have been good for your career."

Paula nodded. Those had been her thoughts exactly.

"But if it were a different position, a promotion to operations, perhaps . . ."

Paula froze as Stephanie's words sank in. What was she saying?

"We better go grab our seats. Why don't you see me at the reception and we'll talk more?" Stephanie suggested with a sly wink.

For the next hour, Paula tried valiantly to concentrate on her dear friend, whose wedding was going on at the front of the small church. In the back of her mind, her thoughts were on what Stephanie had hinted. If there was any chance at all she could come back to Orlando without risking her future at Weller Regent, she was ready to do it.

Two weeks passed after the mysterious Paula sighting at her mother's condominium complex, and Wynne was unable to get Paula out of her mind. On a hunch she might be headed back this way, Wynne called the Weller Regent in Denver, only to learn from a staffer that Paula was off on Wednesdays but was expected in the next afternoon. So that was all it was, just a visit to Orlando, and probably a chance to see her family and check on her property, which apparently, she still owned.

Each time Wynne drove over to visit her mom, she was compelled to check out Paula's end unit. The red sedan was no longer around, and it looked as though the place was unoccupied. That got her wondering if perhaps Paula was heading back to Orlando. Maybe the Denver thing was just a temporary assignment.

She got her answer in late August, when she happened upon the "On the Move" column of the *Orlando Business Review*. It was only a tidbit and she might have missed it, but the bolded name leapt out at her.

The Orlando Weller Regent is pleased to announce that Paula R. McKenzie *has been promoted to the position of Manager, Hotel Operations. An 11-year veteran of the Weller Regent Corporation, Ms. McKenzie returns to her native Florida from Denver, where she served as senior shift manager in the Weller Regent's newest hotel property.*

"Okay, it took me a while, but I finally met someone really nice

151

that made me think of you. You interested?" Cheryl stood in her doorway, an expectant look on her face.

"Huh . . . ?" Her thoughts elsewhere, Wynne was startled by the sudden appearance of her boss. What the hell was she talking about?

"I'm thinking a small dinner party next Saturday. The two of you could have a chance to meet and chat informally. If you hit it off, great. If you don't . . . hey, it didn't cost you anything."

"Uh, you mean . . . a woman?"

"Uh, yes," she mocked her assistant VP. "Isn't that what you ordered?"

Wynne couldn't stifle the laugh that erupted at the thought of her boss scrounging for her potential dates. But the thought of making small talk with a stranger under Cheryl's watchful eye held no appeal at all. "I, uh . . . I'm sort of seeing somebody," she lied, glancing back at the *Business Review*.

"Oh yeah?" Cheryl certainly seemed intrigued by this pronouncement. "Anyone I know?"

"I don't think so. We haven't been seeing each other long."

"Well I'm glad to hear that, Wynne. You'll keep me posted, won't you?"

"Sure." She hoped to be seeing someone very soon—now that Paula McKenzie was back in town.

For the first year she had been in Orlando, Wynne had kept her nose to the grindstone, doing the best work of her whole career. It hadn't been a hardship, since she enjoyed her job so much.

All she had done on the social front was send Heather a note after she got settled in Orlando, followed by a Christmas card. Both went unanswered. Wynne had learned from a friend in Baltimore that she was seeing someone new and seemed happy. If anyone deserved happiness, it was Heather.

Then something clicked inside her when she saw Paula in Denver five months ago, and she hadn't been able to stop thinking about their all-too-brief affair last year. It was a yearning like she had never known, not only for romance, but for forgiveness she knew she didn't deserve.

"You wouldn't believe how good it is to see you back here. Now how do I get bumped to day shift?" Jolene asked her mentor.

"That should be easy . . . three to five years on the night desk gets you to catering or the business center. Then another two years after that gets you to the daytime desk."

Jolene groaned. "I don't think I can stand Belinda for three to five more years."

Paula chuckled softly, looking about to see if the woman who had replaced her over a year ago was nearby. "You were just spoiled because I was such a pushover. You know, it takes a while to build a rapport with somebody, and she might be struggling with it as much as you are."

"I don't think so, Paula. She just doesn't seem to try very hard to get along with people."

"Let me give you a little advice here, okay? This is how things work at the WR. If your boss does something that breaks the rules, you file a grievance. Everything's spelled out in the handbook. But if it's just a personality clash, then you're more likely to be the one that gets judged when it gets resolved. I know that sounds unfair, Jolene, but that's the way it is. Weller Regent loves it when everyone on the staff gets along, but it isn't realistic to think it's going to happen all the time. If Belinda is doing her job, the WR is going to throw her all the support she needs."

"I know you're right. And I know that I can always count on you to tell it just like it is."

Paula smiled and chucked the woman's arm gently. "Like I said, you're spoiled. And I know it probably makes you feel better to get it off your chest, but I would also suggest that you try not to do that at work or at the bar down the street with the rest of the staff. It just gives it a life of its own, and makes everything worse."

Jolene nodded, clearly embarrassed.

"But that doesn't mean you shouldn't speak up if you think you're being treated in a way that's against our employment practices. And if you aren't sure about it, you can always come to me. Just try to be discreet, okay?"

Paula was finishing up her first day back on the job in Orlando. What Jolene didn't know was that Stephanie had already briefed her on what she considered an alarming number of informal complaints regarding the night shift manager, and with Rusty's post now open, the WR needed to follow up on those, as the person just hired to take his place was now Belinda's immediate supervisor. Without a moment's thought, Paula offered to fill in a few nights to help smooth the transition and Stephanie immediately took her up on it.

But right now, it was four-thirty, a half hour since her shift ended, and Paula was eager to get home. For the next few days, home was her parents' house in Cocoa Beach. Her furniture was en route, and while the WR was willing to put her up for free, she had Slayer to consider. The thirty-hour drive in the small convertible had traumatized him, and it didn't feel right just to leave him on his own with her parents.

Paula had to admit it was pretty fabulous to walk into a house filled with lively conversation and the aroma of dinner at the end of a work day. The last year in Denver had left her feeling lonely and isolated, and she had finally admitted to herself that she had overreacted to the dismal ending of her short affair with Wynne Connelly. She needed to give her social life a little attention, and now that she was working the day shift, she might even be able to get out and meet people.

Chapter 15

"You're getting to be a fixture here, Wynne. What's the matter? Didn't pay your light bill?" Kitty asked, her teasing tone evident.

"Very funny," Wynne answered. "Did you ever stop to think that I might just enjoy your company?"

"I'm not complaining. I like seeing you this much."

The transformation to independence that had begun when Kitty took over Wynne's care after her last surgery had continued after her move to Orlando. It wasn't just that the condo association now took care of many of the things that worried her so back in Baltimore. It was also that she had left behind the reminders of the pain and sorrow that had shrouded her after losing her beloved husband. Here in Orlando, she had started to make friends again, friends who hadn't known her only as Dr. Connelly's wife.

Wynne felt a little guilty at her mother's questions, and vowed to come clean about her interest in Paula eventually. But for now, she kept to herself the purpose of her frequent visits. The sight of the moving van as she pulled into the complex today made her spirits soar, but it was the white sedan in the garage instead of the green Miata and that worried her. It belonged to that woman who had come by with Paula that day Wynne and her mother had been out at the pool. Wynne couldn't make out what she looked like, but it was obvious that she and Paula were very close. Was it possible that the two were moving in together? That was certainly disconcerting.

"Look at all you've done!" Paula was ecstatic to walk in and find her furniture in place, the kitchen and baths set up, and both of her beds dressed in crisp clean sheets. The closet by the entryway held a stack of cardboard boxes, broken down flat for the recycle bin.

"I didn't know what you wanted to do with all your books and pictures, so I left them in their boxes on the porch. Oh, and I hate to tell you this, but everything you own needs to be ironed." Maxine was sprawled on the couch, the red-stained paper plate nearby a telltale sign of the pizza she had ordered.

"Mom, I can't believe you did all this. You must have worked all day."

"Not all day. The truck didn't get here until about two o'clock."

"What did you do all morning?"

"I scrubbed the bathrooms and the kitchen . . . swept out the garage. Oh, and I cleaned all the windows."

"You're kidding. And I thought I had a rough day." Paula had worked a double shift, filling in as promised in the senior shift manager post while the new hire settled in. "You get to name your reward."

"You mean that?"

"Anything you like. You want a professional massage? A manicure and a pedicure? Name it."

"Okay. What I want is for you to start spending more of your life away from that hotel."

Paula looked at her mother perplexed. "You mean not work as much?"

"Yes, but more than just not being there. Now that you're working on the day shift—at least as soon as you get through this temporary duty—I'd like to see you start having more fun, start doing things with friends, maybe even meet somebody."

"From your lips to God's ears, Mom," Paula said sincerely.

Maxine sat up, surprised at her daughter's easy agreement. "Really?"

"Yeah, really. I've been thinking about it, even back in Denver." She kicked off her shoes and sat down in her favorite chair, tucking a foot underneath her. It was almost midnight and both of them were beat, but ever since their talk when she had come back for Rusty's wedding, Paula realized she really wanted to start sharing more of her personal life with her family. It felt good to be able to connect with her mom this way, and she liked to think when she did meet somebody special, they would be happy for her. "I'm going to make a real effort to get out and meet people."

"Do you have a lot of . . . women friends?"

"You mean lesbian friends?"

Maxine nodded.

"A few, but not many that I'm very close to. I think the most important thing is just to make friends—all kinds of friends. Eventually you start to meet people you have things in common with, and then you meet their friends, and their friends, and so on. But I'm serious, Mom. Now that I have nights and weekends off, I'm not going to live every minute of my life for the Weller Regent. This last year has really taught me the consequences of not having a life outside of work."

Her mother smiled. "I can't tell you how glad I am to hear that, honey. I guess all parents want to see their kids happy, but I've been a little selfish about that. I've wanted to see you happy with somebody, not just at work. Your dad and I are really proud of what you've accomplished at the Weller Regent, but it would pale next to seeing you in love with somebody."

For some reason, Paula blushed as she thought about being in love. Clearly, she had further to go with feeling completely comfortable talking about this stuff with her mom, but it was freeing in

157

a way. That said, she hoped her mother would never ask about her sex life.

"We should go to bed. Don't you have to be at work early?"

"My shift starts at seven," Paula answered, standing wearily. "I really appreciate everything you did today. You should sleep in tomorrow, okay? I'll come down and pick up Slayer after work."

"I might take you up on the sleeping in part, but don't worry about Slayer. He can stay with us as long you need."

"But I miss him, and besides, he'll be excited to get back to his old haunts. I bet the lizards line up on the window to see him. They'll all be fat, though, because they haven't had any exercise in a year."

The white car left yesterday. A green Miata with Colorado tags sat in the open garage, and Wynne caught a glimpse from afar of Paula lugging flattened cardboard boxes across the parking area to the recycle bin. After one more trip, she backed out of the garage and was gone.

"What do you keep watching out there?" Kitty asked, peering over Wynne's shoulder.

"Just . . . somebody moving in."

"Somebody in particular?"

Wynne knew it was silly to pretend her frequent visits were only because she enjoyed spending time with her mother. Lying to and about Paula McKenzie had already caused her enough problems. If there was any way to pull Paula back into her life, everything needed to be in the light of day.

"Yeah, it's somebody I know," she confessed. "You remember when we first looked at this place I told you that I knew someone who used to live here?"

Kitty nodded.

"That's who it is. She moved to Denver right after I got the job here, but I guess she held on to her place. I read not too long ago that she'd been promoted and was coming back."

"Is she a friend of yours?" her mother asked.

Wynne sighed. "She used to be. But I screwed things up."

If Kitty was surprised at this, she didn't show it. "Why don't you tell me about her?" Pulling a chair up to the window, she waited for the details.

Wynne and her mother had grown so much closer over the last year and a half, especially after Kitty moved to Orlando. During the time she was recovering from surgery, they talked about personal things in a way they never had, including how Wynne had come to spend two years with Heather Bennett. It was more than just having family nearby that Wynne liked. It was Kitty herself, who was an interesting and loving woman when she wasn't so frantic about how she was going to manage her life.

"Okay, her name is Paula McKenzie and she works downtown at the Weller Regent. That's where I used to stay when I was coming back and forth. We got to be friends and we . . . went out a few times." She hoped her mother wouldn't press for more than that.

"So what happened?"

"We just . . . What happened was that I didn't really expect to have the feelings that I had, or for her to feel the way she did about me. It started as something casual and it took off."

"Isn't that what you wanted to happen?" Kitty asked, not yet getting the picture.

"Well, there was Heather," she added quietly, as if that explained it.

"Oh," Kitty said simply, as she started to comprehend. "So this was going on while you and Heather were still . . . together." Her tone was one of understanding, not judgment.

"Yeah," Wynne confessed. "But then when I found out about the VP job, I realized that I'd screwed up by not being more upfront about my situation. It wouldn't have mattered if we'd kept things on just a friendship level, but we didn't."

"Why was that was a problem? You split up with Heather before you moved down here."

Wynne shifted uncomfortably. "That's right, but the things between Paula and me happened when I was coming down here, when I was still living with Heather. They didn't know about each other. Before I got the job offer, I never figured we really had any possibility of making anything out of it, so I just didn't see the point. But then she called the house one night and Heather answered the phone . . ."

"And that ruined everything," Kitty finished.

"Well, it was certainly the last nail in the coffin. I'd already made up my mind that I had to tell her everything, no matter what happened, but I was hoping that we could maybe step back and start over. But when she found out on her own, things just sort of fell apart, and the next thing I knew, she'd moved to Denver."

The two women sat quietly in the living room, both reveling somewhat at the unusual closeness they felt. The last time they had a heartfelt conversation like this was when Kitty had asked her daughter if she had done something to cause such a problem for Heather. Wynne had tried to explain away her lover's rudeness as a product of her upbringing, but in the end, she had conceded there was no legitimate reason for Heather to treat her family that way. But she had assured her mother Heather would never come between them.

"So does the fact that you're watching her again mean that you're still interested?"

Wynne nodded solemnly. "It's been a year and I haven't been able to get her out of my mind . . . or stop kicking myself."

"I can't believe how out of shape I am," Val wheezed as they rounded the final turn and headed back toward Paula's condo.

"You and me both. This air seems so heavy," Paula complained, out of practice with running in the heat and humidity. She had gotten used to Denver's mile-high climate, even though that meant running indoors on a treadmill for much of the winter.

"You sure you don't want to go back to the night shift? It would be better for my health and body image."

"Not a chance. This is what I've been working toward for eleven years."

"Yeah, I envy you. But I guess as long as I stay in the sports bar business, I'm never going to have a normal life."

"Then switch jobs," Paula advised, puffing as her tired feet continued to pound the paved jogging trail.

"Easy to say, but what would I do?"

"Are you kidding? You could manage a restaurant anywhere in town. You might not make as much to start as you do at Flanagan's but you'd get to have friends, and go out at night. What's the point of making all that money if you can't ever do the things you want to do?"

"I really like Flanagan's, though."

"Yeah, I know, and I like the Weller Regent. But I'm not going to let it take center stage any more. I want more out of life than just a good job."

"Yeah, me too, I guess. Turning thirty really made me start thinking about it more."

"You could always wait like I did until you start pushing thirty-five, but then you'll have lost another five years with nothing to show for it." The women reached the end of the path, where they both gratefully stopped, bending over with their hands on their knees. "You want to come up for a drink?"

"No, I have to go. Some of us still have to work Saturdays," Val groused.

"You really ought to think about finding something new. Did I tell you that I joined a women's volleyball league?" That was in fact Paula's first step at creating a social life.

"Yeah, that's cool." Val held her car door open a moment before getting in to allow cooler air to circulate inside. "So when do we have to do this again?"

"I'm off every weekend. It's going to be hard to get on a schedule to work out together, unless you can come over on the nights you're off."

"We'll see. I've missed seeing your red face nearly every day."

"I've missed you too, Val. I'd give you a mushy hug, but you're all sweaty," she said, making a face.

"Call me."

"You got it. Maybe I'll stop by Flanagan's some night."

"Do that. Your drinks are on the house."

Paula wearily climbed the stairs and entered her condo. A shower would feel great, but first she needed something cold to drink. Had she not stopped in the kitchen, she would have missed the small knock on the door.

"Forget something?" she called as she returned to the entry. The sight of Wynne Connelly on the landing nearly stole her breath.

"Hi."

"Wynne." It was all she could say as the shock registered. The face before her, tanned and relaxed, was one she never thought she would see again.

"I, uh, moved to Orlando while you were gone," Wynne said sheepishly. "And I read in the paper last week that you were back at the Weller Regent."

"You moved here?" This was unbelievable.

"Yeah, right about the time you left. Eldon-Markoff made me an assistant VP."

If it were anyone else, Paula would have invited her in, but not Wynne Connelly. "This is . . . I don't know what it is."

"It's good to see you again Paula. Really good."

"Wynne, I can't believe you're standing here."

"In the flesh," Wynne said, offering a tentative smile. "Anyway, the reason I stopped by was to make sure you knew about this." From the pocket of her shorts, she pulled a folded blue flyer announcing a Labor Day picnic next weekend for those living in the condo complex.

"You live here?" This conversation was growing more bizarre

162

by the minute. Paula was starting to think she was taking a nap and this was her dream.

"No, I live across the highway, in a house off Terrell Drive. But my mom lives here . . . right over there in Building Four," Wynne said, pointing to the building nearest the community pool.

Paula remembered that she was wringing wet with sweat and her face was probably splotched. Not her best look. But she didn't have to look good for Wynne Connelly.

"She moved down here last March, and I thought she would like it here," Wynne continued. "She does. She likes it very much. So I was hoping that you were planning on coming to the picnic so you can meet her, now that she's your new neighbor."

Paula took the flyer and studied it. She had gotten one in her mailbox and made a mental note to put in an appearance, if only for a few minutes. Labor Day was usually a day for family things in Cocoa Beach. "I, uh . . . I think I have other plans."

"Well, I understand. Maybe we can work out another time. I'd like for my mother to meet you." On that note, Wynne smiled and turned back toward the stairs. "And it's really good to see you again," she said again as she slowly descended.

Finally assured that she wasn't hallucinating, Paula watched as Wynne made her way back to her mother's building. Her limp was much better, and she looked fabulous.

Chapter 16

Wynne scanned the complex anxiously to see if Paula would show. She was still spending a lot of time at her mother's home and had seen Paula twice from afar. On both occasions, she was coming out of the condominium's fitness facility in the direction of the jogging trail that circled the adjacent golf course.

The Labor Day picnic at the complex was underway, with more than a hundred residents and guests milling about between the pool and the clubhouse. The caterers had laid out a buffet line of side dishes while two men watched over the grill.

"Tell me again what she's like," Kitty asked.

Wynne suspected that her mother's curiosity went beyond just wanting to see who had her in such a state. Kitty wanted her own assurances that this Paula McKenzie was nothing at all like Heather Bennett.

"She's . . . right there." Wynne beamed with excitement as she watched Paula bound down the steps toward the party. Paula apparently knew many of the people in attendance, and she stopped to greet one group after another. Eventually, she found her way to the table where the Connellys waited.

"Hi! I'm glad you could come." Wynne stood immediately and pulled another chair to their table.

"I try not to miss these things. It's a good chance to see my neighbors."

Wynne didn't care why she was here.

Paula turned to Kitty and introduced herself. "Hi, I'm Paula McKenzie. I understand you're my new neighbor."

"I am, and I understand you and my daughter are friends."

Wynne nervously completed the introductions as the two women shook hands. Paula remained standing until Kitty insisted that she join them.

"So how do you like Orlando, Mrs. Connelly?"

"Please call me Kitty. After all, we're neighbors now. We like Orlando just fine, don't we, Wynne?"

"Very much."

"I like it, too. I'm really glad to be back." Paula was quite deliberate about addressing her remarks to Kitty rather than Wynne. "And I like this complex too. The facilities are nice and the people are friendly. Do you like it here?"

"Oh, yes. The complex is very nice."

Wynne squirmed at realizing that Paula was avoiding her altogether.

"Wynne tells me that she met you at the hotel."

"That's right. We used to be pretty good friends."

Used to be? Wynne hadn't expected this to be easy, but she was surprised to hear Paula twisting the knife.

"Well, I know she's been very excited about you moving back to town. She hasn't made many new friends here, and I hate to think of her spending all that time by herself at home. It'll be nice to see her start getting out more now that you're here."

Wynne's face burned with embarrassment at her mother's blatant insinuations.

Paula stood suddenly and stepped back from the table. "I should be going. I have something planned with my family, but I wanted to stop by and say hello. It was very nice meeting you, Mrs. Connelly."

"I told you to call me Kitty. And it was nice meeting you. Wynne, if you want to walk your friend back to her place, I'll be fine here."

With her face still glowing red, Wynne stood and fell in beside their departing guest.

"Your mom is certainly subtle."

"Like multiple gunshot wounds," Wynne agreed sheepishly.

"I know the way home. You don't have to walk with me."

"I know, but I was hoping we could talk a little." Wynne shoved her hands in her pockets, slowing her gait so Paula would do the same. Paula's demeanor today was far from warm and friendly, but at least she had come to the party, and that counted for something.

"Fine," she answered noncommittally. "Your mom said you were spending all your time alone these days. What happened to the little woman?"

Another zinger. "I split up with Heather right after I got back to Baltimore."

Paula rolled her eyes in apparent disbelief.

"Yeah, I know. My timing left a lot to be desired."

"Now there's an understatement."

Plainly, forging even a friendship was going to be a challenge. "Look, I know you told me in Denver that it didn't matter, but I want you to know how sorry I am that I made such a mess of everything."

"You don't have to apologize," Paula answered, looking straight ahead as they walked.

"Then don't think of it as an apology. Think of it as a statement of how much I regret what I did because it caused me to lose your friendship, and because it cost me a chance to maybe have even more than that. I know I should have spoken up, but I never really thought things would go that far between us."

166

"That's no excuse, Wynne. No matter what you thought would happen to us, you and I started out just being friends, and even friends would think to say something like 'Oh, and I live with someone back in Baltimore.' But you deliberately left that out. You told me about your mom, your sister, and your niece. Why didn't you tell me about your girlfriend?"

She had no excuse. So how could she admit that and win forgiveness? "Paula, you and I started flirting with each other the first night we met. We were having fun. It didn't seem like it was going anywhere, but it was the first time in five years I could remember having fun with anybody." She heaved a big sigh, worried that she might be digging herself into a deeper hole. "Look, I'll say it again. What I did was wrong. I should have told you about Heather. But at the time, I didn't think there was any chance of you and me being anything more than friends."

"We had sex, Wynne. That was you, wasn't it?" Paula sneered sarcastically, still not making eye contact.

"I didn't set out to have sex with you. I never thought it would go that far, honest to God."

"It never should have gone that far, and if you'd told me about this Heather, it wouldn't have. I'm not in the habit of borrowing someone else's girlfriend for a roll in the sack. And just so you know it, I don't happen to like to share either."

Wynne walked in silence for a few steps, acutely aware of the ache in her chest as she absorbed Paula's angry words. But they both needed to vent their feelings, so she plowed ahead.

"Paula, everything I did was wrong, and I knew it. I told myself over and over that I shouldn't be spending time with you like that, and especially when I started to realize that my feelings for you were growing every time I came down here."

Paula looked at her in disbelief.

"Don't look at me like that. Didn't you feel it too?"

"I was free to feel that way. You weren't."

Wynne sighed. "I knew it was wrong, but I didn't want to stop. I figured my job would end soon and both of us knew that would be the end of it. I never thought it would go that far. I lost control."

"So did I," Paula confessed.

"When I left your house that day, they offered me the assistant VP job. All I could think about was you and how I had screwed everything up. Then you found out about Heather before I had a chance to tell you. And I would have told you, Paula. I swear. I realize how convenient that sounds, but it really is the truth."

"Did you tell Heather?"

"No. I hurt Heather enough just by ending our relationship. There was no reason to add to that."

"Would you have broken up with her if it hadn't been for me?"

"There's no way I would have asked her to come to Orlando. That would have been like making a commitment to her and I never thought what we had was strong enough for me to do that."

"If you felt that way about her, why were you even with her?"

Wynne turned up both palms as if defeated. "For all the wrong reasons. I'll tell you about it one of these days if you really want to hear. Heather's a good person. We just weren't right for each other. I hated hurting her, just like I hated hurting you."

As they climbed the steps, neither woman spoke. Out of habit, Wynne grasped the rail and started to pull herself up. Then she caught Paula watching her and let go of the rail to show off her progress.

"You had the surgery?"

"Yeah, about a year ago. I think this is as good as it gets."

"It looks like it's a lot better. Does it hurt much?"

"Not like it used to." They reached the landing and stopped. Wynne finally gathered her nerve to ask for what she wanted. "Paula, I know I don't deserve your friendship, but if we can work it out to start over, I promise I won't lie to you again."

Paula turned her back on Wynne and inserted her key in the door. Without even looking at her, she answered sternly, "Wynne, you need to get it out of your head that we can ever start over. We might be able to be friends someday"—she emphasized the word

168

"might" almost viciously—"if I ever feel like I can trust you again, but we won't ever go down that other path. If that's what you've got in mind, do us both a big favor now and just let it go."

Despite all those qualifications, Paula's response was enough to keep the hope alive in Wynne. If they could be friends again, that would be enough.

Chapter 17

Wynne smiled to herself as she turned into the condominium complex where her mother—and Paula McKenzie—lived. Cheryl was right about how important a personal life was to one's overall mental health. Sure, Wynne loved her job and didn't mind the long hours when they were necessary, but it was nice to have a whole weekend ahead of her when she didn't have to think about her inbox.

Instead, she would think about Paula, who seemed to invade her consciousness at every turn since their talk two weeks ago at the Labor Day picnic. She had been looking for an opportunity to see her again, and that moment was presenting itself right now— Paula was washing her small sports car in her driveway.

Wynne stopped at the curb and got out. "I always assumed you washed that car in the tub. Maybe a little car bassinette or something."

"Very funny." Paula smirked as she grabbed the hose to rinse her windshield, intentionally spraying the ground very close to where Wynne stood.

"Hey, you're dangerous with that thing."

"You better believe it."

"You don't scare me," Wynne said with a smirk of her own, not caring at all if Paula took her up on her dare.

"Haven't you heard? My bite is worse than my bark." With that, she swung the hose again, deliberately soaking Wynne's sneakers.

Undaunted, Wynne walked closer, ignoring the sloshing of her shoes.

"You're pretty brave," Paula said. "What brings you out this fine day?"

"I was coming to see my mom, but then I spotted an opportunity to get my car washed."

"What, you don't have water over at your house?"

"Yeah, but I'm just not as good at this as you. I keep getting water on the car, not other people."

Paula reached into a bucket and tossed her a soapy rag, which she caught, but not without soaking her T-shirt. Wynne shook her head and began scrubbing the Miata's fenders.

"Does this mean we can do mine next?"

"Sure." Paula continued to spray as Wynne scrubbed. "You missed a spot."

Wynne sighed and shot her a sidelong look. "Maybe we should trade jobs. You scrub while I play jokester with the hose."

"That would be stupid on my part, wouldn't it?"

Wynne could tell that Paula was fighting to keep from grinning. She tossed her cloth in the bucket and stood up straight. "I think it would be an excellent opportunity for me to demonstrate my trustworthiness."

Paula's face went dead serious. "You have a long way to go."

Defiantly, Wynne stepped forward and took the hose from Paula. "Gotta start somewhere."

ಊಾಲ

Wynne knocked on her mother's front door as she entered, calling out to announce her arrival. "Mom? Anybody home?"

The condo was quiet, surprising since the front door was unlocked and Wynne had called earlier to say she was coming.

"Where are you?"

Suddenly, a three-year-old burst from the guest room with her arms as wide as her smile. "Auntie Wynne!"

"Sophie!" Wynne scooped her up and twirled her. "Where did you come from?"

"In there." She pointed to the bedroom, where her mother and grandmother now leaned in the doorway.

"Ew, I don't want to hug you. You're wet," Janelle said, making a face.

Wynne ignored her and wrapped her sister in an embrace anyway. "I didn't know you were coming."

"That's because it was a surprise."

"How long are you guys staying?"

Janelle shrugged. "That depends. I got laid off."

"You what? How could somebody get laid off in a field like yours?"

"Our practice got bought and the new owners think they can get by with fewer people working X-ray. I just happened to be the last one hired."

"But you'll find another job, right?" Wynne sat on the couch and pulled Sophie into her wet lap.

"Yeah, but I thought I might look around here, since all of you abandoned us to cold, snowy Baltimore."

Kitty beamed. "Won't that be wonderful?"

Wynne hugged Sophie hard. "You mean I get to see this little squirt whenever I want to? Yes, that's very wonderful."

"You're all wet, Auntie Wynne."

"Yeah, what's that about?" Janelle asked.

"I just washed my car."

"Since when do you wash your own car? I always thought you were afraid to break a nail."

Wynne elbowed her sister.

"Since that cute blond woman moved in across the way," Kitty volunteered, much to Wynne's embarrassment.

"You have a new girlfriend?"

"I wish," Wynne said.

"Will you come swimming with us?" Sophie tugged on her wet shirt.

"I don't have my swimsuit, but I'll come watch you. Would you like that?"

Sophie nodded as her mother took her hand. "Let's go get changed."

Kitty walked to the window and looked out. "I saw you and Paula out there. Are things going well?"

"It was okay, but don't get your hopes up. She's barely speaking to me." She felt her mother's hand rest on her shoulder and looked up to see an encouraging smile.

"That will change. She seems like a very sweet young woman, Wynne."

"She is. Now all I need is a chance to make things up to her."

"Be patient. People like that . . . their hearts are good."

"I don't know, Mom. Two days in a row might be pressing my luck."

"So press it. The worse she can do is say no."

Wynne looked out the window. Paula's garage door was open and her Miata sat in plain view. "I don't even have her number."

"I do." Kitty opened the drawer of her end table and handed her daughter a booklet. "It's the homeowner's directory."

Wynne blew out an uneasy breath. "What time?"

"Why don't we cook out down by the pool? The Shumachers will like that. Let's say five-thirty." Kitty left her alone to make her call.

Wynne gathered her nerve and finally dialed the number.

"Hello?"

"Paula? It's Wynne."

Silence.

"Uh, my sister and her daughter got in from Maryland last night. Mom wants to have a cookout tomorrow and invite some of her friends from the neighborhood. We hoped you might come."

"I don't remember giving you this number."

"My mother looked it up in the homeowners' directory." *Sheesh!* Paula certainly had a gift for putting the screws to her.

"A cookout?"

"Yeah, about five-thirty down by the pool. My niece just loves the pool. She's been down there all day."

"How old is your niece?"

"Three and a half."

"I have plans for tomorrow already," Paula said flatly.

"Then I guess—"

"But we should be back by five-thirty. Can I bring someone?"

Wynne swallowed hard. Seeing Paula with a date wasn't exactly what she had in mind. "Okay."

"All right. Four of us. Should we bring something?"

"No . . . no. Just yourselves. See you then."

"I can't believe they still have energy after a whole day at Sea World," Paula said. "What do you feed them?"

Her sister-in-law chuckled. "You've been with them all day. You've seen what they eat—ice cream, cotton candy, sugar-coated pretzels and more ice cream."

"That's what I'm going to eat from now on."

Josh and Jordan took off down the stairs, already wearing their water wings.

"Watch for cars!" Adrienne shouted. "Get her hand, Josh."

Obediently, Josh took his sister's hand and stopped at the curb, looking both ways before skipping across the street to the fenced-in pool area. Kitty met them both and opened the gate.

Paula scanned the group looking for Wynne. A woman with wet hair was sitting with her back to them but Paula couldn't make out who it was. As they walked closer, the mystery person got up and walked down the steps into the shallow end, her identity now unmistakable. Paula lowered her sunglasses from the top of her head to cover her stare. Wynne was a gorgeous woman. Wynne in a bathing suit was indescribable.

"Paula, I'm so glad you made it. Who are these adorable little ones?" Kitty handed the two women a cold drink and gestured to Josh and Jordan, who had joined Sophie and Wynne in the shallow end of the pool.

Paula answered a wave from the Schumachers and introduced Kitty to her family. Then she and Adrienne met Janelle. It was easy to see the resemblance between Kitty and Janelle, but Wynne didn't look much like either.

Paula turned back to get another look at Wynne, who was now standing in thigh-deep water near the children. Her one-piece black bathing suit showed off her figure very well. What was underneath that suit was lovely also, Paula remembered.

"Glad you could make it," Wynne called, though she didn't seem particularly enthusiastic.

"I'd better go help her with the kids," Adrienne said.

Paula took the chair Janelle offered, a perfect position from which to watch the activity in the pool. She was a little surprised that Wynne hadn't come over as soon as she got there.

"I hear you wield a mean water hose," Janelle said.

Paula grinned. "It pays to stay on my good side."

"Sounds like it." Janelle looked over her shoulder at the group in the pool. "I wish I had their energy."

"I was just telling Adrienne the same thing. We were at Sea World all day and those two still look like they've just been shot out of a cannon."

"I'd love to take Sophie to Sea World. We're thinking about moving down here. Wynne and Mom both love it . . ."

Despite her best efforts to pay attention, Paula couldn't take her eyes off Wynne. She and Adrienne were sharing a laugh, probably something about the kids. Wynne had a captivating smile.

" . . . have any idea about that?"

175

Janelle was giving her a questioning look. "Excuse me? I was . . . I was watching Jordan and Sophie. They seem to like each other."

Janelle turned around again. "Yes, they do. I was asking if you knew anything about the local schools. Sophie has a couple more years before she goes to kindergarten, but if I buy a place here, I want to be in a good school district."

"I don't think you can go wrong with the schools around here, if you want to buy in this area of town."

They talked casually for another half hour before Saul Schumacher announced that the hotdogs and hamburgers were ready. Wynne and Adrienne coaxed the children out of the pool and helped them dry off.

"Josh, Jordan, come tell me what you want to eat," Adrienne said.

"You too, Sophie," Janelle added.

Wynne slumped into a chair at one of the covered tables and began to massage her knee. "I wish my mother would fix my plate."

"My poor, helpless child. What can I get you?"

"Anything. I'm so weak with hunger I can't decide," Wynne answered dramatically.

"Let me do it, Kitty," Paula offered. "Serve yourself."

Wynne groaned. "Something tells me I'm in trouble now."

Paula prepared two identical plates, stopping at the end of the table. "Do you want your ice tea on your hotdog or in a glass by itself?" The children squealed with laughter as she held the pitcher precariously over the bun.

"By itself, please."

"Very well." She brought the plates over and took the vacant seat next to Wynne, noting with disappointment that she had covered up with an oversized T-shirt.

"I hear you all had fun today at Sea World."

"We did. It's not so crowded now that the kids are back in school."

"I haven't gotten out to see much."

"You've been here a year. What's keeping you?"

176

Wynne looked her square in the eye. "Things aren't much fun solo."

Paula knew she was being baited. With a teasing grin, she answered, "Now that Sophie's here, you won't have that problem, will you?"

"I was hoping I might engage a local to provide a tour."

"That shouldn't be difficult. You're the travel agent."

"So if I come up with the right package, can I count on your tour services?"

"You'll have to find something really special. I've been to every single attraction in Orlando more times than I can count."

Wynne tilted her head and in a small voice said, "I suppose an overnight trip is out of the question."

Paula nearly spewed her drink.

"You never really know these things unless you ask," Wynne said, apparently enjoying her turn to tease. "Want another hotdog?"

Paula watched in disbelief as Wynne walked back toward the grill. Either Wynne hadn't heard a word she had said at the Labor Day picnic, or she was yanking Paula's chain. It was an interesting game, she decided, but one that she would win. Stringing Wynne along with an occasional flirt to let her know what she was missing would be sweet vengeance.

An hour later, all three children were exhausted to the point of crankiness. Paula and Adrienne thanked their hosts and started home with Josh and Jordan.

"You're lucky to have such nice neighbors," Adrienne said. "I really enjoyed talking to Wynne."

"Yeah, she makes a good first impression," Paula said, her tone mildly sarcastic but not malicious.

"What, you mean you don't like her?"

"Yeah, I like her," she admitted with a shrug. "We had a thing before I went out to Denver, but it didn't work out. It's always a little uncomfortable after something like that, but we should get through it."

"She's very pretty."

"She's definitely that."

"Any chance you two will see each other again?"

A few days ago, Paula would have answered no in an instant. But that was before she had accepted Wynne's invitation to a cookout and then surprised herself by looking forward to it all day. "I don't think either of us wants to go there again, Adrienne."

"Funny . . . I would have guessed just the opposite."

Wynne pulled into her driveway and pressed the button on her sun visor to activate the automatic garage door opener. "See, it's not very far from Mom's. I can be over there in five minutes if she needs anything."

"Nice neighborhood," Janelle said.

"I guess. I don't get out in it very much. I know more people over at the condo than I do around here."

"So that's the woman that's got your tongue hanging out," Janelle said.

Wynne slapped her steering wheel as she turned off the engine. "Man, there's no such thing as a secret when it comes to the Connelly women, is there?"

"Hey, don't get on your high horse. You're just as guilty of it as we are. We're so thick in each other's business you can't tell where one ends and the other one starts."

With a crinkling of her nose, Wynne let her sister know her assessment was on the mark. "In case you were wondering, this is the garage."

Janelle got out and closed her door. "So no comment on Paula, huh?"

"I'm sure Mom gave you all the important details."

"You didn't even act like you were glad to see her. I thought you'd never get out of the pool."

"That's because I thought Adrienne was her date." Wynne opened the kitchen door and turned on the lights. "My gourmet kitchen."

"This is where you microwave all those box dinners, right?"

"You know me so well."

"I finally had to learn how to cook when Sophie got too big to eat out of a jar every day." They passed the dining room and Wynne turned on the chandelier. "Uh, excuse me, but don't you have any furniture?"

Wynne shrugged. "There's a couch in the living room." She led the way and flipped a switch, which turned on a small lamp that sat on the floor.

"Just a couch?"

"It's Mom's fault. When she came down here with me last year, she said I ought to hold off buying things until it started to feel like home."

"And it doesn't feel like home yet?"

"It's just a house."

"Do you at least have a bed?"

"I have two."

Wynne led her down the hallway turning on lights as she passed each room. The first was furnished with the bedroom suite her mother had picked out when she came to Orlando to help after the surgery. "This is the guest room and it has its own bath. And here's my office." An L-shaped desk with a leather executive chair sat in the center of the room.

"Knowing you, this is your favorite room."

"I appreciate my bedroom more than I used to," Wynne said.

"You mean now that Heather's not in it?"

"I mean because I'm traveling so much, but now that you mention it . . ."

"You hear anything from her?"

"Not much." Not any. Another flip of a light switch revealed a stationary bike, a compact home gym, and a small television. "My exercise room."

"How's the leg, by the way?"

"Mostly okay. It always gets sore when I'm standing for a long time." Wynne turned on the lights in the enormous master bedroom. Her king-sized brass bed sat diagonally in the opposite corner. Antique tables and chests and a love seat completed the ensemble.

179

"Wow, my last apartment would have fit in here."

Wynne led her into the huge bathroom, which had a marble shower stall and a whirlpool tub underneath a skylight. "This tub is the reason I bought the house, and also why I don't care if I ever get any furniture or not."

"Speaking of my last apartment, I need to talk to you about something."

They sat down on the love seat.

"What is it?"

"Mom offered to cash in a couple of CDs for me so I can get my own place."

"She wants you here in Orlando."

"I think we need to be with you guys too. But Mom wanted to be sure it was okay with you."

"Of course it's okay with me. Why wouldn't it be?"

"The money."

"What about the money?"

"You know how she is, always trying to treat both of us equally. You should take half of it."

"I don't need it, Janelle. I have a great job and no time to spend what they pay me."

"Then I don't think I should take it."

"Yes, you should take it." Wynne shifted on the loveseat and took her sister by the shoulders. "Look, I knew Heather was coming between us and I didn't try hard enough to stop it. I had no idea we were all so far apart until she was gone and I got to see how things should have been. If you won't take it from Mom, take my half from me. I want you and Sophie close enough that I don't ever lose you again."

"Aw, that's so corny."

"I know. I've turned into a hideous mushball."

"You ought to try that out on Paula."

"It's going to take more than that, I'm afraid."

Chapter 18

"I can't believe you scored these tickets," Paula exclaimed. "All the home games are sold out."

"You said I had to come up with something special," Wynne answered smugly. Great connections and a fat checkbook sure came in handy, she thought to herself. Ever since the Buccaneers won the Super Bowl, they were the hottest ticket in Florida. But some of Eldon-Markoff's agencies held tickets back that were part of travel packages, and the seats often became available at the last minute. Wynne knew this from having gone to a game last year with Cheryl and her husband.

"You definitely win the prize. This is about as special as it gets."

That settled that, as far as Wynne was concerned. She would put in for all the home games from now on if it meant Paula would come with her.

Climbing the stairs to their upper level seats in Raymond James Stadium, the women quickly became caught up in the game day excitement. Paula snagged a passing vendor and bought them each a hot dog and a cold draft beer in a souvenir cup.

Wynne was really happy with the way the day was going. It had taken her a while to get up the nerve to call, afraid that Paula would refuse or say that football tickets weren't "special" enough. This was their first time alone together since they reconnected. Things had started out awkwardly in the car, with both women struggling a little with what to talk about. But eventually, they settled down on the drive over to Tampa and lapsed into a casual discussion of the hotel business, the travel business, and the Buccaneers' chances of returning to the Super Bowl.

"Does it feel weird to be cheering against the Ravens?"

"A little," Wynne admitted, though she had transferred her loyalties from the Baltimore team when she started following the Buccaneers. "I still pull for them when they're playing someone else, but the Bucs are my team now."

"I couldn't bring myself to pull for the Broncos in Denver. I think I knew I wasn't going to be there very long, so I didn't get too comfortable. Does that sound silly?"

"Not at all. I probably would have done the same thing if I hadn't been so sure I was going to stay. But when I took the job in Orlando, I knew it was going to be for the long haul, so I wanted to be a part of it."

"You really feel at home here?"

"Yeah. I don't think home is a place as much as it's a state of mind. All the people I care about are here. And I like my job. That makes it home."

With the game in hand by the start of the fourth quarter, they slipped out of the stadium early to beat the traffic. Paula offered to buy dinner and directed Wynne to Flanagan's, the sports bar in downtown Orlando where her friend Val worked. Elbowing their way through the crowded bar, the women claimed a tall round table and two bar stools.

"I'll go grab a couple of menus," Paula offered. When she got back, Wynne was talking to a handsome, forty-ish man who had

182

set his beer on their table. "Here you go," she interrupted unceremoniously, tossing the menu across the small table.

"Thanks. What's good here?"

Paula was about to answer when the man jumped in. "I like the burrito. Say, do you mind if we pull up a couple of extra stools? There seem to be lots of stools, but not many tables."

"Actually, if you'd like to have this table, we can move on over to the bar," Paula offered flatly.

Wynne turned away to shield the smile that crept onto her face. She was usually more subtle when it came to rebuffing men's advances, but Paula's method was much quicker and a lot more fun to watch.

"Well . . . no," he stammered awkwardly. "You don't have to move. I think there's plenty of room here for all of us."

"I'm sure you're right, but my friend and I haven't seen each other in a long time, and we'd sort of like to talk—to each other." Paula stared at him sternly.

The man looked at Wynne, apparently hoping she would overrule and invite him to stay. Instead, she smiled at Paula and reached for her purse. "Two seats just opened up. If you hurry, we can grab them."

"So that's her, the woman from Baltimore that broke your heart . . . left you shattered in a million pieces . . . stomped on you and left you for dead." Val sputtered between leg lifts.

"That's her, the one and only." Paula stood before the mirror working her triceps with the dumbbells.

"She seemed really nice."

"She is really nice."

"You never mentioned that she looked like a model."

"I told you she was beautiful."

"Yeah, but I thought those were just 'I'm in love' words. Everybody says that when they're in love. But she really is."

"Yep, she certainly is."

"So what were you guys arguing about?"

Paula chuckled. "The bill."

"There had to be more to it than that. You were really bent out of shape."

Paula sighed, setting the dumbbells back in the rack. "I was going to pick up the check because she got the tickets to the game. But she tried to pay it instead. She said she had invited me out so she should pay."

"Sounds fair. Can't you just pay next time?"

"That wasn't the point. The point is that she and I are just friends. It wasn't supposed to be a date and she knew that, so I didn't want her picking up the tab saying it was because she had asked me out. You and I wouldn't have had any argument at all. We'd have split everything down the middle because that's what friends do."

"Sounds to me like you're making a pretty big deal out of nothing. So what if she wanted to pay? So what if it was a date? You did spend the whole day together, and you're both attracted to each other."

"We're not attracted to each other. We were, but that's in the past." Paula couldn't honestly deny that the attraction was still there, but saying it was in the past helped to harden her resolve. "You and I go places together and we don't call it a date. I'm not interested in playing with that fire anymore, thank you."

"Could've fooled me," Val muttered.

"What?"

"If you're not interested, why do you go out with her at all?"

"Because she's nice. Because I like her. Because she's fun."

"So what's the problem with calling it a date? It's obvious that you two have chemistry together."

"Val, I can't go through that again. I don't trust her after what she did."

"Are you sure you're not just punishing her?"

"What difference does it make? Either way, I'm not going to give her the chance to do it again."

"I think it makes a big difference. If she's the kind of person who always treats people badly, that's one thing. But if she's somebody you really like who just made a mistake, maybe you ought to think about it before you throw it away."

Paula shrugged. "How can you separate the two? Only a certain kind of person makes a mistake like that, and if she'll do it once, who's to say she won't do it again? What if we got together and then she went off on one of her business trips and met somebody else?"

"People aren't perfect, Paula. But maybe there's more to it than what it looks like. From what you told me, she's not a bad person."

Paula reached again for the dumbbells to complete her final set. "It's just . . . I know now that Wynne has the power to hurt me a lot if I let her too close."

"Look, I don't blame you for being wary after what happened. But any time you start to care for somebody, you give them the power to hurt you. It's a risk you have to weigh. And in this case, I think you should ask yourself if this woman's worth another chance."

Paula returned the dumbbells to the rack and turned for the door. "Are you ready to run?" As far as she was concerned, the discussion was now closed.

Wynne flipped on the kitchen lights with her elbow as she stumbled into the dark house from the garage. With a sharp tug, she rolled her suitcase over the threshold, the wheels clacking across the tile floor. She would have two days in her office before her next trip, this one to San Francisco on Sunday afternoon.

But it was Paula's weekend to work, so she might as well go into the office for a few hours.

The last two days in Miami had been busy, but fruitful, as she worked with Eldon-Markoff's cruise partner to draft a winter campaign. She was working these days with a lot of autonomy, except on the San Francisco project. The potential acquisition involved three of the corporate officers and a director from human resources.

Despite her exhausted state, Wynne enjoyed her job more every day. It was turning out to be everything she had hoped for—challenging, fun, and interesting. She was lucky also to find herself working with a team of people she really liked. Indeed, she could see herself at Eldon-Markoff for many years.

While she was grateful for Cheryl's advice not to let the job become her life, she was frustrated by not being able to fill her time away from work with what she wanted. And what she wanted was more time with Paula. The small window Paula had opened gave her a glimmer of hope they might someday restore their friendship to one of mutual trust. But there was definitely a barrier to more. She could feel it, especially after that silly argument over the bill at Flanagan's.

Kicking off her shoes, she grabbed the portable phone and collected her mail from the floor where it had fallen through the slot. The first two messages were hang-ups, but the third made her heart race.

Hi, Wynne. I had a great time at the football game and now it's my turn to offer something special. I was wondering if you'd be interested in going to a shuttle launch at the press site next week. I know you probably have to work, but it's scheduled for Friday at twelve-thirty. If you're interested, I need you to call me with your full name, your social security number, and your date of birth so I can get your credentials ahead of time. Of course, this could just be a hoax and I need that information to clean out your bank account. So I guess the question is, do you trust me?

"Are you kidding? I'd go with you to the moon," Wynne said aloud. She wanted to call right away but common sense stopped her. It wasn't quite eleven, but Paula's morning shift started at seven, so she was probably already asleep.

A celebration was definitely in order, though, as she took a wine glass and poured from a corked bottle of cabernet sauvignon. This was the first invitation from Paula. It would have been special had it been for dinner at a fast food restaurant. But Wynne knew how important shuttle launches were to Paula, and that made this invitation exceptional.

Paula pulled up to the gate and passed the guard two sets of press credentials and identification. The soldier recognized her as Ray McKenzie's daughter and knew she wasn't officially employed by a media agency. Still, the head of public information had cleared her and the woman beside her, and he wasn't going to question McKenzie's authority.

As the long flat road continued forward past a line of trees, a giant structure appeared in the distance.

"What's that?"

"That's the Vehicle Assembly Building."

"Where they assemble vehicles?"

Paula laughed. "Good guess. That's where they attach the rockets and get the shuttle ready to mount on the launch pad. That building's so big it has its own weather inside."

Wynne looked at her with skepticism.

"Well, not really. But the condensation gathers at the top and when it gets heavy enough, it falls just like rain."

Wynne was still unconvinced, not so much because the story lacked credence, but because she wouldn't put it past Paula to pull her leg. "How do they get the shuttle from there to the launch pad?"

"It goes on a giant flatbed with treads like a tank. The road out to the pad isn't paved, because it would just collapse under all that weight. Instead, the road is made out of crushed seashells because they give a little. But every time they move one of the shuttles out there they have to rebuild the road for next time. What really sucks is if the window closes and they have to bring it back in and take it apart."

"That sounds like a lot of work."

"Believe me, they hate it." Paula pulled into the grassy parking area and cruised though the rows until she found a space to accommodate her small convertible. Among the two hundred or so autos were a couple of dozen press trucks, easily identified by the satellite dishes affixed to their tops.

A grandstand looked across an open area to the launch pad. Wynne noticed right away the familiar view of the large digital clock and the flagpole in the foreground. Just past those landmarks were water and marsh, wetlands that were home to thousands of birds, fish, and reptiles. Seven miles away was the shuttle Endeavor.

"My dad works in here," Paula said, leading the way to a dome-shaped building that hosted rows of press terminals, walls of charts, racks of brochures, and speakers that carried every official word of the launch process. Ray McKenzie sat behind a desk in a glassed-in cubicle, his raised finger indicating to Paula that his interview was nearly complete. "We should wait here for him."

The physical resemblance between Paula and her father was striking. Their coloring was identical, and hers was the softer, feminine version of his handsome face. She even had his smile, Wynne noted. Perfect teeth and small dimple on one side.

"I'm glad you could come today. Did either of you have any trouble getting off work?"

"I didn't," Paula answered. "I traded tomorrow, though."

"I didn't either. I haven't had a day off in months, so I dared anyone to try to stop me," Wynne explained. "Mr. McKenzie, thank you for getting me in today. This is something I won't forget."

"Call me Ray, please. Paula told me you understood what things here at NASA were really about, so I was glad to do it."

"What's the status, Dad?"

"It looks like all systems go and we're less than an hour away. The weather looks great. I'd say we're going to launch."

Paula turned to Wynne. "It's a drag on everyone to come out here and get all pumped up and not go."

"And it happens more times than I'd like to say," Ray added.

188

"It must be very hard on the crew."

"Yeah, but they're pros. Everybody in the program knows how to adapt."

Paula took Wynne's elbow and steered her toward the side door. "I think we'll go out to the grandstand, Dad. We'll come back in after she goes up, okay?"

"Okay, have fun."

Wynne's excitement about seeing the launch was magnified by being with Paula. This was a once in a lifetime event for someone like her—someone not connected to the space program—so she was thrilled to get such a special invitation. But even more than that, she felt honored that Paula was letting her close enough to be part of something that meant so much to her on a personal level. It gave her a glimmer of hope that they might be able to one day put their unfortunate past behind them and be not just friends, but more.

Once on the grandstand, Paula produced a stack of press releases and read aloud interesting tidbits about the mission and crew. Wynne listened and watched as the grandstand came to life with journalists and VIPs. A voice over the loudspeaker announced T minus five minutes.

"Let's go to the edge of the water to watch it go up." Paula pointed ahead, where contractors were already lining up on the bank.

A voice on the loudspeaker ticked off the final thirty seconds. Wynne gazed intently at the rocket in the distance looking for movement. The first sign of the launch was a large mountain of white smoke billowing at the base of the launch pad. The mountain grew rapidly wider, but only slightly higher. The shuttle's initial lift was barely perceptible.

As the rumble reached their outpost, hundreds of birds took to the air from the glades in front of them. The water rippled fiercely as the whole earth shook.

"It's cleared the launch pad," Paula shouted over the deafening roar. "Now it's over to Houston."

"It's awesome!"

189

The shuttle appeared to hang in the sky momentarily before its climb accelerated. Wynne was shaking with excitement as the shuttle turned on its back and arced to trace a path directly above their heads. In less than three minutes, it was beyond the naked eye.

"I've never seen anything so amazing in my whole life!"

"I know. It gets me every single time."

"What did you say about Houston?"

"Kennedy only handles the launch. Once it clears the launch pad, it goes over to Mission Control."

"So what do these guys do then?"

"Exhale."

Wynne looked back at the grandstand to see journalists and photographers collecting their gear, ready to file their launch stories. "It's over in a hurry, isn't it?"

"Yeah, but they're already starting to get ready for the next one." They walked back into the dome where Paula hugged her dad.

"Great job, Ray," Wynne said, offering her hand in congratulations. She was surprised when he took it in both his hands and gave her what felt like a fatherly squeeze.

"Thanks, Wynne. I'm really glad you could make it."

They said their goodbyes and headed out to the car.

"Paula, I can't thank you enough for this. I don't think I've ever witnessed anything more exciting. I really appreciate you and your dad inviting me."

"I knew you'd like it. This is why I called you that night."

"What night?"

"That night in Baltimore, when Heather answered the phone. I was calling to see if you could come to a launch that weekend. I had to know the next day so I could put in for your credentials."

Wynne's stomach churned as she recalled that night. In only an instant, her feeling of exhilaration was washed away by the memory of one of the worst nights of her life. No longer confident in what to say, she pulled a cap low over her forehead as they started out, looking off to right at the scenery on her own side of the car.

"I guess I shouldn't have brought that up, huh?" Paula asked sheepishly.

"I deserved it, I suppose."

"No, you didn't. We were having a good time together. I should have just let it go."

"It's not your fault. Friends should be able to talk about anything. I think . . ." She shook her head and looked away again. "Forget it."

"You think what?"

"I think we could be great friends, but you're going to have to forgive me for that to happen."

The security gate appeared up ahead and Paula waited until they had passed through to respond.

"I want to forgive you, because I don't want either of us to feel bad about our past anymore," she confessed. "But I haven't really been honest with you about my feelings."

Wynne tipped her cap up from her eyes and shifted in her seat to face Paula.

"What happened between us wasn't just me losing control. I thought you and I had something that could have been special. Instead, I ended up feeling cheap and used, and I was angry for a long time, but not just at you. I was angry at myself for being such a fool in the first place, and I was angry at every woman I met at the hotel for a whole year afterward."

Wynne bit the inside of her lip. This was hard to hear. She had known about the anger, and didn't blame Paula one bit. But she hadn't known that Paula had real feelings for her. Wynne never thought she deserved to have someone care about her that way. And it was especially difficult to realize what her duplicity had cost her.

"I'm so sorry, Paula. I'd give anything to be able to go back and do it right."

"I know. I believe you when you say that. But I've been carrying

191

this around for a while and it's going to take a little longer to get past all of it."

"I'll give you all the time you need if it means we can really be friends again."

Paula gave her a half smile and pushed her bangs from her eyes. "I'm going to try harder, okay? I had fun with you today. I even had fun washing cars a couple of weeks ago, but I didn't want to give you the satisfaction of saying so."

Wynne blew out a breath of relief as she shook her head. "I'm not surprised you had fun, since I was the one who went home soaking wet."

"I'm not above a little vengeance."

"I'll remember that."

"No need. I'll remind you."

"I'm sure you will." At that point, Wynne relaxed. She wanted to reach over and cover Paula's hand as it rested on the gearshift, but the potential for rejection was higher than she was willing to risk.

Chapter 19

Wynne pulled her Volvo into the circle of the Weller Regent and rolled down her window.

"Checking in, ma'am?" the valet asked.

Before she could answer, her passenger arrived.

"Never mind, Joey. That's my ride," Paula said as she let herself into the front seat. "I appreciate this, Wynne."

"No problem at all. Where are we headed?" Paula had called earlier in the day to ask for a ride to pick up her car from the shop. Wynne never once considered saying no, instead asking Denise to reschedule two meetings so she could leave early.

"The Mazda dealer on Semoran. They called about an hour ago and said it was ready." She clipped her seatbelt in place. "How did you manage to get off so early?"

"I worked all weekend. I gave myself the afternoon off."

"Good deal. I'm starting to learn that I don't get much back for the overtime I put in, at least not in the form of extra pay or time off."

"No one can work like that for long, you know. You'll burn out. My boss runs me out of the office if I stay too late."

"I think I'm going to start following my boss out the door at five o'clock. How do you like working at Eldon-Markoff?"

"I absolutely love it. I always feel challenged but never over my head. That's a good balance. And the people I work with are just great."

"I think I'd say the same about my job too—except the over-my-head part." She nodded toward the intersection ahead. "If you turn left up here, I'll show you a shortcut."

Wynne put on her signal and moved into the turn lane. "I have a hard time picturing you over your head at the Weller Regent. You always seemed to be right on top of everything."

"Yeah, but working in Operations is different. It's not like managing emergencies and overflow. The executive office is where you learn everything you need to know about directing a hotel."

"Is that still what you want, your own hotel?"

"One of these days, maybe."

"You're not sure anymore?"

Paula shrugged. "The job's pretty demanding. And when you're the boss, there's no one to run you out when you stay too late."

"Who says that has to be someone at work?"

This time, Paula didn't answer right away. When she finally did, she sounded almost frustrated, as if she had given the issue a lot of thought without finding a resolution. "How can you have both a good job and somebody worth coming home to? If you're pouring yourself into one, the other one's going to get the shaft."

"That doesn't have to be true. People just have to find the right balance."

Paula pointed to the driveway ahead. "There's my car. I appreciate the ride."

"You want to grab dinner?" Wynne blurted out her invitation, trying her best to sound casual. Despite their growing comfort as friends, she was still nervous about being shot down.

"All right. What do you have in mind?"

"How about Buck's?" The barbecue restaurant had become one of Wynne's favorites.

"Okay, but not like this." Paula gestured to her suit. "I want to change first. Can you pick me up at home in an hour?"

As she pulled off the lot, Wynne smiled to herself. Little by little, she was working her way back into Paula's life. On their trip home from the Cape, they had crossed the hurdle into what seemed a solid friendship, but Wynne knew it wasn't going to be enough to have Paula as only a friend. With every minute they spent together, her heart went further down that forbidden path.

It was ironic that Wynne had suggested Buck's, Paula thought. She had always thought of the barbecue place as the scene of Wynne's first crime, since it was at their first dinner Wynne should have told her about Heather. "I'm impressed that you remembered how to find this place."

"I swing by here once in a while for carry-out. Ribs this good are hard to find."

"I know. I thought the ribs in Denver might be better, but nothing comes close to Buck's." Besides the food, Paula liked the casual atmosphere.

"Right this way, ladies." They followed the hostess through the noisy dining room to a booth in the corner.

Paula thought about Wynne coming into Buck's alone for carry-out. "Your mom said you hadn't made a lot of friends here. Why is that?"

Wynne shrugged. "At first I was working all the time. When Mom came down I started spending most of my free time with her. And I have to travel at least once a week, so I don't always feel like going out."

"Have you met anybody? Any friends?"

"Not really. I've been to a few parties with people at work. But they're mostly couples. The only single women at work are some of the clerical staff."

195

Paula nodded in understanding, but Wynne seemed to sense she had said something wrong.

"That probably sounded snobbish, but I didn't mean it that way."

"I know what you mean. You have to maintain your distance if you're going to be an effective supervisor. I'm the same way at the hotel."

"That's it. So there really isn't anyone from work to do things with. I went to a block party last spring and met a few of my neighbors. Most are couples with children."

Paula knew as well as anyone how difficult it was to meet friends, especially other lesbians. Her life was centered on the Weller Regent just as Wynne's revolved around the travel company. "I joined a women's volleyball league at the rec so I could get out and meet people."

"I bet that's fun."

"It probably would be if I hadn't missed so many games because of work."

"That defeats the whole purpose, doesn't it?"

"Yeah, I guess I should have waited for the spring league. I was working nights when I first got back because the new person was having a hard time."

"So how is the volleyball league? Have you made friends?"

"Sort of. They're nice but most of them are a lot younger than me. They usually go out clubbing afterward and I have to go home to bed."

"We've become our parents."

"I think my parents had more fun."

"Probably."

The waitress stopped by to take their order and bring drinks. When they were alone again, Paula decided it was time to broach a subject they had both been avoiding. As they rekindled their friendship, they would have to lay the past to rest. "You said you'd tell me about Heather one of these days."

Wynne looked at her and frowned. "Did I say that? That doesn't sound like something I'd say."

"Yep, you said you'd tell me the whole sordid story if we got to be friends, and I think it's safe to say we're friends again." Paula was pleased to see the smile that lit up her companion's face.

"I'm glad you feel that way. So do I."

"So tell me about Heather."

Wynne sighed and folded her hands on the table. "Heather is a very complicated story."

"I promise I won't judge you, Wynne. I just want to know about her."

"Okay." Wynne flattened her palms and leaned back. "I met her at a party and we went out a couple of times. I didn't think it would go anywhere so I—"

"Why not?"

"We just didn't have a lot in common. Heather was pretty . . . and also very nice, but I found her hard to talk to. She was eight years younger than I and didn't have many opinions, other than what shoes looked best with what jacket, that kind of thing."

Paula had little interest in fashion. She probably couldn't have spent ten minutes with Heather. "I have to admit, I have a hard time picturing you with someone like that."

"So did I. But then I had my accident and she was there when I woke up in the hospital. She came every single day for ten weeks to keep me company and help me with the physical therapy. She once told me she felt responsible because I had just dropped her off after what I thought would have been our last date."

The waitress interrupted with their dinner.

"Wouldn't you rather eat ribs than hear more about Heather?"

"I can do both," Paula answered, digging into her heaping plate. "Besides, you haven't told me how you ended up being a couple."

Wynne blew out a breath. "We became a couple because I felt guilty. She offered to move into my house when they let me out of the hospital. I should have said no, but I couldn't do anything for myself, so I let her. She was kind and generous, and I couldn't believe she gave so much of herself. Then she told me I was her whole life and all she wanted was for me to love her like she loved me."

"And you didn't want to hurt her feelings."

"I felt like I owed her so much. I thought I should at least try to be who she wanted." Her eyes became clouded with tears as she told the story.

"You can't make yourself love someone when it's not there."

"No one knows that better than I do. I loved her, but not like you want to love someone special. I knew it was a mistake as soon as we went down that path. I was miserable but I didn't have the guts to talk to her and tell her how I felt. So I just kept going through the motions, day after day, hoping something would click. But then I started spending more time at work. And I'd go to bed as soon as I got home . . . whatever I could do to avoid being with her."

Paula could see the conversation was upsetting to Wynne, but she had needed to hear this to understand why Wynne had kept Heather a secret. The details didn't justify her deception, but they certainly made her more sympathetic. Wynne's efforts to do right by Heather were good-hearted, if misguided.

"Why didn't you tell me about her?"

"I just . . ." Wynne pushed her plate away and folded her arms. She looked as if she might bolt any second under this pressure. "I just didn't, Paula. I have no excuse. I was unfaithful to Heather. And I deliberately misled you. I was selfish and wrong about everything."

"Whoa!" Paula stretched across the table to take Wynne's hand. "Don't pull away. I said I wasn't going to judge. It's just that . . ."

"What?"

Paula sighed. "The more I get to know you, the harder it is to imagine you would do something like that."

Wynne shook her head. "I've never done it before. It's like I was somebody else when I came down here. But when it hurts to live with something you've done, you learn you don't want to be that way."

"And now?"

"Now I've . . ." Paula was surprised to hear Wynne chuckle in

198

the midst of their otherwise gripping conversation. "I've learned so many lessons I ought to have a PhD."

"So you're done with doing stupid stuff, Dr. Connelly?"

"Mostly." Her appetite obviously renewed, Wynne dug in with both hands to tear apart her plate of pork ribs. In a matter of seconds, she had barbecue sauce all over her hands and face. "I'm done with secrets, but I reserve the right to make much smaller mistakes."

Paula took her napkin and wiped a smudge of the red sauce from Wynne's chin. "I can live with that. I don't expect perfection from my friends, even though it's the example I set."

"And you're so humble too."

"Shhh . . . I don't want everyone to know." Paula leaned back and grinned with satisfaction. It was nice to finally have everything out in the open with Wynne. Now that she understood how things had been back in Baltimore, the whole situation seemed a lot less awful than it had a year ago.

Paula spotted a familiar group of women on Court 3 and hurried over, dodging several volleyballs that sailed through the air as teams warmed up. Their captain, Dee Hobart, was huddling the team with some last-minute instructions.

"Hi, guys. Sorry I missed the last couple of weeks."

"We missed you too," Dee said as six of the women took the court. "At least I did."

Paula recognized a flirt when she heard it and she acknowledged it with a friendly smile. Dee was a nice woman, attractive . . . not pretty, really, but striking. She was tall and slender and had chiseled looks that seemed to match her personality. Paula had no doubt Dee ran the show, no matter what the arena.

"I've been working double shifts for a while," she explained as they stood alone on the sidelines. "But I think I can make the last three games."

"Are things that busy at the Weller Regent?"

"I've been training someone on second shift. But I kicked her out of the nest last week and she's doing just fine."

"I'm not surprised. If I had you training me, I'm sure I'd knock myself out to impress you."

Paula could feel it coming, the inevitable hit.

"Would I be off base if I were to invite you to dinner on Friday night?"

There wasn't any part of Paula that wanted to go out on a date with Dee Hobart. It wasn't that she was put off by the idea. She just didn't feel any sort of attraction. Yet, her whole purpose for joining the league had been to meet people and make friends. You couldn't build a social network by turning down your first dinner invitation.

"Sure, I'd like that."

Dee flashed a dazzling smile. "Fantastic. How does eight o'clock sound?"

"Good." Suddenly a nervous wreck, Paula turned her focus to the action on the court, where her team had just earned the serve. "Do I get to rotate in?"

"Go get 'em."

Paula slapped the departing player's hand as she entered the game. With a quick glance toward a smiling Dee, her stomach dropped. Why on earth had she said yes?

Chapter 20

"Excuse me, Wynne?"

Claudia Sanchez, Markoff's administrative assistant, stood in her doorway.

"Yes?"

"Mr. Markoff wants a meeting right now with all the officers and assistant VPs. We're linking up Cheryl and Wendell by speaker phone."

"I'll be right there." Wynne glanced at her watch. Friday afternoon meetings were unusual, but this was probably about the San Francisco project. Moments later, she joined the caravan of busy executives as they filed into the conference room. All had dropped what they were doing to answer the urgent summons of their CEO.

Ken Markoff opened the meeting with two announcements: Eldon-Markoff would acquire San Francisco-based Western Travel, a smaller company with a solid network of Asian contacts.

Cheryl and Wynne would leave first thing on Tuesday to meet with department heads at Western's headquarters on the west coast to begin the transition.

Markoff's second announcement was more surprising. Effective immediately, Cheryl Williams was leaving her post as vice president for sales and marketing to assume the title of president of Eldon-Markoff, the number two position in the company.

One by one, the executives passed on their congratulations to the disembodied person on the speakerphone.

"I really appreciate all of your votes of confidence. I'll stop by your offices and thank you in person when I get back on Monday. But right now, I need to cut this short so I can get to the airport and get home."

Markoff adjourned the meeting, but stopped Wynne as she walking out. "May I see you in my office for a few minutes?"

"Of course." She was already thinking about how this move would impact her workload. Until they got a new VP in place, she would probably have to absorb more of the sales administration. She was already handling virtually all of the marketing.

Once inside the plush corner office, Markoff closed the door and offered her a chair. Buzzing Claudia, he asked her to put the call through.

"Wynne, this is Cheryl again. I've only got a minute."

Wynne was startled to hear her boss's voice. Evidently, they had worked out the quick adjournment and planned this additional call in advance.

"I'm here. Congratulations again."

"Thanks, and congratulations yourself. If you say yes, you're going to be the new vice president for sales and marketing."

Surprise didn't come close to describing what Wynne was feeling. She was flabbergasted. It had never occurred to her that she would be promoted so soon after coming on board. But she had no doubts she could do the job. "Yes!"

"That's wonderful." Markoff stood to extend a hug. Cheryl was right when she said the company was a lot like a family.

"Thank you. Thank you both. I promise not to disappoint either of you."

"We already knew that. That's why we asked. Now I really have to go, so I'll see you all on Monday morning."

"Safe travels, Cheryl."

Wynne turned to her CEO to reiterate her thanks. "Those are some tough shoes to fill, but I promise to do my best."

"They are, Wynne, but we all believe you're the right person for the job."

She walked back to her office as if on a cloud. The first thing she wanted was to call Paula and share the great news. More than anyone, Paula would be able to appreciate how important this promotion was. Swinging into her swivel chair, Wynne dialed Paula's home number, which she knew by heart.

"Hello."

"Hi there. It's Wynne. I know it's short notice but I got some great news today. How about having dinner with me so I can tell someone before I explode?"

"Uh . . . I can't tonight. Maybe this weekend?"

"Aw, come on. We'll go wherever you say and I'll get you home early."

"I can't, Wynne," she said again. "I'm having dinner with a friend from my volleyball team. Can we do something tomorrow?"

Wynne tried to hide her disappointment. "Sure. I'll give you a call in the morning." Tomorrow would have to do, but it would be worth it, because Paula would be as thrilled for her as she was for herself.

Wynne pulled into the condominium complex, eager to give her mother and sister the news. The VP job came with an obscene salary, which meant Sophie was headed to the Ivy League if that's what she wanted.

As she passed Paula's condo, she noticed a black Jaguar parked in the drive. That volleyball friend sure did drive a fancy—

Then she saw them together, Paula and some . . . lipstick dyke. They were dressed smartly in heels and the stranger was holding the door for Paula to get in. This wasn't just dinner with a volleyball friend, as Paula had put it. This was a date.

She continued around the drive, not stopping at her mother's building. This was humiliating enough without having Paula see her. She parked as far away as she could to give them plenty of time to leave. Then she started her car again and left the complex, turning back toward her office, the one place where she was in total control. The last thing she wanted to do tonight was celebrate.

The building was mostly dark and she used her key card to enter. The cleaning crew would be upstairs for another hour or so but that wouldn't interfere with what she wanted to do.

When she reached her desk, she pulled out her notes on the Western Travel merger and began to draft a plan for incorporating their current marketing assets into those of Eldon-Markoff. There was sufficient equity in the Western brand to warrant a gradual co-branded campaign.

Determined not to think about Paula, Wynne completely lost track of time as she worked. The outer offices had been dark and empty for hours, and the lone lamp on her desk kept her from seeing the figure fill her doorway.

"This is ridiculous, Wynne!" Cheryl's voice was tinged with obvious irritation.

Startled, Wynne jumped back from her desk, knocking a pile of papers into the floor. "God, you scared me."

"It's after ten o'clock. Even the cleaning crew is long gone. What the hell are you doing here that can't wait until Monday?"

"I'm . . . I've started to work on the co-branding plan for Western."

"And why does that have to be done tonight?"

In all her time at Eldon-Markoff, Wynne had never seen Cheryl so angry, at least not at her. "I just started on it and things were falling into place. I didn't realize it was so late." Suddenly it occurred to her that she wasn't the only one in the office after ten. "So what are you doing here?"

Cheryl's lips tightened and she sighed. "I . . . admit that I came by to pick up some things to read over the weekend. I have to do that when I'm out of the office for a week or I'll never catch up."

Wynne nodded in agreement. She took things home almost every night.

"But I plan to do my reading from a deck chair at our beach house, not cooped up in this office."

Wynne studied Cheryl's annoyed expression as she dragged a chair around the desk and sat down, effectively pinning Wynne in her seat. "I've said this to you a dozen times. I think your work is wonderful. I also think you're capable of getting it done during regular hours. I really want you in this VP slot, but you have to live your life too. I want twenty or thirty years of solid, steady contributions from you, not five at breakneck speed before you give out."

Wynne began to put her things away to let her boss know she was getting the message.

"Look around. You don't see any of the other officers here after six-thirty or seven at night. Everybody goes home to their real lives, the ones that matter. Didn't you tell me you were seeing somebody?"

"That . . . didn't work out." Despite Wynne's attempts to conceal her emotions, she knew Cheryl read her disappointment.

"Is that why you're here? Are you trying to bury yourself in your work so you won't feel lonely?"

Stung by the truth, Wynne looked away.

"Here's what we're going to do. You go home tonight and pack a suitcase. Casual clothes. Jim and I will pick you up at nine o'clock in the morning. You're coming to the beach house with us."

"I can't do that. You and Jim deserve your time together."

Cheryl waved her hand in the air. "He's going fishing with his friends. He won't even notice either of us. And we can talk about whatever's on your mind or you can just forget about it for a couple of days. Your choice."

That made getting away sound like a good idea. "Are you sure?"

"Absolutely. And besides, I think it's high time you and I got to know each other better outside of Eldon-Markoff. I'd really like for us to be friends, Wynne."

"I'd like that too."

"So let's get out of here and get packed."

Wynne dropped the folder in her in-basket and pulled her purse from the bottom drawer. "Okay, Cheryl. I'm right behind you."

Paula feigned interest as Dee Hobart walked her through how she had set up her own law practice after leaving a harried job as associate in one of Orlando's largest firms. It seemed important to her that Paula understand what a bold decision it had been to give up the security of a good-paying job to strike out on her own.

Dee was stylishly dressed in black slacks with a tunic top. Her short red hair was perfectly coiffed, locked into place with a generous supply of product. Paula had planned on wearing a denim skirt and sweater, but when Dee had called to say they were going to Norman's, arguably Orlando's finest restaurant, she took out the cocktail dress she worn to Rusty's wedding.

"I just got tired of working my ass off seventy hours a week so the partners could make more money. Now I work about fifty and take home three times as much as I used to. I sold my condo and bought a ninety-year-old house in Winter Park. I'm having a ball with the renovations. I imported Spanish tiles for the pool . . ."

It was during Dee's explanation of her remodeling plans that Paula became aware of how hard she had to concentrate in order to pay attention. Her internal thoughts were louder than Dee's excruciatingly detailed descriptions of the hand-painted crown molding and variable-width, mahogany-pegged, hardwood floors.

Paula set her wine glass down, worried she might drink too much and say what she was thinking . . . that she wished she had broken her date with Dee to go with Wynne and hear her big news. Even if Wynne's story had been the discovery of ancient Lithuanian travel vouchers, it would have been preferable to Dee Hobart's litany of all that was important in her life.

"So tell me what you like about the hotel business."

Grateful for the reprieve, Paula began to talk about her job, how she had started at the Weller Regent right out of college and worked her way to her current position. Dee listened intently, interrupting from time to time ask questions or add comments.

" . . . and coming back to Orlando means stretching out my long-term plans. I probably won't have a shot at my own hotel for another seven or eight years, but at least I know I'll be ready by then."

"I don't think I could stand to work for someone else that long, especially if I was the one doing most of the work."

"Believe me, everybody in the hotel business works hard."

"Still, the serious money is in ownership, not working for somebody else."

"It's nice to be paid well, but it's not the most important part of the job."

Dee grinned. "Yeah, everybody says that, but nobody means it."

Paula bristled but bit her tongue. Nothing like having your date call you a liar. She glanced discreetly at her watch and wondered what was taking so long with dinner.

"You hungry?"

"Starving."

"I told you we should have ordered an appetizer." Dee motioned for the waiter.

"No, I don't want to spoil my dinner."

"We won't. We'll just eat a couple of bites. That way, the chef can take his time. At these prices, I expect everything to be perfect."

"I really don't want anything before dinner, but thank you." Paula hoped her smile didn't look as fake as it felt. In truth, she was ready to wolf down her meal as soon as it came so she could go home. Even before she learned of Dee's apparent obsession with money, she was already feeling as though they had little in common. And there was no chemistry at all. First impressions on the arousal scale were usually pretty reliable for her, and this one was barely registering.

207

This must have been how Wynne felt those first few times she went out with Heather, Paula thought. She almost shuddered at the prospect of accidentally ending up with a woman like Dee. The sooner one shook free from a situation like this one, the better for everyone.

What had always made her time with Wynne so special was their undeniable chemistry. Whether laughing and joking or talking seriously about the state of the world, or just relaxing together over dinner on paper plates, her awareness of everything about Wynne was overwhelming, even as friends. Paula shook her head and chuckled with dismay as the realization struck her—no matter what she told herself, she and Wynne Connelly would never be just friends. Why was she being so stubborn about it? Wynne made a mistake and apologized. That should be the end of it. No more nights like this looking for someone who was never going to measure up.

" . . . You don't think so?"

Paula was caught off-guard, her head miles and months away. "No, it isn't that." She had no idea what Dee had been talking about. "I was looking at something behind you. The waiter almost dropped a tray."

Dee looked over her shoulder. "Oh, good. Here's our dinner."

Paula breathed a sigh of relief. She was one step closer to the end of the evening, and the opportunity to do something that might change her life forever. For the first time since she had returned to Orlando, she admitted to herself that Wynne deserved a second chance.

Satellite Beach was a quiet oceanfront community of condominiums and houses built just beyond the dunes. The park-like beach was almost deserted, though it was a gorgeous December day.

"It's beautiful here," Wynne said. "Do you come every weekend?"

"As often as we can. We love it. Ken Markoff has a house here

208

too, about a mile down the beach. His makes ours look like a caretaker's cottage."

"It's so quiet." Wynne tugged off her sandals to walk along the water's edge. "I can see why you love it."

Cheryl buried her hands in the pockets of her hooded sweatshirt. "You know, you don't get your permanent Florida resident card until you start shivering with the rest of us when it gets down to sixty."

"People keep saying that, but I still remember what winter feels like in Baltimore." She felt invigorated by the cool waves that lapped at her feet.

"I thought you might want to talk about what had you so upset last night."

Wynne shrugged. "There isn't much to tell. It's a pretty classic case of unrequited love."

"So it's love, is it?"

The revelation came as a surprise, but it was as strong as any conviction Wynne had ever felt. "Yes, I love her, and I'm in love with her."

"Does she know how you feel?"

"She . . ." She waved her hand in the air. "It's complicated."

Cheryl walked along quietly, clearly indicating her willingness to listen.

"I met her last year when I was coming down to work on the strategic plan. We hit it off but . . ." Wynne ran both hands through her hair. "God, this is embarrassing."

"You don't have to say anymore if you don't want to. But I'll listen if you want me to."

They slowed their gait as Wynne watched the sand go dry around her feet with each step.

"I have a hard time talking about my mistakes."

"I think that's true for everyone. Is this a mistake you can fix?"

"I doubt it. She's seeing somebody else and I don't know if I should step aside gracefully or fight for her."

Cheryl took her shoulders and spun her around to face north. "If you head in this direction, you can go for over two miles. Why don't you start walking and empty your head? See if your heart has anything to say."

Wynne felt a soft push in her back and she began to walk, looking over her shoulder after twenty yards to find Cheryl already strolling in the other direction. Maybe it was a good idea to explore her feelings for a change instead of chasing them away with work. It couldn't make things any worse.

She had been foolish in allowing herself to believe Paula's romantic interest in her had been rekindled. That was just wishful thinking. Paula had been up front right from the beginning that she wasn't going to go there again. Wynne had conveniently pushed that to the back of her mind because she hadn't wanted to accept it.

They were destined to be no more than friends. Someone else would be Paula's lover, a thought that made Wynne physically ill.

None of that was Paula's fault, though. This was all because of the reckless decision Wynne had made to ignore that little voice almost two years ago telling her not to let go. She didn't deserve someone like Paula—not then and not now.

Paula deserved better, because she had proven her generous heart by forgiving the betrayal. And now, it was unthinkable to refuse her offer of friendship.

Wynne had taken Cheryl's advice and listened to her heart. She would be the best friend she could be, even if that meant supporting a new love interest. Nothing was more important to her than Paula being happy.

With that now resolved, she felt like shit.

This wasn't going to be easy. Thank goodness she was going out of town on Tuesday. She wouldn't have to deal with it for at least a week. Maybe her heart would be ready by then.

Paula listened for the beep before leaving her second message of the day.

"This is me again. I guess I misunderstood you on the phone. I thought you said you were going to be around this weekend."

Slayer jumped onto the counter, insisting she turn the water on so he could drink from the sink.

"Anyway, if you get this before dinner, call me. There's a new Japanese restaurant in the shopping center by Publix. Maybe we can go for sushi. Bye."

Paula checked through her window one more time to see if Wynne's car was at her mother's condo. It wasn't. But Kitty was out by the pool with her granddaughter, so Paula hurried down to see if she knew where Wynne was today.

"I haven't heard from her. But it's such a pretty day. She's probably working on her tan in the back yard."

"I thought she usually came over here to do that," Paula said.

"Well, she's got that tall fence. I think she prefers the all-over look, if you know what I mean."

Paula knew exactly what she meant, and the mental image of Wynne lying nude in the sun sent a glorious surge of heat to her midsection. "You think it would be okay if I drove over there?"

"Sure."

"Uh . . . I don't know exactly where she lives."

Kitty gave her detailed directions, which Paula easily committed to memory. But as she walked back to her condo, she decided to wait for Wynne's call. As tempting as it was to just go over there, they didn't need a repeat of last time, when they both had lost control and rushed into having sex without even talking about what it meant. If they were going to renew their relationship, this time wouldn't be only about sex.

As she started up the stairs, a delivery van pulled into her driveway.

"Paula McKenzie?"

"Yes."

"These are for you." The driver presented her with a beautiful arrangement of orange roses.

Paula's first thought was of Wynne, but the card jolted her back to reality.

I had a lovely time last night—Let's do it again soon, Dee

211

It was exactly what Wynne said Heather had done after their first date. This couldn't go any further.

Paula wasted no time locating Dee's phone number on the volleyball schedule. She dialed and a cheery voice answered right away.

"Hello, Dee? It's Paula . . . Yes, they just arrived and they're lovely." She waited anxiously as Dee explained her choice of color, a cross of yellow for friendship and red for love. "They certainly are beautiful. But I thought it would be a good idea for us to talk about last night . . ."

Chapter 21

Denise leaned her head into the doorway of the break room, where Wynne was rummaging in the refrigerator for something she could eat at her desk. "I have Paula McKenzie on line one. I offered to take a message but she said she'd hold."

Wynne stiffened. She wasn't ready for this conversation. As soon as she opened her mouth, Paula would know it was eating her that she was seeing someone.

"Do you want me to tell her you're in a meeting?"

"No, I'll talk to her." She returned to her office and closed the door, warily eyeing the blinking line on the phone. "Hello, this Wynne Connelly," she said formally.

"Hi, I missed you this weekend."

"I went out of town for a couple of days . . . with Cheryl. We were working on some things." Even though it wasn't quite a lie, Wynne felt a pang of guilt about her implication that her weekend had been filled with work.

"Maybe I can tempt you away from your desk tonight. The concierge has a couple of tickets to the Magic-Lakers game. You interested?"

"I can't. I have to go to San Francisco."

"You leave tonight?"

"First thing in the morning. But I have a lot of work to finish and I'm not packed yet."

"Okay, maybe a rain check. When do you get back?"

"Friday night . . . late."

"I think they're on the road next week. Want to do something else?"

"I can't say right now. Things at work are pretty crazy with the new acquisition."

"What new acquisition?"

"We bought up that agency in San Francisco we've been looking at for so long. It was in the paper today." Along with the press release about the new vice president for sales and marketing.

"Well, congratulations, I guess. Will you call me when you get back?"

"Sure."

Paula stepped off the elevator and walked straight to the concierge desk.

"Hey, Carlos. Thanks for scraping up those basketball tickets, but I don't think I'm going to be able to use them tonight after all."

"Too bad. The Magic's on a run."

"Yeah, maybe later in the season."

"Just let me know. I'll get you the best seats in the house."

"Thanks. I know you will." She wasn't nearly as disappointed about the game as she was about missing out on the chance to do something with Wynne. It was unusual to go this long without getting together, especially over a weekend.

Paula hoped things would go well for Wynne in San Francisco. She had sounded distracted on the phone, like something was bothering her. And with having to work all weekend, she was probably under a lot of stress.

Already, Paula was thinking ahead to next weekend. Maybe they could do something that would help Wynne relax and get her mind off work. Paula chuckled to herself. She had a few ideas of what that could be. Now that she had her head on straight, she was eager to—

"Hey, boss. Are you pulling another double shift?"

Paula smiled when she saw Jolene behind the front desk. She was going to have to find a way to get her favorite clerk moved up to the day shift.

"No, but I promised to cover for Belinda until six. She has a parent-teacher conference this afternoon. Speaking of Belinda, has that situation gotten any better?"

"Yeah, now that you mention it, it has. After she took that week off, she just came back a whole different person."

"Sometimes, all you need is a little time away," Paula said. Jolene didn't know it, but Belinda's time away had come in the form of a personnel management seminar in New York. Paula and Stephanie had determined that retraining was the last hope and if Belinda didn't get it, she would likely be demoted and transferred.

"I think it made a real difference. Maybe I should have a week off too and see if it improves my attitude."

Paula masterfully raised a single eyebrow before laughing. "Oh no, it doesn't work that way. What is that old saying? 'The floggings will continue until morale improves.' That's the way we do things here."

"Was it good for you to spend a year in Denver?"

"What do you think? Am I a better boss?" She grinned at Jolene, as if daring her to say no.

"I don't know, Paula. It's so hard to improve on perfection."

"You are so insightful. I like that about you."

"It's just that you didn't seem very happy when you left, but you do now."

"That's because I—" She had never been unhappy in her job.

215

Disappointment about Wynne was the sole reason she had left Orlando. "It was a good year at the WR out there. But I missed this place and I was just incredibly lucky to find my way back. That's why I'm so happy now."

There was another reason, but not one she would talk about with Jolene.

"I'm glad you're back. But I already sucked up to you and you still didn't let me move to first shift."

Paula chuckled and slid the door open to the cabinet beneath the front desk. "Good lord! Look at this mess."

"Whatever it is, I didn't do it," Jolene said quickly.

"I'm going to clean this out while we're not busy. You watch the desk."

Paula dragged a trashcan over to where she crouched and began to extract wayward items from the shelves below. Her haul included several cell phone adapters and laptop power cords, loose batteries, an empty backpack, a half dozen registration packets from conferences held months ago, and a stack of old newspapers.

"How does all this stuff get in here?"

"Lost and found, probably. People bring it to the desk when we're busy and we forget about it," Jolene explained.

"You're probably right. Who reads all these newspapers at the front desk?" she asked with irritation.

"I don't know. Maybe just when people are on break. Hey, isn't that the woman that used to come in here?" Jolene grabbed a section of the paper Paula was pulling out.

"Now, don't you start too. I trained you not to have bad habits."

"Well, isn't it?" Jolene turned the paper around to show Paula the picture of K. Wynne Connelly.

"I'll be damned . . . That's what it was." She stared open-mouthed at the news story on the front page of the business section. This was the big news Wynne had wanted to share last Friday night. Instead, Paula had gone on that disastrous date with Dee.

"She's a friend of yours, right?"

"Yeah, she moved here while I was in Denver."

"Maybe you should give her a call and congratulate her."

"Good idea," Paula agreed without looking up. She folded the paper and set it aside, her thoughts racing about their telephone conversation the day before. No wonder Wynne had seemed so distracted. Her feelings were hurt because Paula hadn't asked about her big news.

"No, I get back on Friday night, Mom. It'll be late . . . Sure, I'll stop by on Saturday." Wynne knew she would have to buck up sooner or later and make an appearance in the condo complex. Keeping her distance from Paula also meant not seeing her family. "Mom, I need to go. There's someone at the door . . . I don't know who it is, but I need to answer it. I'll call when I get back in town, okay?"

Wynne lowered the flame underneath the soup she was heating and hurried to the front door. Expecting to find one of the neighbors' kids selling something for school, she was taken aback by the sight of Paula, leaning against the pillar on the porch, her arms crossed in an accusing posture and a folded newspaper in her hand.

"I can't believe I had to read this in the newspaper."

"I got the news on Friday." *When you were getting ready for your date.* Wynne stood aside as Paula stepped into her living room.

"Wynne, this is fabulous. I'm so proud of you." Paula gave her a hearty hug, which Wynne tried to return.

"Thanks."

"Why didn't you tell me?"

"You were busy." Wynne heard the edge in her voice. She wasn't ready for this yet.

"You were gone all weekend. I left you three—" Her eyes grew wide. "Wait a minute. Are you mad at me about something?"

"No."

"But something's wrong. I can tell."

Wynne sighed. It was impossible to brush aside her feelings when she knew she was wearing them on her face. She walked back

217

into the kitchen to turn off the burner. "You want some soup and crackers?"

"Stop it, Wynne. Talk to me."

Wynne turned around, crossing her arms as she leaned on the counter. This time, she tried her best to smile. "I'm not mad. Honest."

Paula stepped closer. "Then what's going on? Why haven't you called me?"

She shook her head, unable to speak. The truth was too humiliating.

"Fine." Paula started for the door but turned back, her eyes flashing with anger. "You know, when you first asked me to forgive you, the one thing you promised was that you would be honest with me from now on. So go ahead and keep your little secrets, but don't expect me to trust you again."

"Paula, wait." Wynne grabbed her elbow and she stopped. She wasn't going to let secrets tear them apart again. "I'll tell you everything."

Paula softened her look, her anger at bay as she waited for an explanation. Wynne hadn't felt pressure like this since the night she broke things off with Heather.

"I did something you told me not to do." She looked up at the ceiling as though the words she needed to say might appear on a script. "I . . . I let myself read too much into us becoming friends again. I was starting to feel like we might have something special, and that you were feeling it too. And then I got upset because you . . . because you went out on a date with someone else."

Paula's mouth was open as if she was going to answer, but all she did was shake her head.

"I know, you said we weren't going to go down that road again. I'm not upset at you. I'm upset because I didn't listen . . . because I didn't want to believe you."

"Wynne, I . . ." Paula took a step closer. "It was a really bad date . . . one of the worst ever."

Wynne chuckled, but without a trace of humor. "That's beside the point. One of these days, it'll be right."

"I hope so." Another step. "Maybe then I won't be checking my watch all through dinner wondering if you're still up so I can ditch this woman and have some real fun. Or looking over at her and thinking about how I wished she was funny like you, and easy to talk to. And realizing there's only one person who's ever made my heart race just by touching my hand."

With one last step, Paula closed the distance between them and brushed her hand against Wynne's.

"Are you saying . . . ?"

"I'm saying I don't want anyone but you."

Wynne had almost given up on her dream of hearing those words. She pulled Paula into an embrace and squeezed tightly. "I love you."

"You love me?"

"Yes," Wynne whispered, lowering her mouth to touch the lips she had missed for so long. She could feel Paula relax in her arms, returning the kiss with all the hunger of their first time. Memories of their night together roared back and Wynne forcibly calmed herself, breaking the kiss but not the embrace. "I promise I'll never hurt you again."

Paula melted into Wynne's arms, not even stopping to ask herself if it was safe to let go. She had made up her mind days ago this was where she belonged.

"We're not going to lose control this time, Paula. I'm going to prove to you that you can trust me."

"I trust you now," Paula said, already working the buttons on Wynne's shirt. "Where's your bedroom?"

Wynne grabbed her hands and squeezed them. "I want you more than anything, but I don't want you to have any doubts."

"Just promise me this is real." Paula tugged her through the dining room in search of a bed. "Don't you have any furniture?"

"I have a great bed. Just keep going."

Moments later, both women were stripped to their waists. Paula tossed her skirt over the trunk at the foot of the bed, unable to take her eyes from Wynne's breasts, which gleamed white against her tanned skin.

Wynne pulled her again into a kiss, this one leaving no doubts about how she felt. Paula succumbed as she felt herself being pushed back gently onto the king-sized bed. She watched as Wynne rid herself of her slacks and thong, gloriously reminiscent of the last time they did this.

Slowly, Wynne crawled over her, settling between her thighs. Paula opened her legs and rested her feet on Wynne's calves. Their bodies melded into mutual warmth as her hips rose in anticipation.

"I haven't been with anyone since you," Paula whispered. She held her breath as she waited for Wynne's reply.

"I haven't either."

"Not even Heather?"

"No, no one." Wynne tenderly nibbled the soft skin below Paula's ear. "How could I?"

Wynne shifted her body to the side so she could run her hand up and down Paula's nude form. The breasts, the hips, the silky curls were all just as she remembered them, just as she had envisioned them so many nights alone in her bed. She lowered her head, sucking a taut nipple into her mouth as her hand wandered to the soft insides of Paula's thighs.

"I've wanted you like this since the day you left," Paula murmured.

"I won't leave again." Wynne swung one leg over to straddle Paula's thigh, using her knee to nudge Paula's legs farther apart. Sliding her fingers through the wet folds, she pressed gently inside.

"I want to be inside you too."

Barely aware of her own body, Wynne somehow crawled up and opened her legs to allow Paula's fingers to find her center.

"Fill me like this."

"God, Paula." Wynne's thoughts of savoring the moment flew out the window as she took Paula's fingers inside. She thrust her own hand deeper but left her thumb to flick against the rigid clitoris.

Paula pumped her hips against the exploring fingers, struggling to match the rhythm with her own hand as her concentration wavered.

Wynne rocked her body up and down, driving toward her peak. "I love you," she gasped. Closing her eyes tightly, she staved off her own climax barely long enough to feel the contraction around her fingers as Paula stiffened in her arms.

From one to the other and back, their throbbing bodies made a circle of heat.

"I've missed you," Paula said, her voice low and serious. Gently, she trailed her fingers across Wynne's collarbone, dipping from time to time to the valley between her breasts. They had spent more than two hours getting reacquainted and now lay temporarily sated.

"Me too. But it's all just as wonderful as I remember it."

"It was better."

Wynne rose up on one elbow so she could look into Paula's eyes. "Why?"

"Because I dreamt about it for so long." Paula nestled closer. "You're not going to believe this, but I have to be at work in about six hours."

"Lucky you. I have to be on a plane at six-thirty, and I'm not even packed."

"Then I should go." Slowly, she extricated her limbs from Wynne's and rose from the bed.

Wynne watched her as she dressed, then she pulled back the covers and climbed out of bed. She had to be sure there were no doubts still hanging in the air. Tying her robe around her waist, she moved behind Paula and wrapped her arms around her waist. "I really do love you."

"I believe you."

❦

221

" . . . Lee Washburn intends to take the retirement package, so we'll need to find someone who can handle the west coast marketing. We should make that an assistant VP position, because it's going to have a lot of responsibility."

For the second time in the last ten minutes, Wynne felt her chin dip as she fought to stay awake.

"Excuse me, Ms. Connelly," Cheryl continued, her voice syrupy sweet. "Should I ask the flight attendant to bring you some coffee or would you prefer I just sit here quietly and let you catch a nap?" The twinkle in her eye told Wynne she was teasing.

Wynne shook her head and sat up straight, unhooking her seatbelt so she could stretch. "I didn't get much sleep. I should probably have another cup of coffee."

"You weren't up working on this, were you?"

"No," Wynne answered, unable to suppress the blush and the smile as she thought back to her evening with Paula.

"Oh, now that's an interesting look," Cheryl said, clearly amused to see Wynne's face turn red. "Does this mean you two are going to work things out?"

"Actually"—her smile broadened as she thought again of her evening—"I think we've worked things out very well."

"That's great news, Wynne. Why don't you tell me about her?" Cheryl closed her folder and leaned back into her leather seat.

"She's . . . her name's Paula, and she's one of the ops managers at the Weller Regent."

"Is that . . . ? Wait a minute . . . I should have realized that's who it was. I remember Ken saying something about running into the two of you at Jack Elam's."

"Wow, there really aren't any secrets at Eldon-Markoff, are there?"

"Hey, I told you from Day One. We're a family. You should bring her to the Christmas party next week."

"You think it would be all right with everyone?"

"Of course. I want to meet whoever it is that has you nodding off in the middle of a briefing. If she doesn't come to the party, I'm going to have to show up at her house."

Wynne laughed aloud at that image, wondering whether Paula would rather face a holiday party or a one-on-one with her boss. "I'll ask her."

"Good. Now why don't you go ahead and take a nap? I'll wake you up when we start to land."

Wynne didn't need to be asked twice. In just a few minutes, she was sound asleep.

For the hundredth time that day, Paula caught herself daydreaming and shook herself to snap out of it. Wynne was due back home tonight. They had spoken by phone several times over the week, each tentatively confirming with the other they were headed in the right direction.

The hotel had been relatively quiet over the last two weeks, the drop-off in holiday business travel evident from the near-empty lounge and restaurant. This gave the staff an opportunity to catch up on end-of-year paperwork and to get the jump on spring cleaning. In three short weeks, their conference season would be in full swing.

From her small windowed office, Paula could see her boss across the hall behind her desk. Something big was going on. She could tell by Stephanie's serious look and the fact that she had been on the phone with her door closed for most of the afternoon. Whatever it was, they would probably all know soon enough.

Paula debriefed with Belinda and Jon, the new senior shift manager, as they started their shift. Ten more minutes and she was out of here for the next two days.

"Paula, can I see you in my office?" Stephanie's face was grave.

"Of course." Paula followed her inside, and the hotel director closed the door.

"I've been on the phone all day with Vince Tolliver."

223

Chapter 22

Wynne hurried off the plane to ground transportation, rolling her bag behind her. She was bursting with excitement to see Paula again. Four days away seemed like an eternity.

The warm air embraced her as she walked outside and shed her coat. Orlando had never felt so much like home.

There was no sign of the familiar Miata, but her flight from San Francisco had arrived early. She was about to call Paula when her cell phone rang.

"Is this my taxi service?" She smiled as soon as she heard Paula's voice. "Don't do that. If anyone understands working late, it's me. I'll just grab a cab and meet you at your place. Of course, I'll probably need a ride home later . . . like early Monday morning." Wynne walked quickly toward the taxi stand and raised her hand. "We'll worry about food later. I'm only hungry for one thing right now."

She closed her phone and climbed into the taxi for the ride to Paula's. Life was suddenly so good.

"Hi." Paula held open the door and reached out to take the suitcase. "Was it a good trip?"

Wynne got a sudden case of nerves. She had expected to be bowled over by a passionate kiss after being gone so long, but Paula was clearly holding back.

As if reading her mind, Paula reached out awkwardly and pulled her close, burying her face in Wynne's neck. "I missed you."

"I missed you too." Despite the embrace, Wynne couldn't shake the feeling that something was wrong. "Is everything all right?"

"Yeah . . . yeah, but we need to talk." Paula took her hand and led her to the couch.

"What's up?" Wynne tried not to show her panic, absently scratching the passing Slayer.

"You remember I told you about the guy that I worked for in Denver, Vince Tolliver?"

"You mean the one who got mad because Stephanie recruited you to come back?"

"That's the one." Paula grabbed the cat and pulled him into her lap. "He called Stephanie today and he wants to return the favor."

"What favor?"

"He's just gotten the director's job at the Weller Regent in San Francisco. He wants me as his senior operations manager. It's the number two job in the hotel."

All of a sudden, Wynne felt nauseated. This was to Paula what the vice president's job had been to her, an opportunity that only fools let pass. "So you'd leave Orlando again."

"It's a very big promotion, Wynne. I could be running my own hotel in two years. If I stay here, it'll be seven years before Stephanie retires, and there are no guarantees I'll get her job."

Wynne nodded her understanding, all the while frowning at the implications. "Is it what you want?"

"I haven't made up my mind yet. I have to let Vince know by Wednesday."

Wynne waited to hear more, but obviously Paula expected her to react to the news. Finally she answered, her voice giving in to defeat. "I just found you again and I'm losing you already."

"You're not losing me, Wynne. If I go, it'll only be for a couple of years and we can still see each other. I've got four weeks vacation and I can request a work schedule that lets me off four days in a row."

"But what happens in two years? If things work out like you say, you'll get your own hotel and you'll go somewhere else."

Paula nudged Slayer off her lap and dropped to her knees, scooting over to kneel in front of her. "I haven't said yes. If we can't work things out, I won't go." She laid her head in Wynne's lap for a few minutes without talking. Then she turned and climbed back onto the couch, leaning back in Wynne's arms.

Wynne wanted to cry. For four short days, her life had been perfect. Now it was slipping away. But she couldn't ask Paula to pass up this opportunity. She wanted no part of another relationship that was built on sacrifice and obligation. "I'll come to San Francisco with you."

"What?"

"We just bought the agency out there. We're going to hire an assistant VP to work on the west coast. Maybe Cheryl and Ken will let me just move into that slot."

Paula sat up and turned around, her eyes full of surprise. "You'd give up your job to come with me?"

"What good is a job if it's all I have?"

"I can't let you do that."

"Why not? My job is no more important to me than yours is to you. You deserve to make it to the top."

"But you've just made it to the top. You haven't even had a chance to enjoy it."

"What I care about is you and I don't want to lose you. Just don't do to me what I did to Heather."

"What do you mean?"

"Be honest with me." Wynne swallowed hard. "If you don't love me, don't let me make a total fool of myself."

Paula wriggled free and shifted on the couch so they were face to face. With both hands, she cupped Wynne's face and looked her straight in the eye. "I do love you and I don't want to lose you either."

Paula awakened to the strangest, most wonderful sensation. She was lying on her stomach draped across Wynne's body. Slayer rested on her pillow, purring softly in her ear. There were no alarms, no planes to catch, nothing to pull her away from the comfort of this embrace.

The awakening muscles underneath her began to twitch and she instinctively drew closer. She and Wynne had made love last night, pouring themselves into one another with a passion she had never known. Long after the deep breathing told her Wynne had fallen asleep, she lay awake, their conversation replaying in her head. Wynne's offer to come to San Francisco had crystallized her decision.

"You awake?" Wynne gently caressed her shoulders.

"Yeah." Paula lifted her head and chuckled at the contented cat. "We have a visitor."

"He's such a doll," Wynne cooed. "So are you."

"You too." Paula cuddled again. "I woke up thinking about you giving up your job and us moving to San Francisco."

"My bags are already packed. You can run, but I'm going to follow you wherever you go."

Paula squeezed her tightly. "You made the decision easy, Wynne. Thank you."

"When do you have to be there?"

"I'm not going."

Wynne blinked and struggled to sit up. "You're what?"

"I'm not going. There are a lot more important things in this world than getting to the top of a hotel hierarchy. I'll get there eventually if it's meant to be, but you're right. If all I have is a job, what's it worth?"

"But a job isn't all you'd have, Paula. I told you I would go."

227

"And that told me what I needed to know."

Wynne shook her head in obvious confusion.

"Before we talked last night, I was afraid to turn it down. I knew if I did and things didn't work out between us, I'd resent you for it, and be angry with myself for making the wrong decision. But with you willing to give up your job to go with me, I realized that you're committed to us, just like I am. I didn't know it, but that's what I needed to hear."

"So we're not going?"

"Nope, we're not going." Paula gently pushed her back against the pillows, settling herself in the crook of Wynne's arm. "This is right for us. Moving up so fast at the WR wasn't all that important to me until I lost you before. Then I started to feel like work was all I was ever going to have. So I wanted it all as fast as I could get it."

"And now you're okay to bide your time and wait for something here?"

"As long as I get to have you in my life."

"Then I'd say we have a deal."

Slayer stood and stretched his long body, hoping in vain someone might offer a scratch. Maybe he would go poke around in the kitchen and see if there was any of that canned beef left over from last night. It was probably going to be a while before anyone would think to ask if he was ready for his breakfast.

WHEN LOVE FINDS A HOME by Megan Carter. 280 pp. What will it take for Anna and Rona to find their way back to each other again? 1-59493-041-4 $12.95

MEMORIES TO DIE FOR by Adrian Gold. 240 pp. Rachel attempts to avoid her attraction to the charms of Anna Sigurdson . . . 1-59493-038-4 $12.95

SILENT HEART by Claire McNab. 280 pp. Exotic lesbian romance.

1-59493-044-9 $12.95

MIDNIGHT RAIN by Peggy J. Herring. 240 pp. Bridget McBee is determined to find the woman who saved her life. 1-59493-021-X $12.95

THE MISSING PAGE A Brenda Strange Mystery by Patty G. Henderson. 240 pp. Brenda investigates her client's murder . . . 1-59493-004-X $12.95

WHISPERS ON THE WIND by Frankie J. Jones. 240 pp. Dixon thinks she and her best friend, Elizabeth Colter, would make the perfect couple . . . 1-59493-037-6 $12.95

CALL OF THE DARK: EROTIC LESBIAN TALES OF THE SUPERNATURAL edited by Therese Szymanski—from Bella After Dark. 320 pp. 1-59493-040-6 $14.95

A TIME TO CAST AWAY A Helen Black Mystery by Pat Welch. 240 pp. Helen stops by Alice's apartment—only to find the woman dead . . . 1-59493-036-8 $12.95

DESERT OF THE HEART by Jane Rule. 224 pp. The book that launched the most popular lesbian movie of all time is back. 1-1-59493-035-X $12.95

THE NEXT WORLD by Ursula Steck. 240 pp. Anna's friend Mido is threatened and eventually disappears . . . 1-59493-024-4 $12.95

CALL SHOTGUN by Jaime Clevenger. 240 pp. Kelly gets pulled back into the world of private investigation . . . 1-59493-016-3 $12.95

52 PICKUP by Bonnie J. Morris and E.B. Casey. 240 pp. 52 hot, romantic tales—one for every Saturday night of the year. 1-59493-026-0 $12.95

GOLD FEVER by Lyn Denison. 240 pp. Kate's first love, Ashley, returns to their home town, where Kate now lives . . . 1-1-59493-039-2 $12.95

RISKY INVESTMENT by Beth Moore. 240 pp. Lynn's best friend and roommate needs her to pretend Chris is his fiancé. But nothing is ever easy. 1-59493-019-8 $12.95

HUNTER'S WAY by Gerri Hill. 240 pp. Homicide detective Tori Hunter is forced to team up with the hot-tempered Samantha Kennedy. 1-59493-018-X $12.95

CAR POOL by Karin Kallmaker. 240 pp. Soft shoulders, merging traffic and slippery when wet . . . Anthea and Shay find love in the car pool. 1-59493-013-9 $12.95

NO SISTER OF MINE by Jeanne G'Fellers. 240 pp. Telepathic women fight to coexist with a patriarchal society that wishes their eradication. ISBN 1-59493-017-1 $12.95

ON THE WINGS OF LOVE by Megan Carter. 240 pp. Stacie's reporting career is on the rocks. She has to interview bestselling author Cheryl, or else! ISBN 1-59493-027-9 $12.95

WICKED GOOD TIME by Diana Tremain Braund. 224 pp. Does Christina need Miki as a protector . . . or want her as a lover? ISBN 1-59493-031-7 $12.95

THOSE WHO WAIT by Peggy J. Herring. 240 pp. Two brilliant sisters—in love with the same woman! ISBN 1-59493-032-5 $12.95

ABBY'S PASSION by Jackie Calhoun. 240 pp. Abby's bipolar sister helps turn her world upside down, so she must decide what's most important. ISBN 1-59493-014-7 $12.95

PICTURE PERFECT by Jane Vollbrecht. 240 pp. Kate is reintroduced to Casey, the daughter of an old friend. Can they withstand Kate's career?   ISBN 1-59493-015-5 $12.95

PAPERBACK ROMANCE by Karin Kallmaker. 240 pp. Carolyn falls for tall, dark and . . . female . . . in this classic lesbian romance.   ISBN 1-59493-033-3 $12.95

DAWN OF CHANGE by Gerri Hill. 240 pp. Susan ran away to find peace in remote Kings Canyon—then she met Shawn . . .   ISBN 1-59493-011-2 $12.95

DOWN THE RABBIT HOLE by Lynne Jamneck. 240 pp. Is a killer holding a grudge against FBI Agent Samantha Skellar?   ISBN 1-59493-012-0 $12.95

SEASONS OF THE HEART by Jackie Calhoun. 240 pp. Overwhelmed, Sara saw only one way out—leaving . . .   ISBN 1-59493-030-9 $12.95

TURNING THE TABLES by Jessica Thomas. 240 pp. The 2nd Alex Peres Mystery. *From ghosties and ghoulies and long leggity beasties* . . .   ISBN 1-59493-009-0 $12.95

FOR EVERY SEASON by Frankie Jones. 240 pp. Andi, who is investigating a 65-year-old murder, meets Janice, a charming district attorney . . .   ISBN 1-59493-010-4 $12.95

LOVE ON THE LINE by Laura DeHart Young. 240 pp. Kay leaves a younger woman behind to go on a mission to Alaska . . . will she regret it?   ISBN 1-59493-008-2 $12.95

UNDER THE SOUTHERN CROSS by Claire McNab. 200 pp. Lee, an American travel agent, goes down under and meets Australian Alex, and the sparks fly under the Southern Cross.   ISBN 1-59493-029-5 $12.95

SUGAR by Karin Kallmaker. 240 pp. Three women want sugar from Sugar, who can't make up her mind.   ISBN 1-59493-001-5 $12.95

FALL GUY by Claire McNab. 200 pp. 16th Detective Inspector Carol Ashton Mystery.   ISBN 1-59493-000-7 $12.95

ONE SUMMER NIGHT by Gerri Hill. 232 pp. Johanna swore to never fall in love again— but then she met the charming Kelly . . .   ISBN 1-59493-007-4 $12.95

TALK OF THE TOWN TOO by Saxon Bennett. 181 pp. Second in the series about wild and fun loving friends.   ISBN 1-931513-77-5 $12.95

LOVE SPEAKS HER NAME by Laura DeHart Young. 170 pp. Love and friendship, desire and intrigue, spark this exciting sequel to *Forever and the Night.*   ISBN 1-59493-002-3 $12.95

TO HAVE AND TO HOLD by Peggy J. Herring. 184 pp. By finally letting down her defenses, will Dorian be opening herself to a devastating betrayal?   ISBN 1-59493-005-8 $12.95

WILD THINGS by Karin Kallmaker. 228 pp. Dutiful daughter Faith has met the perfect man. There's just one problem: she's in love with his sister.   ISBN 1-931513-64-3 $12.95

SHARED WINDS by Kenna White. 216 pp. Can Emma rebuild more than just Lanny's marina?   ISBN 1-59493-006-6 $12.95

THE UNKNOWN MILE by Jaime Clevenger. 253 pp. Kelly's world is getting more and more complicated every moment.   ISBN 1-931513-57-0 $12.95

TREASURED PAST by Linda Hill. 189 pp. A shared passion for antiques leads to love.   ISBN 1-59493-003-1 $12.95

SIERRA CITY by Gerri Hill. 284 pp. Chris and Jesse cannot deny their growing attraction . . .   ISBN 1-931513-98-8 $12.95

ALL THE WRONG PLACES by Karin Kallmaker. 174 pp. Sex and the single girl—Brandy is looking for love and usually she finds it. Karin Kallmaker's first *After Dark* erotic novel.
ISBN 1-931513-76-7 $12.95

WHEN THE CORPSE LIES A Motor City Thriller by Therese Szymanski. 328 pp. Butch bad-girl Brett Higgins is used to waking up next to beautiful women she hardly knows. Problem is, this one's dead.
ISBN 1-931513-74-0 $12.95

GUARDED HEARTS by Hannah Rickard. 240 pp. Someone's reminding Alyssa about her secret past, and then she becomes the suspect in a series of burglaries.
ISBN 1-931513-99-6 $12.95

ONCE MORE WITH FEELING by Peggy J. Herring. 184 pp. Lighthearted, loving, romantic adventure.
ISBN 1-931513-60-0 $12.95

TANGLED AND DARK A Brenda Strange Mystery by Patty G. Henderson. 240 pp. When investigating a local death, Brenda finds two possible killers—one diagnosed with Multiple Personality Disorder.
ISBN 1-931513-75-9 $12.95

WHITE LACE AND PROMISES by Peggy J. Herring. 240 pp. Maxine and Betina realize sex may not be the most important thing in their lives.
ISBN 1-931513-73-2 $12.95

UNFORGETTABLE by Karin Kallmaker. 288 pp. Can Rett find love with the cheerleader who broke her heart so many years ago?
ISBN 1-931513-63-5 $12.95

HIGHER GROUND by Saxon Bennett. 280 pp. A delightfully complex reflection of the successful, high society lives of a small group of women.
ISBN 1-931513-69-4 $12.95

LAST CALL A Detective Franco Mystery by Baxter Clare. 240 pp. Frank overlooks all else to try to solve a cold case of two murdered children . . .
ISBN 1-931513-70-8 $12.95

ONCE UPON A DYKE: NEW EXPLOITS OF FAIRY-TALE LESBIANS by Karin Kallmaker, Julia Watts, Barbara Johnson & Therese Szymanski. 320 pp. You've never read fairy tales like these before! From Bella After Dark.
ISBN 1-931513-71-6 $14.95

FINEST KIND OF LOVE by Diana Tremain Braund. 224 pp. Can Molly and Carolyn stop clashing long enough to see beyond their differences?
ISBN 1-931513-68-6 $12.95

DREAM LOVER by Lyn Denison. 188 pp. A soft, sensuous, romantic fantasy.
ISBN 1-931513-96-1 $12.95

NEVER SAY NEVER by Linda Hill. 224 pp. A classic love story . . . where rules aren't the only things broken.
ISBN 1-931513-67-8 $12.95

PAINTED MOON by Karin Kallmaker. 214 pp. Stranded together in a snowbound cabin, Jackie and Leah's lives will never be the same.
ISBN 1-931513-53-8 $12.95

WIZARD OF ISIS by Jean Stewart. 240 pp. Fifth in the exciting Isis series.
ISBN 1-931513-71-4 $12.95

WOMAN IN THE MIRROR by Jackie Calhoun. 216 pp. Josey learns to love again, while her niece is learning to love women for the first time.
ISBN 1-931513-78-3 $12.95

SUBSTITUTE FOR LOVE by Karin Kallmaker. 200 pp. When Holly and Reyna meet the combination adds up to pure passion. But what about tomorrow?
ISBN 1-931513-62-7 $12.95

GULF BREEZE by Gerri Hill. 288 pp. Could Carly really be the woman Pat has always been searching for?
ISBN 1-931513-97-X $12.95

THE TOMSTOWN INCIDENT by Penny Hayes. 184 pp. Caught between two worlds, Eloise must make a decision that will change her life forever.
ISBN 1-931513-56-2 $12.95

MAKING UP FOR LOST TIME by Karin Kallmaker. 240 pp. Discover delicious recipes for romance by the undisputed mistress. ISBN 1-931513-61-9 $12.95

THE WAY LIFE SHOULD BE by Diana Tremain Braund. 173 pp. With which woman will Jennifer find the true meaning of love? ISBN 1-931513-66-X $12.95

BACK TO BASICS: A BUTCH/FEMME ANTHOLOGY edited by Therese Szymanski— from Bella After Dark. 324 pp. ISBN 1-931513-35-X $14.95

SURVIVAL OF LOVE by Frankie J. Jones. 236 pp. What will Jody do when she falls in love with her best friend's daughter? ISBN 1-931513-55-4 $12.95

LESSONS IN MURDER by Claire McNab. 184 pp. 1st Detective Inspector Carol Ashton Mystery. ISBN 1-931513-65-1 $12.95

DEATH BY DEATH by Claire McNab. 167 pp. 5th Denise Cleever Thriller. ISBN 1-931513-34-1 $12.95

CAUGHT IN THE NET by Jessica Thomas. 188 pp. A wickedly observant story of mystery, danger, and love in Provincetown. ISBN 1-931513-54-6 $12.95

DREAMS FOUND by Lyn Denison. Australian Riley embarks on a journey to meet her birth mother . . . and gains not just a family, but the love of her life. ISBN 1-931513-58-9 $12.95

A MOMENT'S INDISCRETION by Peggy J. Herring. 154 pp. Jackie is torn between her better judgment and the overwhelming attraction she feels for Valerie. ISBN 1-931513-59-7 $12.95

IN EVERY PORT by Karin Kallmaker. 224 pp. Jessica has a woman in every port. Will meeting Cat change all that? ISBN 1-931513-36-8 $12.95

TOUCHWOOD by Karin Kallmaker. 240 pp. Rayann loves Louisa. Louisa loves Rayann. Can the decades between their ages keep them apart? ISBN 1-931513-37-6 $12.95

WATERMARK by Karin Kallmaker. 248 pp. Teresa wants a future with a woman whose heart has been frozen by loss. Sequel to Touchwood. ISBN 1-931513-38-4 $12.95

EMBRACE IN MOTION by Karin Kallmaker. 240 pp. Has Sarah found lust or love? ISBN 1-931513-39-2 $12.95

ONE DEGREE OF SEPARATION by Karin Kallmaker. 232 pp. Sizzling small town romance between Marian, the town librarian, and the new girl from the big city. ISBN 1-931513-30-9 $12.95

CRY HAVOC A Detective Franco Mystery by Baxter Clare. 240 pp. A dead hustler with a headless rooster in his lap sends Lt. L.A. Franco headfirst against Mother Love. ISBN 1-931513931-7 $12.95

DISTANT THUNDER by Peggy J. Herring. 294 pp. Bankrobbing drifter Cordy awakens strange new feelings in Leo in this romantic tale set in the Old West. ISBN 1-931513-28-7 $12.95

COP OUT by Claire McNab. 216 pp. 4th Detective Inspector Carol Ashton Mystery. ISBN 1-931513-29-5 $12.95

BLOOD LINK by Claire McNab. 159 pp. 15th Detective Inspector Carol Ashton Mystery. Is Carol unwittingly playing into a deadly plan? ISBN 1-931513-27-9 $12.95

TALK OF THE TOWN by Saxon Bennett. 239 pp. With enough beer, barbecue and B.S., anything is possible! ISBN 1-931513-18-X $12.95

MAYBE NEXT TIME by Karin Kallmaker. 256 pp. Sabrina has everything she ever wanted—except Jorie. ISBN 1-931513-26-0 $12.95

WHEN GOOD GIRLS GO BAD: A Motor City Thriller by Therese Szymanski. 230 pp. Brett, Randi and Allie join forces to stop a serial killer. ISBN 1-931513-11-2 $12.95

A DAY TOO LONG: A Helen Black Mystery by Pat Welch. 328 pp. This time Helen's fate is in her own hands. ISBN 1-931513-22-8 $12.95

THE RED LINE OF YARMALD by Diana Rivers. 256 pp. The Hadra's only hope lies in a magical red line . . . climactic sequel to *Clouds of War.* ISBN 1-931513-23-6 $12.95

OUTSIDE THE FLOCK by Jackie Calhoun. 224 pp. Jo embraces her new love and life. ISBN 1-931513-13-9 $12.95

LEGACY OF LOVE by Marianne K. Martin. 224 pp. Read the whole Sage Bristo story. ISBN 1-931513-15-5 $12.95

STREET RULES: A Detective Franco Mystery by Baxter Clare. 304 pp. Gritty, fast-paced mystery with compelling Detective L.A. Franco. ISBN 1-931513-14-7 $12.95

RECOGNITION FACTOR: 4th Denise Cleever Thriller by Claire McNab. 176 pp. Denise Cleever tracks a notorious terrorist to America. ISBN 1-931513-24-4 $12.95

NORA AND LIZ by Nancy Garden. 296 pp. Lesbian romance by the author of *Annie on My Mind.* ISBN 1931513-20-1 $12.95

MIDAS TOUCH by Frankie J. Jones. 208 pp. Sandra had everything but love. ISBN 1-931513-21-X $12.95

BEYOND ALL REASON by Peggy J. Herring. 240 pp. A romance hotter than Texas. ISBN 1-9513-25-2 $12.95

ACCIDENTAL MURDER: 14th Detective Inspector Carol Ashton Mystery by Claire McNab. 208 pp. Carol Ashton tracks an elusive killer. ISBN 1-931513-16-3 $12.95

SEEDS OF FIRE: Tunnel of Light Trilogy, Book 2 by Karin Kallmaker writing as Laura Adams. 274 pp. In Autumn's dreams no one is who they seem. ISBN 1-931513-19-8 $12.95

DRIFTING AT THE BOTTOM OF THE WORLD by Auden Bailey. 288 pp. Beautifully written first novel set in Antarctica. ISBN 1-931513-17-1 $12.95

CLOUDS OF WAR by Diana Rivers. 288 pp. Women unite to defend Zelindar! ISBN 1-931513-12-0 $12.95

DEATHS OF JOCASTA: 2nd Micky Knight Mystery by J.M. Redmann. 408 pp. Sexy and intriguing Lambda Literary Award–nominated mystery. ISBN 1-931513-10-4 $12.95

LOVE IN THE BALANCE by Marianne K. Martin. 256 pp. The classic lesbian love story, back in print! ISBN 1-931513-08-2 $12.95

THE COMFORT OF STRANGERS by Peggy J. Herring. 272 pp. Lela's work was her passion . . . until now. ISBN 1-931513-09-0 $12.95

WHEN EVIL CHANGES FACE: A Motor City Thriller by Therese Szymanski. 240 pp. Brett Higgins is back in another heart-pounding thriller. ISBN 0-9677753-3-7 $11.95

CHICKEN by Paula Martinac. 208 pp. Lynn finds that the only thing harder than being in a lesbian relationship is ending one. ISBN 1-931513-07-4 $11.95

TAMARACK CREEK by Jackie Calhoun. 208 pp. An intriguing story of love and danger. ISBN 1-931513-06-6 $11.95

DEATH BY THE RIVERSIDE: 1st Micky Knight Mystery by J.M. Redmann. 320 pp. Finally back in print, the book that launched the Lambda Literary Award–winning Micky Knight mystery series. ISBN 1-931513-05-8 $11.95